FACING THE MUSIC

FACING THE MUSIC

TIM THOROGOOD

Matador
9 Priory Business Park
Kibworth Beauchamp
Leicestershire LE8 0RX, UK
Tel: (+44) 116 279 2299
Fax: (+44) 116 279 2277
Email: books@troubador.co.uk
Web: www.troubador.co.uk/matador

ISBN 978-1783064-304

British Library Cataloguing in Publication Data.
A catalogue record for this book is available from the British Library.

Typeset in Aldine by Troubador Publishing Ltd
Printed and bound in the UK by TJ International, Padstow, Cornwall

Matador is an imprint of Troubador Publishing Ltd

To Katie and John for being my Glastonbury companions over so many years and to Deirdre for all her constructive comments, advice and patience.

ONE

Sunday morning, 2.30 a.m.

A battered drumstick flew from the stage and shot over the boiling turmoil of sweaty heads. A wave of open hands rose from the crowd and tried to snatch it from the air.

'It's mine!' Gary yelled, leaping with his arms and fingers outstretched.

The stick twisted furiously sideways, crossways, handle-over-tip. It rotated in and out of a beam of dazzling white light, disappearing for a moment, then flashing back into sight and tracking along the purple rays of a distant spotlight. Tiny droplets of sweat scattered in all directions along its trajectory and sprayed off into the vast expanse of the dance tent.

A tremendous roar followed the drumstick, a primeval sound even louder than the crashing music itself. Like an earth-tremor the vibrations of the crowd expanded outwards into the surrounding hillside, startling nocturnal animals and disturbing the cold bones of ancient druids buried deep within Glastonbury Tor.

But the drumstick was too high and too fast to be caught by anyone. It was too unruly and its spin too chaotic. In less than five seconds, it had vanished into darkness, to hit an unknowing stranger on the shoulder. It fell to the ground unseen and was trampled into the damp grass. The roar of the

1

crowd subsided, as disappointed bodies fell back to earth in a communal thump of muddy rubber boots. The drummer on stage grabbed a replacement stick from the quiver at his side and carried on with the roll, hardly missing a beat.

Gary was still jumping and pushing, bouncing off other people's backs and shouting in their ears. He felt as spontaneous, unrestrained and free as the drumstick. He could feel his heart pounding, sometimes matching the beat and sometimes overtaking it.

He thrust both fists triumphantly above his head, as if praying to the god of electronica, and began to punch the air. The giant psychedelic mobiles hanging from the rafters of the tent whirled and bobbed with the heat generated by the dancers below; and Gary stared at their bright fluorescent colours.

As the tablet he'd swallowed began to dissolve into his bloodstream, Gary danced even more furiously, stamping his feet and waving his arms. He looked forward to the stage and was hypnotized by the bright screens behind the band; strange pixelated images exploded into his field of view, pulsating with the rhythm, changing shape and size and evolving before his eyes. His brain pounded as the music became clearer and more insistent, the colours on screen deeper and brighter, and his thoughts sharper.

Who cares if I'm twice the age of anyone else around here? Gary asked himself, as he bounced and jerked in the crush of youthful bodies.

Kareena was dancing at his side, gyrating and shaking her long hair to the beat. Gary held her head in his hands and gazed into her deep brown eyes. He kissed her and she pressed herself against him. Gary grabbed her buttocks with his hands and pulled her close. He was hot, hard and excited. He felt that his energy was boundless. He was rocking, trip-hopping, raving! It was beautiful, Kareena was beautiful, he was beautiful!

Gary cast all thought of Natalie aside; and he was sure that the kids would be asleep in their tents by now and would never know. He squeezed Kareena again: here was someone new – a fresh, young, feisty woman. He knew that she wanted him and his body told him that he wanted her.

Gary felt elated, and free of all commitment or responsibility. He had no idea if it was one or two or three in the morning. It didn't matter: he was dynamic, powerful and in control.

Not just in control, he yelled to himself, but *completely* in control; and Gary knew in his heart that his life was about to change for the better and that this feeling, this bursting, lusty, energetic feeling – and the band, and the music and Kareena – would all last forever.

'Let's go,' Kareena shouted unexpectedly into his ear.

Gary wasn't sure that he'd heard her properly. He wasn't even sure that it was Kareena. He was only aware that he was losing all normal sense of time and space, and there didn't seem to be anything he could do about it. The combined effect of the drugs and alcohol were irresistible. He didn't bother responding to her suggestion, but jumped once again and landed gently back on his feet, his fall having been cushioned to an exquisite softness by his boots.

He was hemmed in on all sides by the thronging mass, but it felt like being in a wide open space, with people moving indistinctly around him at the faraway edges. He was no longer thrashing the air with his hands, nodding his head rhythmically or pumping the ground. He was standing still, being pushed in all directions by the people still dancing next to him. Gary was spellbound by the light show on stage and the never-ending images, which changed unremittingly with the beat: now intensifying, now degrading and then disappearing.

Gary's brain throbbed and he groaned with pleasure. He reached forward, as if in a trance; and tried to touch a huge grinning yellow face, which had materialised on the screen before his eyes. The face began to turn, slowly at first; then faster and faster until it was spinning like a wheel. It increased and decreased in size in time with the music. The face seemed to catch Gary's eye as it span and he was riveted to the spot. The face was howling with laughter, but whether it was at him or with him, Gary was unsure.

His mouth was now open and he felt himself dribble: a slow, hot snake of saliva that drooled over his slack lower lip. He wiped his chin with the back of his arm. He was shaken by the dryness and the roughness of his skin. Without warning, the wide space around him contracted, so that once again he was confined on all sides by close, squirming bodies. He grabbed Kareena around the waist and together they danced, squeezing tight, dissolved in one united movement.

The guitars wailed their final riffs and the singer screamed his last, deafening the audience. As the band left the stage, bellowing spectators surged forwards and backwards, euphoric and angry altogether, demanding more.

'Let's go,' Kareena shouted again.

'They might come back,' Gary croaked, his throat sore from shouting.

'Maybe; but I want to go now.'

Kareena moistened Gary's parched lips with her tongue. 'Don't you want to come with me?' she asked suggestively, raising her eyebrows and running her hand down his spine. 'I'm really high, you know.'

Gary gazed at her face. Her cheeks were red with exertion, her brow and fringe sweaty, and her large eyes open wide and clear. Kareena rubbed her thigh against his groin. 'Come on,' she urged.

Gary smiled and kissed her gently on the nose. 'No contest,' he said.

Holding hands, they pushed their way out of the tent, turning their backs on the encore which the band had begun to deliver to its grateful and ecstatic fans.

'I'm thirsty,' Kareena said as they cleared the tent and found themselves in the dance field again, standing in a soup of mud.

Gary gasped as fresh air and a cool dampness filled his lungs. He knew that it must have rained again, but couldn't tell how long ago. He suggested that they find somewhere for a drink but, even then, he knew that Kareena would have to lead the way. His mind and body had become detached and he was no longer capable of co-ordinated action.

Kareena pointed at some bright lights far away. Gary peered into the darkness. It was as if his head had been wrapped in a black sheet, because he could only perceive tiny pinpricks of light. Kareena took his hand and pulled him in the direction she had chosen.

Gary felt a numbness creep over his body. He stumbled along, sloshing mud with his boots. The music from the dance tent played over and over in his head. Although he hadn't known any of the songs, he could recall them all in crisp perfection. Occasionally, he would try to bypass the noise and confusion in his head and reach for normal thoughts like: Who am I? Where am I? What am I doing? Each time these thoughts began to form, a mysterious force blocked their path towards his conscious mind, until they dissipated and were quietly lost in some unknown part of his brain. It was as if his thoughts had been hijacked by something alien that he couldn't control. It made him feel sick.

Kareena led them into a large circular tent at the edge of the dance field. The inner walls were fitted with mirrors, which reflected the high, mounted spot lights and sent shards of rainbow colours everywhere. It was much less crowded than the dance tent, though a DJ was mixing tracks near the bar and several dozen people were on the dance floor.

Gary waited at a table while Kareena bought the drinks. He tried to work out where he was, but he had no real idea. All he knew was that he was glad of the rest.

Kareena returned with a can of lager for Gary and a bottle of water for herself. 'I didn't know you were married,' she said with surprise, as she sat down at the table. 'I mean, didn't you tell me your wife had died?'

Gary frowned. He followed her gaze and looked at his ring finger. His wedding ring was back where it belonged – or rather, he reasoned, where it no longer belonged. He didn't know when or how he had put it back on.

Instinctively, he wanted to hide his hand but managed to limit his reaction to a soft drumming of fingers on the table top. He hadn't wanted Natalie to intrude into this night and he resented the feeling that somehow she was present and watching him.

'I'm not; and yes, she died three years ago,' Gary said, taking a swig of lager. He could sense that Kareena was expecting a fuller explanation. He shifted uneasily on his seat. 'I should've taken the ring off but it's too hard. It's been there for nearly half my life, you know. I'll take it off one day, but not yet. I'm not ready.'

'Can I see it?'

Gary shrugged and eased the ring off his finger. Kareena tried it on several of her fingers, but it was too large to fit snugly. She caressed the smooth flat inner surface and the fat, curved outside edge between her finger and her thumb, gazing at the distorted reflections on the shiny gold. Suddenly, she clenched her fist around the ring, hiding it from view.

'I'll look after it for you, if you want,' she said, smiling sweetly.

'There's no need,' replied Gary, with panic in his voice. He held out his hand, barely noticing how it shook.

'I'll keep it safe,' Kareena said, looking at Gary with doe eyes. She took his hand in hers and added: 'Until tomorrow morning.' Gary knew he was unhappy, but he couldn't think clearly enough to say so. He frowned again. 'Don't you trust me?' Kareena asked, with a feigned tone of being hurt. 'I'll look after you, too… if you'll let me.'

Kareena passed the tip of her tongue enticingly across her lips. Gary didn't want to think about the ring any more. He only wanted to think about Kareena and the growing bulge in his trousers.

'OK,' he said. 'I'd like that. I'd like both.'

He drank some more lager. He felt a strong gurgling in his

stomach, but put the turbulence down to the fizzy drink. He looked at Kareena. Although he desired her, he was having trouble articulating his thoughts.

'What were we talking about?' he asked, scratching his head.

'You said you wanted me,' Kareena giggled. She leant over and whispered lightly in his ear, so that goose pimples ran down his neck: 'But you didn't say how.'

Gary adjusted his trousers to contain the mounting pressure between his legs. He was at least clear that the time for thinking – or trying to – was now over.

'Let's go then,' he gasped. 'Is it far to your tent?'

They walked arm in arm and hip by hip to the end of the field, their rubber boots squelching on waterlogged grass.

'My tent's just over there,' Kareena said pointing to tens of thousands of tents stretching into the darkness.

'I need a slash first,' Gary said. He lurched towards a fenced-off urinal at the entrance to the campsite.

'I'll wait for you over there,' Kareena said, pointing to a wooden gate. 'But don't be too long.'

Gary waded through a sea of mud and water into the urinal. Several men were relieving themselves along the side of a metal trough. Although it was dark everything was bathed in an eerie blue light, which radiated through the tarpaulin fastened to the fence. Gary stumbled to the far end of the trough, as far away from anyone as he could stand. He unzipped his trousers, pulled out his swollen penis and held it in his hand. He needed to urinate badly, but couldn't so long as it stubbornly refused to relax.

Gary stared at the soggy cigarette butts and half-empty

lager cans rolling gently in the trough, in the stream of other people's urine. He screwed up his nose at the acrid smell. A man came near and added to the flow of steaming orange liquid. Gary turned his back to him in embarrassment. As he listened to the sound of urine on metal, he felt his organ soften and, eventually, he too was enjoying the relief brought on by a full bladder steadily emptying itself.

As he zipped up his trousers, Gary's heart began to beat loudly. He imagined Kareena's probing tongue playing with his own and his groin began to swell up again. He imagined caressing her breasts, then her buttocks, then her breasts again as her body quivered beneath his. His hand slid between her legs and made her moan.

His heart was pounding as he stepped out of the urinal, clutching himself through his trouser pockets. He could see Kareena, smiling and holding out her hands, inviting him to join her. Gary felt as if he were in a dream. He squared his shoulders and marched to claim his prize. His heart was now racing and crashing music seemed to fill his head.

'Quick,' he read from Kareena's lips. 'I want you. I want you now!'

Gary would never know what made him slip. He was within a few yards of the gate when he saw his arms fly out in front of him. Kareena's expectant face disappeared from view and everything was obliterated, as his head landed in liquid mud.

Gary's first impression was the absence of light. The second, a complete silence, as muddy water filled his ears, nose and mouth. The third was the instantaneous absorption of water by his clothes, soaking his skin. Finally, he felt the cold.

With his head in the water Gary couldn't breathe; and he

didn't try to. His brain registered that a catastrophic change had taken place, but it wasn't able to explain to him what it was. Unable to process these sensations, his mind stalled altogether, leaving Gary lying in the water feeling strangely tranquil, as if he were asleep.

His will power having failed him, instinct kicked in to force air out of his lungs, expel water from his nostrils and wrench his face explosively out of the mud. He spat out the water and gasped for air, coughing and spluttering and propping himself up on submerged elbows. He shook his head and tried to wipe the muck from his eyes.

He coughed again and searched for Kareena. She stood there, only feet away, looking shocked. He pleaded with his eyes for her to help him, but she didn't move. Instead, he saw her face change to a look of pity, then horror and finally disgust. Gary tried to call for help but his mouth would hardly open.

'Do you know him?' Gary heard a voice ask. He peered into the darkness and saw a man standing next to Kareena, with a thin, curved scar down the side of his right cheek. Gary recognised him from the dance tent; he must have followed them, but he couldn't work out why. He looked quizzically at Kareena. Even from where he lay he she looked very beautiful.

'No,' she said, with some hesitation. 'I don't know who he is.'

'Then come with me,' the stranger said. 'I won't let you down.'

As Kareena disappeared from view Gary had the sensation that he was falling. His grasp of reality began to fade quickly, as he tumbled further and further into blackness.

When he had stopped falling Gary felt as though he was

now sitting in cold water at the bottom of a deep well. Even with his eyes fully open, Gary could see nothing, not even the hands that he held before his face. The only light was a tiny circle at the top of the well shaft and Gary had to crane his neck to see it. He shivered with cold, but continued to lie with his head in the muddy water.

If he drowned, he thought, the children would be orphaned. His mind filled with a stream of connected memories: playing in a garden, a rubber mask, a sore, sore throat, Amy the Labrador, Miss Graham, musical chairs, frilly frocks, sweet sherry, Suzanne Fuller, bras, breasts, Miss Nightingale, exams, the first day at college, Natalie, the miscarriage, graduation, Natalie, the gold ring, Hannah, Treyarnon bay in the rain, Suzanne Fuller, smashing glass, Marc, number twenty-three Ashley Road, black smoke at the crematorium, Frank, France, Natalie up, Natalie down, Natalie gone.

TWO

The previous Thursday

It seemed a lifetime away, though it was only three days before. Gary was sitting in a road-side café and it was eleven o'clock in the morning. The warm aroma of brewed coffee mixed uneasily with the heavy odour of fried food. The place was full and they'd been lucky to get a seat. He tried to shut out the sounds of voices everywhere, of cups on saucers and of metal lids on tea pots. He was concentrating hard to remember his lines.

Gary clenched his fists tightly under the scuffed yellow table. Hannah and Lucy sat opposite, casting glances over their shoulders and giggling. At his side, Marc jabbed away on an electronic game, oblivious to the activity around him.

'Hannah,' he said quietly. When there was no response, he cleared his throat and repeated her name more loudly.

Hannah looked up at her father with bleary eyes. Gary hardly knew how to begin, despite having spent the last hundred miles composing his little lecture.

'I've got something really important to say,' he continued; 'to both of you.'

He took a deep breath but fell silent as a waitress arrived at the table with their all-day breakfasts. Hannah and Lucy picked up their cutlery and attacked the sausages on their plates. Marc grabbed his cheeseburger with both hands and sank his teeth into it. Gary looked at the under-cooked fried egg on his own plate and felt queasy.

'It's about Glastonbury,' he said firmly. Hannah nodded, as if to say 'what else?'

'Well, I mean, it's a big place and I won't always be with you; so we've got to get the ground rules sorted out.'

Hannah shrugged her shoulders and crunched a piece of toast.

'It's going to be hot, according to the forecast, so you'll have to wear your hats and drink lots of water.'

'And… ?'

'And it's important to look after yourselves. You know, lots of sun cream and that sort of thing.'

Hannah looked unimpressed and Gary felt a rising panic. He knew that he had to get to the point quickly. He brought his hands onto the table and began to tap his fingernails on the Formica. He licked the salt from his upper lip.

'The main thing I want to talk to you about is alcohol.' Hannah groaned and tried to clear her mouth of food. Gary held up his hand to stop her interrupting. 'I've mentioned this before, but you know I'm not happy about your underage drinking. No, no, listen: I've tried to be as relaxed as I can about it, but this is different and I've had more thoughts.'

Hannah shook her head and let out a long 'Boring…' under her breath.

'Look, you two, there's going to be lots of lovely people at Glastonbury and the atmosphere's going to be great; but you should know that some people are out to take advantage. I don't want you or Lucy to be fooled; you've got to keep your wits about you.'

Hannah furrowed her brow to show that she was beginning to get annoyed.

'Glastonbury's not a place where you'd want to get drunk or sick. But it's not just that. There's one area that I need to speak to you about really seriously.'

Gary's voice sounded so high-pitched that he hardly recognized it. Hannah and Lucy held their forks in mid-air, with looks of fearful anticipation.

'The one area is… ' Gary hesitated before taking the plunge; 'well… it's the realm of sex.'

Gary watched for a reaction; and when he saw none he forged ahead with a torrent of well-rehearsed advice.

'Basically, it's boys that are the problem. You can't afford to get drunk and go back to one of their tents. Boys are only after one thing; and you can't even rely on them to use a condom. Anyway, you know that boys don't wash at the best of times, but can you imagine how smelly – how *unhygienic* – they'll be after a few days' camping? So, the message is really quite simple: no alcohol, no going back to boys' tents and no sex!'

Hannah and Lucy were silent. Gary felt triumphant.

'Respect your bodies,' he added for greater emphasis, 'and drink lots of water. Then you'll be fine.'

Lucy's face was bright red. Her knife and fork were lodged in a sausage, but she wasn't trying to cut it anymore. She stared at her plate, as if nothing else in the world existed. Hannah was also flushed, but her eyes blazed with fury. Gary sensed that an elderly couple at the next table had also stopped eating; indeed, it felt as if the whole café had frozen momentarily.

Hannah laid her knife and fork slowly on her plate and she swept her head back defiantly.

'So,' she said with contempt in her voice, 'the great Expert of Life has spoken. All bow down before him and hark his mighty words. In the fabled Land of Glastonbury, we can go anywhere we like, except for the Realm of Sex.' She leant forward and added in low, staccato tones: 'I don't think I've heard anything so pathetic in all my life. I can't believe you said that in front of me and Marc, let alone in front of my friend. Dad, you are such a loser!'

She stood up and pushed her plate towards Gary, sending cutlery clattering onto the floor. The café froze again and heads turned.

'C'mon, Lucy, let's go to the toilet. I think I'm going to be sick – even without alcohol!'

As the girls fled from the table, Gary saw Marc smirking at him.

'Nice one, dad. You handled that really well.'

'It had to be done.'

'Don't you think they teach us that stuff at school? And why say it to Lucy, if her mum's coming tomorrow?'

'Two girls together… '

'Dad – that wasn't just sad; it was gross!' Marc shoved the last of the gooey cheeseburger into his mouth and with the back of his hand wiped drizzling fat and tomato ketchup off his lips. '*Gross!*'

'I did if for your mother.'

Marc shook his head, then took his father's hand. 'You've got to get over her some time, dad. You can't go on like this forever.'

Back in the car, they drove on in silence. Gary tried the radio, but Hannah's constant sighing persuaded him to switch if off again. In the hour it took to reach the festival, Gary's mind revisited the pep talk he'd given the girls. He winced several times at the way things had come out and wished he'd done better. He gripped the steering wheel tightly with his taut and clammy hands; and felt any remaining hope for the weekend being sucked out of the car through his partially open window.

When Gary spotted a hitch-hiker he decided immediately to give her a lift, if only to stop Hannah kneeing him repeatedly through the back of his seat. The girls protested loudly, but Hannah soon undid her seat belt and moved over to the let the young woman clamber in beside her.

'Hi, girls,' the stranger said, in a soft American accent. She placed a green plastic petrol container at her feet and held out her hand. 'I'm Kareena.' Lucy reached over and shook hands, but Hannah just smiled weakly.

Gary looked at the newcomer in his rear-view mirror. Late twenties, he thought; with gorgeous eyes that reminded him of Natalie and gave him an unexpected thrill. He asked her where she'd run out of petrol.

'On site,' she replied, 'just as we arrived at the parking lot.'

'Are we that close?' Gary asked with surprise.

'Oh, yeah. It's only a few miles away.'

Gary hummed with pleasure at the thought that their journey was nearly over. As he scoured the road ahead for signs of the festival, he saw several other cars laden with people and camping equipment. 'I think you must be right,' he said, more to himself than to Kareena, pushing the accelerator down with new-found enthusiasm.

After her initial hesitation, Hannah introduced herself to Kareena and asked which bands she wanted to see. When

Kareena replied 'None in particular' Hannah pulled a face. 'Why have you come then?' she asked.

Kareena laughed. 'I'm here with some friends, just for the vibe.'

In the mirror, Gary saw Hannah roll her eyes at the v-word and he looked anxiously at Kareena in case she noticed. He lingered on her eyes for several seconds and he became aware of a faint attraction towards her. Immediately, he suppressed the feeling: she might be nearly twice Hannah's age, he thought, but it was still inappropriate.

His attention was drawn to a flashing indicator light ahead. He followed the car in front and pulled off the main road into a country lane. Soon, he was directed into a field, where he came to a halt. Several marshals in fluorescent yellow tabards were checking tickets, so Gary wound down his window.

He was nonplussed to see an elderly Caribbean pirate approach, complete with three-cornered hat, black eye-patch and a brightly-coloured stuffed parrot on his shoulder.

'Welcome, all of you, me hearties!' the old man said with a broad grin. 'Are you dropping this lot off?' he asked Gary, nodding towards his passengers.

Gary gave a nervous laugh. 'Well, I've got a ticket, so I suppose I'm going in with them.'

The pirate chuckled and his parrot wobbled precariously. Gary caught its beady black eye, which looked straight back at him. 'I hope you've got the stamina,' the pirate said, as he handed back the tickets, 'because there's no time for cocoa and slippers in there, me old hearty.'

'I'm not that old, so I think I can handle it,' Gary said, sounding slightly irritated and thinking that the older man had a bit of a nerve.

'I'm sure you can, but watch out: a lot of unexpected things can happen in a place like this.' The pirate brandished a curved plastic cutlass, which he had whipped from his baggy trousers. 'Along with you!' he commanded.

As Gary reached for the handbrake, the pirate pointed the cutlass at him. 'And don't let me catch you sleeping at night, matey,' he added, with mock menace, 'or I'll run you through and feed you to the sharks!'

As they pulled away, Kareena asked if Hannah and Lucy were sisters, because they looked so alike. 'No, we're not,' Hannah giggled. 'We're best friends, and Marc's my younger brother.'

'So where's mom? At home?' Kareena asked.

The giggling was snuffed out like a candle, leaving an awkward silence swirling in the air. The car jolted suddenly, as one of the wheels ran over a small boulder and dropped into a pothole behind it. There was a chorus of complaint as the bump rolled from the front to the back of the car, bouncing everyone in their seats. The garden wheelbarrow, which Gary had strapped to the roof rack along with their camping equipment, jumped and crashed onto the roof of the car with a loud bang.

As the car regained its balance, Marc explained: 'Mum's dead,' he said.

The young teenagers' eyes were fixed on Kareena. Even Gary found himself gazing at her through his mirror. All he could see were her deep brown eyes, but now it pained him to recall their familiarity. He longed to say something; some tender words, perhaps, but nothing came.

Kareena had obviously not foreseen Marc's response, but she continued with hardly a moment's pause. 'Sorry, guys,' she said. 'How could I have known? I guess it's really hard for you all; especially your pa.'

Gary crashed the gears as he slowed to avoid another pothole. The teenagers shouted at him, but Kareena just looked into his rear-view mirror and her eyes seemed to be full of sympathy. Her gaze stayed on him rather longer than he would have expected, as if she were trying to communicate something to him. Gary felt a frisson of excitement.

'Our mum fell down the stairs,' Marc said in a subdued voice. 'She was in a hurry and she tripped.'

Gary winced. He then flung the wheel round to avoid a large rock, sending his passengers first to the left and then back to the right.

'But it was nobody's *fault*,' he said a little too firmly.

'It was just an accident,' Hannah said. 'Three years ago.'

'That's a long time,' Kareena said thoughtfully. 'I know it's really sad, but I hope you're managing to get over it by now.'

'*We* are,' Marc replied softly.

Gary grunted loudly to show his disapproval of what Marc had said. He now regretted giving Kareena a lift. It was alright for the teenagers, but life just can't go on for everyone, he thought. He touched his shirt pocket and felt the photograph nestling there. It was a snap of Natalie and the children, when they were young; smiling in the sun on a beach. He often carried it as a reminder of happier times. It gave him reassurance that he was not alone or misguided in what he was doing. This, after all, was a joint venture.

They parked in a field already full of cars glinting in the bright sunlight. Kareena thanked Gary for the lift and offered him her hand. It was a strangely formal gesture and it took Gary aback. He still felt put out by the conversation in the car and, at first, he resisted the offer; but Kareena just stood before him, her hand outstretched. Gary tried to read her face but couldn't see beyond her knowing, enticing smile. He didn't want to make friends with Kareena but, at the same time, he didn't want to be rude. He shook her hand and, as he pulled away, he let his fingers stroke hers.

THREE

A yellow sun beat down from the cloudless blue sky, as Gary and the teenagers marched through fields of parked cars. Gary felt the strain of pushing the wheelbarrow containing their tent, but he was happy to be there. He breathed deeply, filling his lungs with fresh country air, which he could sense was charged with promise. They joined a stream of people in bright summer clothes, who were chatting and laughing as they worked their way to the entrance of the festival. Everyone was carrying a bag, a rucksack or a piece of camping equipment. Children in pushchairs were also doing their bit, clutching pillows, sun hats or wellington boots. Gary began to absorb the excitement all around him and his mood lifted.

The grassy track led to the crest of a hill, where they stopped to take in the view. The teenagers gasped when they saw the vast festival site sprawling before them in the valley below. 'It's absolutely massive,' Marc said, throwing his arms wide to demonstrate what he meant.

Gary nodded in agreement as he struggled to take it all in: thousands upon thousands of small tents packed into the fields and up both sides of the valley; a dozen blue and red big tops standing proud of the tall green trees and bushy hedgerows; and innumerable colourful pennants flapping lazily in the warm sun, intertwined with spirals of wood smoke. 'Unbelievable,' Gary replied eventually, his eyes following the glinting curves of a metal security fence that encircled the whole site. Natalie would have been amazed.

Beyond the festival, the long, wide valley stretched away for several miles. In the distance a rectangular tower stood on top of a small, round hill. It was like a sentinel watching over them, Gary thought, and he felt safe. 'That's Glastonbury Tor,' he said to no one in particular. He could smell the wood smoke now and it somehow felt very primeval. Gazing at the trees, the peaks of the tents and the flags on their tall poles, all he could see was colour and movement. It was as if the whole, huge encampment belonged to a lost mythical age; something straight out of Arthurian legend. He wouldn't have been surprised if a couple of mounted knights in armour had come charging up the hill.

'It's like something from a fairy tale,' Lucy said.

'Don't be stupid; not with all that noise,' Hannah replied, referring to a rhythmic drumming that filled the air. 'I hope that's not the music we've come all this way to hear, dad,' she added, frowning with disapproval. 'What is it, anyway?'

'Hippies doing a rain dance,' Marc suggested unhelpfully.

'I hope not,' Gary said, picking up the wheelbarrow again. 'That's the last thing we need.'

'Well, I hope it doesn't go on for much longer,' Hannah said. 'It's giving me a headache.'

Having passed through a turnstile Gary led them along a gravel track to the family camping field, through a forest of shimmering white and orange silk flags. Privately, Gary was horrified by the number of tents; and he wondered out loud if they'd find any room for theirs.

'It's because we've arrived so late,' Hannah complained.

Gary ignored her and pulled a mobile phone from his pocket. 'It's no use,' he said after short while, 'I can't get hold of Frank and Sam. We'll just have to put our tent up on its own, wherever we can find space.'

It took them half an hour to find a clear patch of grass. It was a misshapen area, bounded by different-sized tents pitched at awkward angles. A fire point marked one corner: a red triangle with a white '44' in the middle, on top of a tall metal pole. Gary negotiated with a few of the neighbouring campers to move their guy ropes to make some more space. When he had done so, he tipped everything out of the wheelbarrow.

The teenagers had fallen on the grass with exhaustion and Gary had to nag them to help him erect the tent. Hannah and Lucy chose the inner tent they wanted to share as a bedroom and threw their sleeping bags into it, leaving a sleeping compartment each for Gary and Marc. They all piled their rucksacks into the middle of the tent, a tall atrium with an entrance.

'I've texted Sam,' Marc said. 'He's coming to see us with his dad and they'll be here any minute.'

'How will they find us?' Gary asked.

Marc arched his eyebrows in astonishment. 'How will they miss us, you mean?'

Before Gary could ask for an explanation, he heard a deep voice outside exclaim 'My God! What kind of tent is this?' Gary looked at the open door and saw it was filled with a man's heavy frame.

'Hi Frank,' Gary grinned. 'Great to see you again.'

'Are you trying to tell us all something, Gary?' Frank asked with mock alarm in his voice. 'A *pink* tent? I mean to say.'

'What's wrong with pink?'

'Attracts the wrong sort, if you know what I mean. I don't suppose Marc'll be too happy with a load of them prowling about at night!'

Marc blushed.

'You can't say things like that,' Gary said. 'Anyway, it was last year's stock and pink was cheap.'

'At least the girls will be safe in a tent like this,' Frank said, ignoring Gary and inviting himself in. 'No hot-blooded males will chase them here!' Hannah and Lucy looked at each other, embarrassed, and Marc gave Sam a pained look. Frank patted Gary on the back. 'I'm sorry. Forget it,' he said. 'It's a pretty colour in here anyway. Who's going to show me around?'

Frank opened the zipped door to Marc's inner tent and called Sam over to come and look. 'There's loads of space here, if you two want to share,' he said. 'That'd be OK, wouldn't it Gary?'

'Yeah, of course; if the boys want to.'

'I imagine they will. It'll be more fun for them and they can come and go as they please. Or they could stay in Sam's two-man tent, but it's a bit small and we're using it for storage at the moment.' Frank bent his knees and reached in for Marc's sleeping bag.

'Good quality,' he remarked, feeling it with his hands. 'And what a big one you've got.' He undid the lace and pulled the rolled up sleeping bag out of its nylon sack. He then fell to his knees and squeezed the bag between them, so that it stood proud, at an angle. 'The girls should be impressed with that,' he laughed.

'Ugh, dad,' Sam said. 'Let me out of here!' Gary heard Lucy mutter 'He's awful' as the girls quickly followed the boys out of the tent. Gary turned to his friend.

'Frank – you've haven't been here two minutes and all you've done is make crude jokes and upset everyone.'

'It was just harmless fun.'

'They don't think so. You should apologise.' Gary left the tent leaving Frank behind.

'I don't apologize to anyone,' Frank called out after him.

'Suit yourself, but don't be surprised if they ignore you all weekend.'

A few moments later, Frank emerged into the sunshine with a scowl on his face.

'I think you're all making a big fuss about nothing,' he said to the teenagers, 'but if I was a bit over the top, I'm sorry. I'm just a bit hungry, that's all. Why don't we all go and eat?'

No one spoke or moved.

'Alright, alright,' Frank said finally. 'I'm buying. It's a free meal; and you can't say fairer than that, can you? So come on, don't spoil things – let's go!'

They wandered in the late afternoon sunshine, browsing numerous stalls along the way. 'It's quite a lot to take in,' Gary said, as they passed a row of busy traders. 'I certainly know where to come if I want juggling balls or a hammock. I wonder if there's anything they don't sell.'

'I know,' Frank replied. 'Natalie would have loved it, especially the jewellery.'

There was a brief silence before Gary agreed. He smiled at Frank but, despite the well-meaning comment, he felt uncomfortable. It just seemed a bit odd to mention Natalie quite so soon. Surely it was down to him to raise that subject first? After all, he was the one who was suffering, not Frank.

'Actually, mum would have hated this,' Hannah said,

having overheard their conversation. 'There are too many people here.'

'Come on, Hannah,' Frank said, responding on Gary's behalf. 'Your mother would've loved this sunshine and seeing so many happy faces!'

It's true, Gary thought: so many smiles and gleaming eyes, all the people ambling along, chatting and enjoying themselves. Yes, Frank is right, Natalie would have adored it.

They turned into a field and the teenagers sprinted towards a large wooden structure, spelling LOVE in white capital letters. Although twice as high as an adult, Lucy and Hannah had soon scaled the side of the letter E like a ladder. They stood on the top, waving triumphantly and taunting the boys who couldn't reach. The boys stepped up onto the base of the L instead and tried to help each other clamber up the outer edge of the neighbouring O, but it was still too high.

'Teenagers drawn to love, just like real life,' Gary said.

'Careful what you wish for, with two beauties like Hannah and Lucy in your charge.'

'I was being philosophical, Frank.'

They watched Sam step into the V and try to lever himself up, but his position became more precarious as the sides diverged. He leant against one slope, crossed his hands and pulled a face. Frank suggested the boys join some other children painting patterns on the side of the letters, but he met with little enthusiasm. 'Maybe,' Sam replied.

'Well, Gary and I are going for a drink in that tent over there. We'll be back soon to look at your artwork, but come over and get us if you finish first.'

The beer tent was light and airy. Sunlight flooded in through the open doorway and filtered through the large brass eyelets, where thick poles supported the canvas. Inside, the sun made the walls glow a bright, creamy white. A host of keen volunteers in red T-shirts stood behind the long wooden bar, pouring foaming pints of real ale from a row of barrels.

'What's yours?' Frank asked. 'Do you fancy a pint of scrumpy cider?'

'Is it any good?'

'It's fantastic; not like that God-awful stuff we drank when we were young.'

Gary grinned at the memory. 'That was twenty years ago. If I remember rightly, they used to put a rat in the vat, to give it a local twist.'

'I never believed that, even then,' Frank said, 'but, really, this stuff's great. You want to try some?'

Gary hesitated: scrumpy had been Natalie's drink and it felt disloyal to her memory to drink it now. He looked at his friend but said nothing.

'Don't worry, mate,' Frank said, putting his hand on Gary's shoulders, as if he could read his thoughts. 'No one's going to mind if you have a pint of scrumpy.'

They sat across a table in the sunny corner of the tent, with their drinks in two tall, pint-sized paper cups.

'Bad journey, eh?' Frank asked.

'Oh, it was OK. Hannah played up as usual. I couldn't do anything right.'

'I bet she had things on her mind. You know what kids are like.'

'Huh!' Gary exclaimed, gulping another mouthful. 'The only thing she had on her mind was boys. I'm amazed she hasn't met one already and run off with him. Lucy's no better: she's completely boy-mad.'

'Did I hear that Claire's coming tomorrow?'

'That's the plan. Her firm's organised some back-stage catering and she's coming to check it all out. I don't think she'll have much to do.'

'Where's she staying?'

'Near us I think, but in the crew camping.'

'So, why didn't you give her a lift in your car?'

'She had to work today… hey, what's with all the raised eyebrows?'

'Well,' Frank said coyly. 'She's a single mother and she's pretty fit, you know.'

'What? Surely you're not suggesting… ?'

'Oh, come on,' Frank replied, sitting back as if he had been pushed there by the force of Gary's reaction. 'You're single too. It's been three years. You're a good-looking bloke. What's the problem? And, you know what, Natalie wouldn't have disapproved.'

Gary opened his mouth in disbelief and put his drink onto the table.

'How dare you say that?' he said in a loud whisper. If they hadn't been friends since college, Gary would have thrown the cider all over him. 'How do you know what Natalie would have thought? It's unacceptable.'

'Oh, please, don't come the raw prawn with me, Gary. I'm entitled to my opinions.'

'And exactly what kind of phrase is that: 'raw prawn'? Frank, where *do* you get them?'

'From the radio. It's Australian, I think. I liked the sound of it so much, I thought I'd give it a go.' He laughed, but Gary crossed his arms and said nothing. 'Look I'm sorry if I've been insensitive. I just thought, well, by coming here you were beginning to get over it.'

'That's *my* business.'

FOUR

The teenagers had exhausted all that LOVE had to offer and came into the beer tent to pull Gary and Frank from their drinks. As they walked towards a nearby Ferris wheel, Gary hung back from the others so that he could take in his surroundings.

The air was still warm and balmy. As the sun descended in the sky, shadows stretched on the ground. People's strides seemed to lengthen too, but no one walked any faster: it was as if the crowd had started to move in slow motion, a sensory illusion heightened by enriched colours in the glowing light.

The gentle hubbub of voices mixed with the dull thud of feet on dry grass and caked mud. The constant movement of people threw up a reassuring dust: a dust which promised a dry evening and a clear night and which told city-dwellers they were now well and truly in the countryside. It was a dust that bound strangers together, in a magical place so very different from home.

Hannah grumbled that grit was getting in her eyes. Before long she and Lucy were coughing in loud repeated rasps, hands covering their mouths. 'Can we can stop for a drink?' Hannah asked. 'Lucy's thirsty, too,' she added, without actually having asked her.

'They'll sell drinks in 'Tantric Chai' over there,' Frank said, pointing to a large, round tent made of multi-coloured panels.

'What does 'chai' mean?' Marc asked.

'Tea.'

'And 'tantric'?'

'It means 'in a tent',' Frank said with a wink to Gary. 'Tea in a tent.'

A faint smell of joss sticks wafted out of the open door flaps, adding an unexpected twist of sandalwood, cinnamon and patchouli to the warm evening air. A middle-aged woman in a faded cotton dress sat to the side, smoking a long, thin pipe. A diamond stud pierced her sunburnt nose and golden rings dangled from each ear, behind straggly blond hair. She tapped her dirty bare feet on the ground and scratched her hairy legs with long, painted fingernails.

'It's a hippy,' Marc whispered to the others as they approached.

'I don't want to go in there,' Hannah said. 'Not if it's full of hippies and…' she paused for a moment '…and drugs…'

Gary smiled to himself: the anti-drugs message was clearly something the school taught well. 'There are no drugs here,' he said. 'They're illegal.'

'I know *that*. What's the smell then?'

'Incense.'

'Well, I don't like it.'

They sat on thick woollen rugs and large patterned cushions. Gary sipped his milky spiced tea and stretched out his legs. It took time for his eyes to adjust to the darkness. All around people were sitting and talking, or reading festival guides. A few were simply curled up, foetal-like, asleep. Gary looked at the tapestries hanging from the walls of the tent depicting scenes of Indian mythology: Hanuman, the monkey-god, he recognised, but who was the blue-skinned flute player with his voluptuous groupies?

At one end of the tent was a counter with a hot water urn. A thin man stood behind it, dressed in a tie-dye muslin shirt and faded jeans, waiting to serve customers. Soft music droned. Gary levered off his shoes and closed his eyes. This is so relaxing, he thought, I could sleep. Just as the lids glided over his weary eyeballs and his brain began to shut down, if not yet for the night then at least for a few minutes, an urgent gasp made him turn his head.

It was Hannah. She was looking directly at Gary, her eyes flickering with anxiety and her bottom lip trembling. Her arms were held straight down at her sides, one fist clutching the rug and the other a tuft of grass. She had knocked over her drink and the liquid was still visible in a dark purple pool on the cushion.

'We have to go,' Hannah hissed through gritted teeth. She repeated her words, with even greater force and urgency.

'What is it?' Lucy asked. Hannah stared into space, holding her head rigidly like a statue. 'Over there,' she whispered. 'Look!' She gave a slight sideways nod to her left, without turning her head in that direction.

Slowly, Gary and Lucy looked towards the end of the counter, past a heavily tattooed man tuning a guitar, towards a narrow opening in the inner wall of the tent. Through that they could see a hidden sanctuary, which was open to the sky. At first, Gary could see nothing but light and shadows. Then he noticed a movement, which at first he took to be a dog rolling onto its side. A closer inspection revealed the truth: three naked people, two men and one woman, all sitting on mats, relaxing in the fading rays of the sun.

One of the men, furthest away, was sitting up, holding his knees with his hands. His eyes were closed and he rocked gently backwards and forwards on his buttocks. The second man was reclining on his back, his hands behind his head and his torso, legs and genitalia stretched out before him. He was talking to the woman, who sat to his side, with a straight back and cross-legged, in a simple lotus position. She was perhaps thirty years old, with remarkably ginger-coloured hair that tumbled about her shoulders and tangled around her breasts.

Gary gazed at her intensely. His eyes caressed her large brown nipples. He followed the line of her inner thighs to the dark triangle of pubic hair at its source. It dawned on him that she was the first naked women he had seen in the flesh since Natalie had died. His interest was only marginally erotic; the very public display of nudity dampened any real feelings of lust or desire. However, he felt a change as he stared at her body: it was as if he had forgotten the beauty, the sheer difference of the female form until now. It was this sudden, unexpected reminder, which reawakened something deep inside him.

'You can see their willies,' Hannah whispered. 'Disgusting old wrinkly ones… Yuck!' Her face was pale. 'Well,' she said as she stood up, glaring at her father, 'are we going to go?'

'We could just look the other way,' Gary suggested.

'You can stay if you like,' Hannah continued, 'but if you're not leaving, I am!' Without looking back she marched out of the tent, with Lucy, Marc and Sam stumbling onto their feet and rushing out close behind her.

When Gary and Frank caught up with the teenagers a minute later, Hannah turned angrily on her father.

'I can't believe you took us to a place like that. First, it was

33

a smelly drugs den, full of dope-heads and crack addicts. Then it turned out to be a nudist colony, full of naked men.'

'And what's wrong with that?' Marc asked.

Hannah ignored him. 'What next?' she cried. 'I suppose you'll take us to a tent where they'll spike the drinks and molest us.' By now she was shaking with indignation. 'I'm just glad mum isn't here because she'd be totally appalled.'

'That's not fair,' Gary countered, stung by her accusation.

"Not fair' is taking us to a place like that.'

Hannah resolutely refused to speak to Gary as they approached the Ferris wheel, but Marc tried to re-live the experience, asking him whether it was legal for people to sunbathe in public with no clothes on. They joined a queue and Gary tried to deflect the question by wondering aloud if they would all get seats.

'I can't go up in that thing,' Frank said unexpectedly. 'I don't like heights much.'

'I don't want to go on it either,' Lucy added. 'It doesn't look safe.'

'Well, we're not frightened,' Marc said as he and Sam clambered into a car together.

'But who'll I go with?' Hannah asked, pulling back from the open car which followed.

'Are you coming, love?' the attendant asked. 'There's a lot of people waiting.'

Hannah glowered at Gary. He understood her reluctance to share the car with him, but she'd have no choice if she wanted a ride. 'I'll go with you,' Gary said gently. 'You don't have to speak to me, if you don't want to. You can pretend that you're on your own.'

After a momentary glance at Marc, who had a mocking grin on his face, she stepped forward, took her seat and folded her arms crossly.

Gary grabbed the safety rail as the wheel's engine roared and they began to rotate backwards. Bare light bulbs fixed on the painted metal struts flared brightly. The car rose slowly and Gary gazed in wonder at the steaming pistons and whirling brass cogs in the centre. As they reached the top Gary could feel his stomach muscles tighten. Hannah gripped the rail too and pulled herself closer to him. They reached the top: nothing obscured their bird's eye view of the tops of the marquees or the fluttering flags beneath them.

The wheel tipped them forward and Gary felt a rush of fear. They plunged downwards and outwards; it was as if the floor of the car had vanished and they were free-falling towards the ground. Hannah screamed and waved one of her hands at Frank and Lucy, who were standing at the foot of the wheel. Gary could see their faces coming even closer and then suddenly receding as the car ran to the lowest point and rushed backwards and upwards to repeat the cycle.

'That was fantastic,' Hannah shrieked, with her hair blowing chaotically about her head. Within seconds they had reached the top of the wheel once again. They were facing directly into the setting sun. Streams of light flooded through the tree tops into the fields below, casting long shadows across the bronze-coloured grass. The nearest tent, which close-up was dark blue in colour, now burned golden orange. 'What an amazing view!' Hannah shouted.

They swung downwards again, as if launching to the very heart of the sun, and again they whooshed backwards and upwards. As they span full circle, two, three, four times, the sun set in a blaze of gold and red behind a distant hill.

Hannah grasped hold of her father's arm and squeezed it tight. 'It's so beautiful,' she mumbled into his ear. 'Maybe it's not going to be so bad after all.'

As darkness fell they returned to the tents for an early night, exhausted from the day. The teenagers were keen to jump into their sleeping bags, treating it like an adventure. Gary was heartened by the way they had settled into their new surroundings. Soon he heard soft snores and whistling from the other compartments and he felt satisfaction with how things had turned out.

His own sleeping bag was surprisingly warm and comfortable and he soon fell asleep, feeling happy and contented.

FIVE

Despite the promising start, Gary slept fitfully. He rolled onto his side, grumbling with discomfort as a sharp stone dug into his shoulder. He turned again and worked his arm onto softer ground, curling up in his bag and placing his hands between his knees. Small noises outside the tent disturbed his sleep and his thoughts began to wander.

He dreamt of Natalie and Hannah: they were fighting and he was standing between them. As they screamed at each other, they both pleaded for his help. He couldn't decide what to do and just stood there, taking the full force of their blows.

His dilemma was forgotten in an instant, when a single ear-splitting peal of thunder broke over the valley. Gary jerked bolt upright in his sleeping bag.

'What the hell was that?' he said out loud. For a moment, he wondered if he was still asleep, but the fear and apprehension that he felt in his bones told him that he was wide awake. He shuddered as a telepathic sense of communal dread spread from tent to tent, like wild fire. This is definitely not good news, he thought.

He sat in the half-light of the approaching dawn and felt last night's euphoria evaporate like ether through the walls of his cotton inner tent. Cold air rushed in to fill its place and he shivered as the temperature dropped.

Gary could feel the weight of the huge clouds now massed

above the tent. He knew the thunder was just a prelude and he counted the long seconds of silence that followed. When it came, the repeat was even louder than the original. A tremendous crash of noise came from directly above his head, and was followed immediately by another. The whole tent trembled with fear, in sympathy with its occupants.

Gary then heard deep rumbles of thunder far away. He couldn't see Hannah or Lucy, but he knew from their absolute silence that they were also awake. He envied the fact they each had someone to hold them tight. For a while, the only sound that punctured the silence was the shallow breathing coming from Marc and Sam. At least, he thought, they had slept through it all.

Suddenly, the inner tent filled with bright pink light as forks of lightning crackled around campsite. Gary rummaged in his clothes and found his wrist watch: it was five o'clock in the morning. He sighed and fell back into his sleeping bag, as the first pitter-patter of raindrops reached the outer tent and ridge-poles.

The air freshened as the rain grew heavier. Gary heard the frame of the tent creak as the guy ropes tightened. Raindrops hurled themselves at the nylon flysheet. Gary could hear water cascading all around onto the narrow ribbons of grass between the tents. The sky boomed and the lightning was so intense that it tore the clouds apart.

'I told you I didn't want to come!' Gary heard Hannah complain to Lucy. 'What did he have to drag us here for, just so we could sit in the dark in the rain; and all my friends at home in bed?'

'I'm here with you, aren't I? 'Lucy replied.

'You don't count, because you're in the same mess that I'm

in. I'm cold and there's something hard under my sleeping bag.'

'Are we actually safe in this tent? We're right out in the open.'

'How should I know? If we're hit by lightning, it'll be a quick death – that's all I can say.'

'I don't want to die,' Lucy moaned.

'At least it'll warm us up!'

The girls' voices were soon drowned out by the hammering sound of powerful rain, which began to force itself through the seams of the tent. A fine mist filled his inner tent and settled on Gary's brow. He pulled the sleeping bag over his shoulders and groaned as he realised that he'd left their wellington boots in the back of the car. As he listened to the onslaught of rain and the renewed explosions of thunder overhead, he prayed that the storm wouldn't last.

Gary closed his eyes and rolled over. He thought about the pep talk that he had given the girls in the café and he felt himself blush at the memory. You must think of something else, he told himself. You're not ready to go over all that again. Anyway, Natalie knows that I did it for her.

He pictured the Natalie of his twenties and, as he did so, the noise of the rain seemed to abate. They were holding hands and smiling at each other. They stood in an empty field, in an empty countryside; it was as if there was no one else in the world but the two of them.

A sharp, silver-blue flash of lightning pierced his eyelids and filled his eyes with a momentary blood-red glow. Gary thought again about the danger presented by their exposed position; but he also knew that there was nothing that could be done about it now, except pray some more.

He remembered an electrical storm in Italy after he and Natalie had married. They had held each other tightly in a campsite outside Pompeii, amid sheets and forks of crackling electricity, booming thunder and raindrops the size of golf balls. The lightning had been so prolonged and intense that it was like daylight. As the vast storm encircled the Bay of Naples, they watched with awe as the ominous, towering presence of Mount Vesuvius became silhouetted against burning orange sides of their tent.

Natalie had screamed with delight at the ferocity of the raging skies, knowing that only Gary could hear her in the chaos that was all around them. She had torn off her T-shirt and pulled him to the ground, thrusting her tongue into his mouth. To the sound of furious airborne drums, in the full glare of earthbound lightning bolts, beneath a barrage of watery missiles, Natalie had made love to Gary like a demented being.

Natalie tried to deny it later, but Gary knew that Hannah had been conceived in that storm. Although unplanned, he was glad of it because he'd always felt that something extra was needed to bind him and Natalie together.

Gary felt aroused in his sleeping bag and stirred, but a final thought – that he and Natalie had not lasted forever, as he had hoped – dampened even nature's ardent response to his memories. He turned onto his other side and opened his eyes, but he could see nothing through the nascent tears. At least the thunder and lightning had died down, he thought, but when will the rain begin to ease off?

He could just about hear Marc's steady breathing next door, even over the sound of the storm, and that gave him some distant reassurance. Slowly, he drifted back into an uneasy sleep.

SIX

The rain was still pouring steadily when Gary woke again, but no longer with furious urgency. It was lighter in the tent and Gary looked at his watch: eight o'clock. It had been raining now continuously for three hours. He could hear muffled voices from nearby tents, all weary and edged with anxiety but, so far as he could tell, the teenagers were still asleep. He dozed on and off for the next hour, when he was disturbed by a loud voice, calling out his name. It was Frank.

'Anyone awake?'

'I am,' Gary replied weakly. 'What's it like out there?'

'Absolutely terrible. The whole place is flooded and it's still pouring like mad.' He paused to allow the regular beat of the rain to confirm what he had said. 'Neither of us have got boots,' he continued. 'I'm not going to buy the basic sort on site. I want proper ones with a lining, so I'm off to Shepton Mallet to buy them. Do you want me to get you some?'

'No thanks. Ours are in the car and I'll fetch them later. How long will you be?'

'No more than a couple of hours. Does Sam want to come with me?'

'The teenagers are still asleep I think.'

'No, I'm not,' Sam called out through the cotton walls of the Marc's sleeping compartment. 'I want to come.'

'Hurry up, then.'

Gary heard the door of the tent being unzipped.

'See you when we get back,' Frank called. 'If your tent hasn't been washed away by then!'

Gary fell back to sleep, but was finally awoken by a cramp in his calf muscle. As he rubbed his leg, he knew that he couldn't lie there any longer. The rain had eased and it was now much brighter. It was nearly ten o'clock and he could hardly believe that there had been five hours of solid rain. He heard stirring noises in the tent.

'Dad, we need a wee,' Hannah called out. 'And we're hungry.'

Gary rubbed his eyes and tried to collect his thoughts. 'And the batteries of my game have run out,' Marc added. 'Right in the middle and I've lost everything. It'll take me ages to do it again.'

'So what? It's only a game,' Hannah said. 'Dad, we're thirsty as well. And there's a huge spider on our side of the tent.'

'Help! He's trying to get me,' Lucy squealed.

Gary extracted himself from his sleeping bag and shivered as he moved through the damp air. His Hawaiian boxer shorts, with their palm trees swaying against a turquoise sky, looked absurdly optimistic and garish in the dull light. He smoothed his hand over the pretty girls in grass skirts and the muscular men with their surfboards. Natalie had bought them for him years ago. He smiled: she's having the last laugh, he thought. He stroked his arms, which were now covered in goose pimples.

His clothes from yesterday felt clammy and his shirt was already beginning to smell musty. He leant out of the sleeping compartment into the centre of the tent and fumbled in his rucksack for long trousers, a long-sleeved shirt and jumper. He put the T-shirts to one side, wondering if he'd ever get to wear them over the weekend. He pulled on his coat and hunted for his shoes in the chaos of bags and clothes piled up high in the middle of the tent.

'How badly do you need to wee?' he asked. 'Do you have to go now or can you wait while I get our wellies from the car?'

'We can wait if you're quick,' Hannah answered, 'but can you bring some food with you when you come back?'

Before he could ask what they wanted, Marc's suggestion of a bacon roll and hot chocolate met with a chorus of approval.

Outside the tent, the drizzle was now very fine and the air smelled of fresh vegetation. Gary pulled the hood of his coat over his head and picked his way between the packed tents towards the farm track. It was a scene of devastation. The sodden grass was pock-marked with boot-prints and every slight depression in the ground was full of murky brown water. Yesterday's dry dust had been transformed into slushy mud.

Tents everywhere sagged, gazebos lay on their side and pennants flapped listlessly from drooping poles. Campers were emerging slowly into the daylight under a sky laden with dense grey clouds.

When Gary reached the track the squelching of his shoes on the wet grass gave way to the slap-slap sound of water on gravel. He noticed that several tents to the side of the track were half-submerged in a vast puddle, which seemed more the size of a duck pond. A slight breeze ruffled the surface of the water and pushed floating debris around the forlorn, nylon islands: a child's beach ball, an upturned umbrella, green water bottles and empty beer cans.

Gary tried to imagine what had happened to those campers, in their sleeping bags as the water had risen higher and higher up the sides of their tents. He shuddered at the thought and realised that, comparatively speaking, his family had got off lightly.

He paused to watch a couple at the edge of the puddle, trying to fish a pair of floating shoes out of the water. They wore black dustbin liners for protection against the rain. Their arms, heads and legs stuck out of holes torn in the plastic, and they had covered their heads with orange plastic carrier bags: they looked for all the world like a pair of monstrous scarecrows.

As he walked on, Gary came across a man in shorts, standing in bare feet with water almost to his knees washing his hair and body with a tube of shower gel. He was smiling and laughing at passers-by, making the most of the disaster which had engulfed them all. As Gary nodded hello, the man pushed his arm up beneath the bulging front canopy of his tent and rainwater poured down over his head, rinsing off the white lather.

'Beats a shower any day,' he called out cheerfully.

It was nearly eleven o'clock when Gary returned to the tent carrying the wellington boots and a bag of bacon rolls; he had no hands left to carry hot chocolate. He was tired, but grateful that the drizzle had stopped. The uniform grey clouds had risen in the sky and it was a little brighter than before.

The teenagers were already dressed. After they had eaten

the food he'd brought, Gary led them through the mud to the portable plastic toilets at the edge of the field. By the time they arrived, all three of them were in discomfort, though only Lucy betrayed the fact by her knock-kneed, shuffling walk.

The toilet cubicles faced each other in two squat rows. Gary and the teenagers joined the queue of campers clutching toilet rolls, wash bags and towels.

'Why are we all waiting?' Lucy asked in desperation. A cubicle door was flung open and a woman stepped out. The queue advanced slowly. 'There are so many people and I really need to go. How do we know they're all full?'

'The doors with green discs are empty, and the doors with red discs are full,' Marc replied.

'But they're all red.'

'Yes, Lucy – that's why we're queuing.'

Suddenly, three or four doors opened at the same time and the campers surged forward. Gary heard a loud complaint from someone about queue-jumping. A man began to push at the locked doors, but they all held fast.

Despite Lucy's obvious need, Hannah was first to an empty cubicle. She jumped up the steps and banged the thick plastic door behind her. She snapped the red 'occupied' disc into place. Almost immediately, Gary heard a cry of despair, then a somewhat louder grunt of revulsion and, finally, a full-throated scream. The red disc on the door switched instantly to green and Hannah jumped out more quickly that she had entered. She ran to Gary holding her nose tightly with her fingers and with a look of horror on her face.

'It's so disgusting in there,' she cried. 'They weren't like that yesterday. What's happened?' Her face was contorted and there were tears in her eyes. 'I can't possibly go to the loo in there. It's all filled up and it really stinks. You can see all the poo down the hole. It's totally disgusting!'

Lucy didn't hesitate, but seized her chance to take Hannah's cubicle, whatever the sensory cost.

'How could you have brought us to such a place?' Hannah asked angrily. '*Are we pigs?*'

Marc smirked and Hannah swung at him with a toilet roll. 'Only pigs live in conditions like this,' she ranted. 'I've never smelled anything like it. I can't go in there – so what are you going to do?'

'It can't be that bad,' Gary said, racking his brain for ideas. 'Lucy doesn't seem to mind…'

'Am I Lucy? No. Mum would never have stood for toilets like this, you know. So why should we? You don't care about us at all, do you?' Hannah burst into tears. Gary felt embarrassed and looked around guiltily to gauge the reaction of the other campers in the queue. He was relieved by the unwavering look of sympathy for his situation. The man behind him stepped forward.

'She's right, they're terrible at this end,' he said, 'but they're much better over there.' He pointed towards the last of the cubicles. 'Here, take this with you,' he added, reaching out his hand to the distraught Hannah. 'It'll take away the smell.'

He gave Hannah a small aerosol can of air freshener. 'I always bring a couple with me when I come to a festival,' he explained in response to the bemused look on Gary's face. He paused for a moment, before adding: 'Honeysuckle and eucalyptus works best, you know.'

As they gathered again, Gary was disappointed when the children's relief proved to be more short-lived than his own.

'What?' Hannah cried, leading a glowering deputation of two, Marc not being remotely bothered, 'No showers? No hot water? How are we supposed to wash?'

'There are some showers, somewhere,' Gary replied, 'but I'm not exactly sure where they are.'

'Well, not anywhere around here,' Hannah said, 'because people over there are washing themselves with cold water.'

Gary followed her accusing finger and saw a queue of people with towels standing by the hedge. An old man in shorts was splashing his wrinkled body with cold water that gushed out of a tap nailed to a post.

Hannah put her hands on her hips. Her elbows pointed left and right, as if to emphasise that they would go anywhere, or do anything, rather than queue for a douse of cold water. 'It's literally incredible,' she seethed. Gary placed his hands over his ears. He felt miserable and was at a loss to know what to do.

'There *are* showers at the bottom of the hill,' said a friendly voice. Gary turned to see the man with the air freshener again. 'But the queues will be far too long at this time of day.' The man delved into a cotton bag slung over his shoulder and produced a small, plastic package, which he gave to Gary. 'Try these instead.'

Gary took the package from his hand and looked at it in wonder. 'I think you'll find,' the man continued, 'that baby wipes are what you need.' He paused and smiled. 'Aloe vera is best for the skin, but these fennel and rhubarb ones smell nicer.'

'I'm not a baby,' Hannah grumbled, when they arrived back at the tent. 'Baby wipes are for bottoms and they smell like sick.'

'No they don't, Han – they smell like rhubarb crumble,' Lucy said. 'And that's my favourite pudding.'

'They're too soapy for me,' Marc declared. 'I don't need them, anyway.'

Hannah put her head out of her sleeping compartment and shouted in Marc's direction: 'That's because you smell like sweat and old socks, just like an old tramp.'

'Well you smell like a cross between dog's pee and vinegar.'

Gary heard the insults and emerged from his own inner tent. He was too late to see who had hit the other first, but he found Marc pulling Hannah's hair with one hand and punching her on the side of the head with the other. Hannah was scratching Marc's neck and kicking his shin. Their high-pitched voices screamed and wailed. The two interlocked bodies fell against the inner walls of the tent dislodging the outer poles in the process.

Gary tried to separate them and received a couple of hefty whacks from each. He slowly prised their writhing bodies apart, as if they were two strong magnets. He held each as best he could at arm's length, bearing the brunt of flailing feet and hands and spitting cries of 'I hate you!', 'You bitch!' and worse.

Lucy stood at the side screeching 'Get him, get him!' and Gary was uncertain whether she was referring to Marc or to himself.

Suddenly, the unzipped door of the tent flew open and Frank marched inside. Clearly horrified by the spectacle before him, he moved forward quickly and pulled Marc off his father's arm. Frank held him tightly around his chest, until the kicking and punching subsided and Gary had subdued his daughter.

'What on earth is going on?' Frank asked.

'You two should be ashamed of yourselves,' Gary spat out, smarting from his facial wounds. He panted for breath, as Hannah shook and gasped in his arms. 'I hate him,' she growled, before finally letting go of the last vestiges of tension in her body.

Frank manhandled Marc out of the tent. Gary manoeuvred Hannah back into her sleeping compartment and Lucy followed in solidarity.

Gary stepped out of the tent, wiping a single tear from his eye. 'What more can I do, Frank?' he asked. 'I'm trying my best, you know. I really am.'

'I don't know, mate. But whatever you're doing, you're doing it wrong. Anyone can see that.'

'Well, thanks a million for that vote of confidence. What a great friend *you* are,' Gary said with irritation in his voice.

'Come on, mate, pull yourself together! Let's split the boys and the girls up between us and meet up again in the afternoon. Things might have cooled down by then.'

SEVEN

It was early afternoon. Despite the dreary blanket of clouds, it was brighter than Gary had dared hope for. As he led Hannah and Lucy across wet, muddy tracks to the market at the foot of the field, he noticed how the distant trees were bleached of colour by a fine white mist. He felt as if the horizon had contracted, so that he could only see the features of objects that were close by. Before, the sheer size of the festival site had been liberating for him; now he felt constricted, hemmed in by it.

'You like Marc more than me,' Hannah muttered, as Gary bought them hot soup and rolls from a mobile kitchen.

'I love you both the same,' Gary replied.

'Why did you pull me off him, then?'

'I pulled you apart,' Gary sighed. 'You know, Hannah,' he added, 'I don't think you're ever satisfied.'

'See what I mean?'

As soft rain began to fall again, the girls shared a conspiratorial umbrella and walked busily ahead. Gary trudged behind them, happy to see the girls take the lead. No doubt they're talking about boys, he thought, but it hardly matters in this weather. At least it keeps them occupied.

When the gentle precipitation became a downpour, they took shelter in a small, open-sided marquee. The girls sat on the rough coir matting and shuffled endlessly, trying to get comfortable. Gary smiled as he watched them fight a losing battle against the sharp bristles, which penetrated their jeans with ease. He decided to stand and he leant against a thick wooden pole supporting the roof.

A young man in a smart white jacket and trousers came onto the low stage, which Gary had barely noticed at the back of the marquee. He took hold of the microphone stand at the front. 'Welcome, ladies and gentlemen, boys and girls. This afternoon, for your entertainment, we have the one and only, the sensational Bash Trash Band!'

As the rain beat down ever more heavily, more people surged through the sides of the marquee. With a broad smile, the young man took the opportunity to thank them all for choosing to come and see their performance.

Hannah pulled a face at Gary to indicate that she was already bored, when a loud, urgent crash of drums and cymbals announced the beginning of the act. Hannah's head swung round involuntarily to face the stage, which was now filled with a dozen young people in white T-shirts and baggy shorts.

The drums were joined by the rhythmic beating of wooden spoons on upturned saucepans. Broom handles added a bass line by thumping the sides of oil drums. Metal bars struck industrial-sized springs and thick wooden sticks smashed down on a supermarket trolley, sounding like a dozen bells all jangling at once.

The multi-layered sound built up to a crescendo. Some children in colourful boots began to dance freely in front of the stage, shedding all concern about the cold and the damp. Gary saw that Hannah and Lucy had started tapping their feet and he was pleased that they had seen some live music at last.

His pleasure lasted only a few minutes before Hannah indicated that the rain had stopped and she wanted to go. She pulled Lucy off the matting and, after a brief discussion of tactics, the two of them departed.

When Gary caught up with them, the girls were huddled over their mobile phones, reading text messages.

'My mum's arrived,' Lucy cried happily, 'and she wants to meet up with us.'

Gary's disappointment at leaving the marquee was lessened by the thought of meeting Claire once again. At last, he had something to look forward to.

'You're late,' Frank said, tapping his wrist watch. 'Nothing changes, eh?' Gary shrugged his shoulders by way of apology. 'Well, anyway, I think our strategy of divide and rule has worked very well, don't you?'

'Hannah's calmed down a bit, but she's still not exactly co-operative. Lucy doesn't help: she's always whispering in Hannah's ear and egging her on.'

'When's her mum coming?' Frank asked.

'She's arrived. Lucy's told her where we are. I expect she'll be here soon.'

Frank grinned and raised his eyebrows. 'I bet you're looking forward to seeing her.'

'Oh, don't start that again, Frank.'

'Sorry, but it really is no secret that she's been to your house a lot in the last six months.'

'Only to drop Lucy off or to collect her. I hardly know Claire.'

'Come on, you must have given her more thought than that.'

'Don't be daft. She's just another parent.'

'Don't *you* be daft! If I wasn't attached and on such a short leash, I'd go after her, and I can't believe it hasn't crossed your mind too.'

'Leave it out,' Gary said, standing up. 'I'm going to get myself a drink.'

Gary felt mixed emotions as he walked to the bar. It was true that he felt a certain attraction to Claire. It wasn't exactly a physical desire, but it was enough to make him feel awkward in her presence. He was still fiercely loyal to Natalie and a little ashamed of any feelings towards Claire.

He sat down again and swallowed a mouthful of cider. 'Well,' he said, 'of course, I do like Claire, but this isn't really the time or the place. You understand that, at least?'

'What?' Frank exclaimed, nearly tipping over his drink. 'You're two attractive, single adults looking for company in a sea of strangers – a sea of anonymity – with tents a stone's throw from one another.' Gary raised the flat of his hand to say 'stop' but Frank continued, now in a quiet but urgent whisper. 'It isn't rocket science.'

Gary shook his head. He couldn't go along with what Frank was suggesting, so long as Natalie was still in his thoughts. He wanted to say so, but was reluctant to discuss her again. 'I'm not sure I'm ready for another relationship yet,' he said. 'It's not that easy, you know. There are kids around and just look at this place: it's all wet and muddy. These are hardly ideal conditions for a romance.'

Frank brushed Gary's knuckles with his fingers to attract his attention and pointed silently at Claire, who had just arrived. She was standing at the entrance, peering into the tent. Gary jumped up and waved his hand. Claire hurried over, with a look of delight and her arms held wide to embrace him.

Gary kissed her on both cheeks. 'It's really nice to see you,' he said enthusiastically. 'How was the journey?'

'Fine, but I had to unload the van myself and now I'm really hot.' She smiled at Gary. 'I could have done with a strong man to help me out.'

Frank introduced himself and shook Claire's hand. They talked briefly about seeing each other at the school their children attended. After some small talk about the weather, Frank offered to buy Claire a drink, winking at Gary as he rose from his seat.

Claire unzipped her jacket and wafted her arms in the air, trying to cool down. Gary looked at her face, which was flushed pink and radiant from recent exertion. Her skin glistened slightly and her eyes appeared bigger and brighter than usual. He cast a quick eye over the opening of her jacket.

Frank returned bearing drinks. 'Well, you haven't missed much, music-wise,' he said. 'The boys took me to see two dreadful new bands. They were so full of aggression you couldn't hear the lyrics for noise. Their only redeeming feature was that they didn't even try to hide their lack of ability. Music wasn't like that in my day.'

'What did you expect?' Gary asked. 'New bands are never going to be as good as established ones.'

'At least they were energetic, by the sound of it,' Claire said. 'Talking of which, where are the kids?'

Gary went to say that they'd gone off on their own, when he was interrupted by a cry of delight. He watched enviously as Lucy rushed past him, flung her arms round Claire's neck and kissed her. 'It's *so* good to see you, mum. What took you so long?'

'I love your sunglasses,' Claire replied.

'Thank you; but they're shades, you know.'

'And they're the only cool thing around here,' Hannah added, as she strode up to the table.

Claire listened to the girls' tale of how they had run the gauntlet of smelly toilets that morning. She stroked Lucy's arm in sympathy. 'Well, what do you girls want to do for the rest of the afternoon?'

'Can we go shopping, mum? Around the market stalls in the middle?'

'Well, I for one am not interested in shopping,' Hannah said, haughtily and a little hastily. 'I thought we had better things to do, Lucy.'

'But I still want to go shopping, even if Hannah doesn't want to come. Please, mum.' Hannah looked crestfallen and Gary guessed she was too proud to change her mind.

'I'm going to take the boys off again,' Frank said, 'to get some exercise in the kids' field. Do you want to come, Hannah, and let your dad have some free time?'

'I'm too old for the kids' field, don't you think?' Hannah said, looking appalled at the idea.

'Your choice,' Frank said shrugging his shoulders and glancing at Gary, as if to say 'I tried'. He produced a map of the festival site and the adults agreed where to meet up later on for tea.

As the others left the beer tent Hannah grimaced with intense displeasure at being separated from her friend.

'Let's get going,' Gary said, abandoning the last of his cider. Hannah stamped the ground hard with the heel of her boot.

'I don't want to go with you.'

'You don't even know where we're going.'

'I don't care.'

'Well, you don't want to stay here, do you? Come on, hold my hand and let's wander round a bit.'

'I'm nearly sixteen years old; what makes you think I want to hold your hand?'

'Hannah…'

'Don't Hannah me,' she said sharply. 'You don't care about me one bit, or you wouldn't have brought me here. Mum wouldn't have brought me to this dump.' She turned on the spot and walked quickly out of the beer tent.

Gary rushed after Hannah but it took him a minute to find her in the crowds. When he caught up with her he was very angry. His first reaction was to shout and even threaten to take her home early; but he managed to hold himself in check when he noticed her red, watery eyes. Instead, he went to hug her and he was pleased that she offered no resistance.

'I'm sorry,' she mumbled. 'I didn't mean to say those things. It was really unkind of me.'

They held each other tight, neither admitting to the other that they were crying; until sniffling and throat-clearing gave the game away.

'Oh dad,' Hannah wailed. 'I miss mum so, so much.'

'So do I,' Gary replied. 'More than you can ever imagine.'

Holding hands in silence, they roamed aimlessly through the festival. For half an hour sunshine butted through the rain clouds, caressing them with warmth and light. The colour of everything around them became absurdly intense. It was as if a whole day's worth had somehow been concentrated into a few minutes, simply by fleeting exposure to the sun's rays.

They came across a collection of conical tipi tents, blazing white in the afternoon sun, in a square field fringed by tall green hedges. Wood smoke swirled out through the spray of poles that burst from their pointed tops. Hannah explored one at the invitation of the owner. When she emerged, she said she wanted to live in one when she was older.

'That would be a bit like living as a hippy,' Gary suggested gently.

'No, it wouldn't,' Hannah replied 'it's not old-fashioned like that, but modern – like being ecological and caring for the world.'

Gary thought that hippies were for all that too, but didn't press the point. 'Wouldn't you be rather uncomfortable living in a tipi?'

'It doesn't look bad to me. It's full of cushions and there's a huge fire in the middle, so it would be warm even in winter.' It looked draughty to Gary, but he didn't argue that point either.

Hannah's mood lightened a great deal as they explored further. She bought some trinkets at a stall and, somewhat optimistically Gary thought, a sun hat. She complained a little about the mud and how difficult it was to walk in some places, but they soon hit a gravel track once again. They went in search of the café where they'd planned to meet the others.

'I hope it's not full of naked people,' Hannah said. 'That was really weird.'

Gary smiled. 'Weird' felt less challenging than her reaction the day before. He was drained mentally and hoped fervently that his luck had turned for the better, at last.

EIGHT

The drizzle started falling again shortly before Gary and Hannah reached the café tent. Gary sighed as he realised that they were the last to arrive.

'They're not naked,' Hannah said, scowling at her father as she scanned the clientele, 'but it *is* full of hippies.' She left his side and hurried over to Lucy, who was showing off her new yellow raincoat to Sam.

Frank and Claire were deep in conversation, pouring over a festival programme. Gary was pleased that they were obviously making plans for the evening, but he felt oddly jealous of their closeness. 'How did it all go?' he asked. They both looked up and moved apart; and not a moment too soon, Gary thought.

'The music was better,' Frank replied, 'but I couldn't tear the boys away from the all-female rock band.'

'It wasn't like that at all,' Marc said. 'We wanted to go and you wanted to stay.'

Frank brushed off Gary's knowing smile. 'They stuck like limpets to the front of the stage,' he insisted.

Claire changed the subject, saying that she'd been to check on her staff in crew camping and everything seemed to be in order. 'But what are we going to do tonight?' she asked. 'Are there any bands you want to see?'

'I'm easy,' Frank replied. 'All music's the same to me.'

'I can't believe you came to Glastonbury if that's your attitude,' Gary said.

'There's loads to do here that doesn't involve music.'

Gary shook his head and suggested a couple of bands that he liked, but Marc said that he and Sam weren't interested. They wanted to go back to the stage where the new bands played.

'How do you know you'll like them?' Gary asked.

'Because I downloaded some tracks, before we came.'

Claire turned to Lucy and Hannah, to ask what they wanted to do.

'If you like, Gary,' Frank said in a quiet voice but with deliberate emphasis, 'I'll take the boys again to see what they want to see… and they can sleep in my tent tonight, or I can take the rucksacks out of Sam's little tent and they can sleep in there.' He paused to let Gary have time to consider this possibility. 'That'll be one less thing for you to think about, eh?'

Gary could read Frank's mind, but felt unable to respond with Claire at his side talking with the girls. He stared at him disapprovingly, but Frank was unrepentant. 'I'm sure the girls will want to go off and do their own thing after the music,' he continued.

Frank's mouth curved into a slight smile. He opened his eyes wide and raised his eyebrows nodding his head suggestively in Claire's direction.

'What do you think, Claire?' he asked. 'I mean about the boys coming with me, and you and Gary taking the girls?'

Claire hesitated, as if she was trying to work something out. Gary was embarrassed by Frank setting him up with a date he hadn't asked for; and he knew that Natalie would've disapproved of his blatant manoeuvring.

'That would be great,' Claire said smoothly. 'But I can't be out too late tonight. I've had a long journey and I've got to get up early in the morning.' She paused and looked at Gary. 'How's that with you?'

'Fine,' Gary nodded, uncertain whether Claire's proposal was as innocuous as it sounded. Frank may have hung him on a hook but, perhaps, an early night would let him wriggle off it.

'Well, let's get going then,' Frank beamed. 'But first we need to eat!'

'Look at those two,' Claire said, as she and Gary walked side by side. She pointed out a couple of people covered in mud from head to toe. 'I think I must be the cleanest person at Glastonbury.'

'How's that?'

'I had a quick shower this afternoon, after we used the *wonderful* flush toilets,' she said. Gary leant over and sniffed her clean hair. 'Hmm – smells of green apples,' he grinned. 'Now I can see why the crew camping is such an attraction.'

'Get off!' Claire said, pushing him away playfully. 'Anyway,' she added softly, 'you can come and have a look yourself, later, if you want.' Gary's skin tingled. 'Maybe after the bands have finished,' he replied, realising at once that Claire could only have meant after the bands. 'We'll have to see what the girls want to do,' he added.

'Oh yes, the girls,' Claire said, as if they were an afterthought. 'And just where are they now?' She called out Lucy's name, but her voice wasn't strong enough to make itself heard above the noisy scrum heading towards the main stage. Gary glanced at his watch: it was seven-thirty. There was a quarter of an hour to the next band and a couple of hours to sunset, though there was little prospect of actually seeing it through the clouds.

'I can see Lucy's new raincoat,' he said, pointing ahead. The girls were standing with a couple of older boys, exchanging mobile phone numbers.

'They haven't wasted any time,' Claire joked, elbowing Gary gently and brushing her arm against his.

'God help us,' he muttered. 'What do you think we should do?'

'Nothing. It's perfectly natural.'

'That's exactly what I'm worried about.'

Gary watched Hannah tickle one of the boys under his arm and then burst out laughing, as he retaliated by pinching her bottom. He was surprised that their contact had become physical so quickly. He also felt a pang of envy: she seemed to find relationships with the opposite sex very easy.

'It's the rain,' Claire said. 'It brings people together.'

'Explain.'

'No one likes to be cold and wet; people are always looking for ways to be to be warm and dry instead. People just don't want to be all on their own…' Her voice halted abruptly. 'Oh, I know what I mean,' she added impatiently.

They caught up with the girls, who had detached themselves from the boys but were still in a state of excitement. Gary decided not to worry: they had unreal expectations, he thought, in a place as vast and crowded as this.

Gary led Claire and the girls up the slope away from the main stage, trying to find a bit more space and a good view. They sat on a concrete bench at the side of the field, covering the wet slab with plastic sheets. The stage occupied the base of a gigantic silver pyramid and looked like something from a science fiction film.

As the band strode into view, a loud cheer rippled from the audience at the front, up to the top of the field and back. Spotlights flooded the stage with green and yellow light, as drum beats and a wail of electric guitars shook the air. A huge close-up image of the lead singer filled the huge screens on either side of the stage.

'Blimey,' Gary said. 'You can even see the stubble on his chin.'

Hannah and Lucy jumped to their feet and started dancing wildly, singing at the top of their voices. They pleaded to be allowed to go closer to the front and, despite advice that they'd be crushed, they soon disappeared.

Gary felt powerless and looked at Claire for support and understanding. He was surprised to find her face so close to his own. A couple of stray hairs caressed his cheek. He could see the speckled pattern of her irises quite clearly and he could smell her warm breath. He smiled nervously, before turning to survey the heaving body of people dancing and jumping before him, and the stick-figures on stage. He looked at the massive screens, which relayed impossibly bright images of the gyrating musicians. So bright, he thought, they might be visible from outer space.

'Well,' he said. 'I can't believe that I'm sitting on a lump of concrete in a field, in the middle of nowhere, cold and damp, and watching a band on a huge TV screen.' He paused as the image on the screen switched from the bass player to the drummer and then back; and as the now blue stage lighting merged into red. 'I might as well be at home,' he added.

'Rubbish! It's all about the atmosphere. You don't get that at home, and think how much the girls are enjoying it.'

As the band played on, a gentle breeze lifted the clouds higher and the sky became brighter. The sun was still obscured but, at least, Gary thought, an interested onlooker could stab a finger in the air and point out its rough location.

He shifted position to find some comfort on the cold concrete. 'I think I have to stand up,' he said, jumping onto his feet and rubbing his backside. 'My bum is frozen.'

'Maybe you should flex it,' Claire murmured suggestively, 'to get the blood circulating a bit.'

Claire was watching him expectantly. Gary smiled and extended his hand to her. 'Would you care to dance?' he asked, with a slight bow.

Claire looked deeply into his eyes and smiled. She took his hand and allowed herself to be pulled up. She kissed the back of his hand. 'It would be my pleasure,' she said and started to sway her hips in time to the music.

Together, they stomped the ground in their wellington boots, twisted their bodies and shook their arms in the air. Occasionally, they sang a line or two of the songs that they knew or, more often, they chanted along to a familiar chorus with a host of other happy voices. Gary began to lose himself in the collective experience that enveloped the field.

For the first time that day he felt truly happy.

When the band came to the end of its set, Hannah and Lucy took themselves off to the toilet. Gary plunged into the crowd and returned with his hands firmly behind his back. Claire looked at him with bemused curiosity. With a flourish, like presenting a bunch of flowers, Gary produced his gift: a clutch of red, green and blue garden candles on wooden sticks.

'They look lovely,' she said.

Gary slowly twisted them into the muddy earth in front of the concrete bench. He lit the wick of one of them in the flames of a small fire, which neighbours were protecting with an umbrella. In a moment there was a row of wax candles flickering joyfully in front of Claire. Gary sat down again and Claire slid her arm into his.

'Did you get them for me?'

'Of course,' Gary replied. 'Well,' he added by way of hurried explanation, when he realised how Claire might interpret his answer, 'they're everywhere and I don't see why we shouldn't have them too. You've got to admit they brighten things up a bit.' He waved his hand at the hundreds of orange flames flickering in the dwindling light. 'They make the field seem really friendly and intimate, don't you think?'

'I love them,' Claire said, pushing her thigh tightly against his. 'You're really thoughtful.'

Darkness had fallen completely by the time the next band had finished. Gary watched powerful lights sweep across the field, bathing the churning mass of heads in deep purple and burnt orange.

As the final note sounded, gentle misty rain began its slow descent onto the crowd below. Gary felt it on his nose first; then it covered the hairs on the back of his hand, like gossamer. By equally minute degrees, the temperature began to drop and a breeze picked up. The mist turned into a light drizzle. Tiny spots of rain raced around the field, blown by small gusts of wind. Gary unfurled the hood of his anorak and pulled it over his head. The soft sound of impacting raindrops echoed in his ears, as he watched the candle flames spluttering before him.

The girls returned to where the adults were sitting and announced that they didn't want to see the next band. Instead, they had decided to go back to Hannah's tent by themselves.

'You won't get lost, will you?' Gary asked.

Hannah gave her father a withering look. 'It's only ten-thirty,' she said. 'I have a festival guide with a map, which, thanks to universal state education, I can read. Should that fail, I am equipped to understand signs – which are only everywhere – and, in case you hadn't noticed, there's no shortage of people if I need to ask for directions.'

'Alternatively,' she continued after taking a short breath, 'I've seen plenty of policemen milling around, and they'll show us the way if we ask. Failing all of these options and if I'm let down by my sense of direction, I have this.' She produced her new mobile phone.

'This modern electronic device allows me to speak to anyone I choose, at the press of a button, so in an emergency I can call for help or arrange a meeting. In short, dad, I expect we'll be OK and you are fussing unnecessarily, as usual.'

NINE

After the girls had left, Gary and Claire found a beer tent to give them shelter from the rain, which was now driving horizontally across the fields. Gary bought them drinks and they sat across a table.

'It's nice to have some adult company,' Gary said, sipping his beer. 'It's dull having to talk to kids all the time.'

'It's been three years, hasn't it?' Claire asked gently.

Gary nodded and took another sip. He didn't really want to talk about Natalie, but it seemed impolite not to. He sighed in the hope that Claire would move the conversation on, but she still waited for an answer. Gary felt a little resentful that he was being pushed into talking about his situation, but Claire was looking at him with such obvious sympathy, that he couldn't bring himself to object.

'It doesn't help,' he said, 'that Marc thinks I should've moved on by now. But, you know, it's just not that easy.' He paused and saw that Claire was watching him very closely. 'I just can't seem to change; or, at least, there's a big part of me that doesn't want to.'

'You can only do these things when you're ready.'

'Yeah, thanks. You're the only person who's said that. You know, I can cope with Hannah's moods, because I know what's she's thinking; but I'm more worried about Marc. He hardly says anything; I think he just bottles it all up inside. To tell the truth, I wish he'd come out with it and, you know, scream and shout a bit like his sister.'

Claire nodded and there was a long silence. Gary scratched the back of his head: this was harder than he expected. Fifteen or twenty seconds passed, but it seemed much longer.

'Are you lonely?' Claire asked at last.

Gary looked at her blankly: she had no idea how lonely he was. He contemplated her soft blue eyes, the straight fringe over her forehead, the round tip of her small, snub nose, her thin, curved lips. Then he focused in again on her eyes.

'Very lonely,' Gary almost whispered. He didn't let his steady gaze drop. Claire reached over her hand and laid it on top of Gary's. 'I know how it feels,' she said warmly, smiling.

'I don't think I'm a very good dad,' Gary said, looking down at their joined hands and breaking the link with her eyes. 'You know,' he said, lifting his head and basking once again in the warmth glowing from Claire's face, 'I thought we might all die in the storm this morning. You were lucky to miss it. I felt so responsible. And when we weren't struck by lightning, I prayed that the tent would stay up despite the wind and the rain.' He smiled at the memory, but it was a half-hearted, wan sort of smile. 'At least it shows I can put a tent up properly!'

Claire smiled back. 'Well, perhaps you could invite me back later to show me your handiwork…'

Gary let out an embarrassed laugh. He saw Claire divert her eyes and streaks of bright pink filled her cheeks. She withdrew her hand and placed it under her thigh. They looked at each other again, smiling but hesitant. Gary was undecided how to react. He felt that he should make some move, but was afraid in case he had misread the signals and Claire wouldn't really be interested. Claire bit her bottom lip, as if she could read his mind.

'Let's go,' she suggested.

'What, now?'

'We can't stay here all night and, anyway, I want to see where you've pitched your tent…' She stood up and tugged at Gary's hand.

'We can't go back to my tent,' he said, hardly daring to believe that he understood Claire's message and, equally, fearing that he had. He also felt a pang of guilt, as if by even considering the possibility of going with Claire, he was betraying Natalie, Hannah and Marc all at once. 'The girls will be back there.'

Claire was already striding to the entrance of the tent, pulling Gary behind her. She threw him a coquettish look. 'Well then,' she replied with a broad grin, 'you'd better come and see where I've put my tent… You can help me adjust my guy ropes…' She plunged into the rain and darkness with a laugh.

'Come on!' she called behind her.

The walk to Claire's tent was like being on a rollercoaster: at times, Gary found the going slow, if there were a lot of other people around; then, a space would open out and Claire would surge ahead so that Gary had trouble keeping up.

They held hands, which Gary took alternatively to be a sign of intimacy or a sign of necessity, so they didn't lose one another. His emotions surged in time to their pace of walking: one moment he was excited and exuberant, full of expectation; the next, cautious, doubtful and – if he was being honest with himself – scared. Claire talked and joked in the slow passages, but called on him to hurry up, when coast was clear ahead.

The rain slackened off, making walking easier. They ducked and weaved their way past people walking more slowly and side-stepped on-comers. Although it was very late, the bright lights of the food tents and clothes stalls on both sides of the path lent a colourful, carnival air to the evening.

As they approached the crew campsite, Gary's arm was already loosely held around Claire's waist. His hand rested lightly above her hip bone. It was an ambiguous gesture, as if its presence there might be taken by either of them as a sign that he was only guiding her along the way; but it was also definite and continuous physical contact. Claire stopped and faced Gary.

'My tent's over there, in the crew camp,' she said in a quiet voice. She pointed over the gate towards a collection of vans, trailers and caravans in a half-empty paddock, which was barely lit by a single dim lamp affixed to a tree.

Her face was very close to his. Even in the semi-darkness he could see light gleaming in the whites of her eyes. He sensed a rush of excitement as he smelled her hair once again. He applied gentle, gradual pressure on her hip with his hand. She began to lean towards him. Her eyes were wide and alert, taking in his every reaction to the slowly evolving events. Gary lent forward and his head stooped slightly; Claire looked up and allowed momentum to bring their lips together.

Gary's heart missed a beat as he kissed Claire, softly and inquisitively at first, then more quickly and urgently, as their lips pressed and parted. Claire's mouth opened and their tongues found each other, entering and retreating in turn. Gary felt Claire's breasts against his chest and, as it hardened, his erection began to make its presence felt.

Fleetingly, Gary thought of Natalie – and of Hannah – but the rush of blood in his head and to his groin took control of his conscious thoughts. He was hardly aware of the photograph in his shirt pocket, pressed between his chest and Claire's. He kissed Claire partly as an act of worship – of her difference and her femininity – and partly as an act of lust. His mind and body were driven by pent-up emotions and frustration – and anger – and his body wanted release, spurring him on and on, as he rubbed her breasts through her jumper and tried, unsuccessfully, to lift it to feel them in the flesh.

Claire pulled back and held his hand in check.

'Not here,' she said. 'Later,' she added detaching herself, 'soon.' Gary's crotch ached and he found himself almost panting with excitement and anticipation. 'Come to the tent,' Claire whispered, as she deliberately brushed her hand across the front of his trousers, sending a spasm of pleasure through his body.

Gary was unable to speak. He let Claire guide him by the hand, to the left-hand side of the metal gate. As she unlatched it, a man in a fluorescent singlet approached from the other side. He stepped up to Claire and Gary and barred their way. 'Passes please,' he said smoothly, but firmly.

Claire started and gave a surprised 'Oh!' She fumbled for the cord around her neck, fished out a plastic coated pass and showed it to the steward. 'Fine, thanks,' he said before turning to Gary. 'And yours?'

'Oh, he's a friend,' explained Claire. Then, seeing that the steward was unmoved by the news, she added: 'He's not staying, just visiting. He's coming to see my tent.'

'Sorry, but you know the rules,' the steward began, with a pained expression on his face. 'No one's allowed into the crew camp without a pass.'

'But he's with me,' Claire protested. 'He's not someone I've just met, he's an old friend. We've known each other for years.'

The steward hesitated, but then pulled back and lifted his shoulders to assert himself. 'Please don't ask me to let him in; you know I can't. The rules are strict and you know there are no exceptions. We can't just let him in, even for a few minutes. This area is for crew and for bands, not ordinary ticket-holders.'

Claire was lost for words. Gary tried to explain that he wasn't interested in the members of any bands, that it was a social visit and probably he'd only be an hour or so, but his intervention only hardened the steward's resolve.

'Look mate,' the steward said to Gary, 'we've already had one minor theft here and the place is full of valuables. It's a question of control – so, I'm sorry, but the answer is no. Please leave.'

The steward must have seen the deflated look on their faces because, as he closed the gate on them, he suggested that they must have at least one other place to go to, if they wanted to get out of the cold.

Gary and Claire walked along the track towards Gary's tent, but they both realised that that was no solution to their situation. As they reached the edge of the crew camping fence, Claire stopped suddenly. 'I know,' she said. 'There's another way in – if we follow the fence, there's a break in it where a water pipe's been routed. We could shift the fence over and squeeze through.'

She grabbed Gary's hand and tried to lead him through the dark hedgerow, along the metal fence. Gary resisted. 'No,' he said, shaking his head. The emergency in his groin was now merely a dull ache. He knew that the moment had passed. What had he been thinking of? 'No,' he repeated. 'I don't want to.'

'You don't want to what?'

Gary didn't know how to reply. Could it be true, he asked himself, that he didn't want to have carefree, casual sex with an excited, attractive woman who clearly did? Was it because he couldn't stop thinking about Natalie? Did he really not want to erase three years of tearful, emotional frustration? Did he really want to continue to wallow in his grief?

Gary was confused and all at once he felt very tired. He looked at Claire and found that the passionate kissing of five minutes before was already a distant memory. In the gloom he could still make out the shape of her breasts, now with two noticeable erect nipples – though, he thought, that could just as easily be the cold – but his urge had gone.

'I don't want to break into the camp,' he said. 'You know, break the rules – and get caught.'

Claire glared at him with an uncomprehending look. 'What about me? What about what *I* want?' Gary detected anger in her voice; perhaps also despair. 'What was all that about, back there, then, if you didn't want to come with me to my tent?'

'It doesn't feel right.'

'It felt fine to me, and I haven't been with a man nearly bursting out of his trousers for two years!'

Gary was silent. They stood for a few seconds, arms outstretched and hands attached before Claire slowly let go. Gary's hand rose to fondle her breast. It was an involuntary, almost instinctive move. Claire flicked his hand away brusquely, but then she stepped forward, so that she was close to him once again. She looked disappointed, but the harsh lines on her face relaxed and she touched Gary gently on the arm.

'It's OK, I understand,' she said with a sigh. 'I suppose it's just not meant to be. I'm sorry I got so carried away.'

'Don't be sorry...' Gary was going to say more, but couldn't find the words and faltered. 'It was a bit of a rush,' he added, denying his own feeling that the rush had brought with it an extraordinary sense of excitement and daring. Claire bit her lip, deep in thought.

'Forget it,' she said rather forcefully. 'Let's just go back to your tent and see the girls; you know, make sure they're OK, then call it a night.'

They walked in silence along the track and across the crowded camp site. Claire kept her hand well out of Gary's reach. The air felt milder, but leaves and pennants still rustled and fluttered around them. They passed groups of people huddled around smoky wood fires crackling under the cover of gazebos and tarpaulins.

Gary was exhausted; no doubt due to the broken night and trudging around in the mud all day. The cider hadn't helped; nor had his unfulfilled sexual exertions. He felt that he'd let Claire down and wasted a wonderful opportunity. He began to feel sorry for himself and soon he longed for two things: that he could crawl into his sleeping bag right now and sleep; and that Natalie was there by his side.

TEN

Sunday morning, 3.30 a.m.

Gary was still lying in the mud; and two days' memories had flashed through his mind in a matter of seconds. As the image of Claire faded, Gary began to hear voices through the thick silence that enveloped him. They were very faint at first, but then became louder and more distinct as they echoed down his imaginary well. Gary looked up and saw tiny figures leaning over the edge of the circular opening far above him.

'Are you all right, mate?' he heard one of them ask.

'He's pissed; just leave him,' said another.

Gary tried to lift his arm towards the figures at the top of the well. 'Help!' he heard himself say, in a voice barely louder than a whisper.

'What a fucking loser.'

'Leave off,' the first voice said. 'Hey, mate, are you all right?'

'We can't leave him like that.' It was a young woman's voice. 'Think if it was you.'

'What can we do?' the second voice asked. 'We'll just get covered in mud. He won't remember a thing in the morning and we'll get no thanks for our trouble. I say, leave him.'

'We could at least stop him drowning.'

Gary heard laughter.

'What a way to go – to drown in six inches of slurry!'

'Oi, mate,' the first voice shouted. 'Can we help you?'

'Help!' Gary cried in a whisper. He could feel the muscles in the back of his neck strain as he lifted his head towards the light.

'Well, I'm not going to leave him,' the young woman said, 'even if I get covered. At least let's get him out of that stuff and clean him up a little.'

Gary heard noises of splashing water, of grunts and of heaving, but he felt nothing. It isn't working, he thought. They can't get me out of here. He tried to call for help again, but could produce no sound.

Suddenly, water started to fall down the well and hit his head. It was a relentless, cold torrent. He tried to hold up his hands to protect himself, but the flow was too furious. He felt as if his head was being shaken by somebody he couldn't see, but it then dawned on him that he was shaking his own head. With that realisation, his perception of the situation changed.

Gradually, the well began to contract and the circle of light became larger and closer. Then the walls of the well shaft fell away and the hole disappeared altogether, leaving Gary on the ground once again. He was sitting beneath a gushing tap, with water pouring over his head and shoulders. He felt strange hands rubbing him all over and trying to wash the mud from his hair.

'Whose great idea was this?' someone asked. 'I'm completely soaked.'

'Stop complaining. You know it had to be done,' the young woman replied.

The tap was turned off. Gary looked about him and saw four young, concerned faces. He tried to speak, but his open mouth was silent; he tried to stand, but began to fall to the side.

'Hold him!' he heard.

'It's no use, we'll have to take him to the medical tent.'

'You're joking, that's miles away.'

'It's not that far. Anyway, we can't just leave him like this or he'll die of hypothermia.'

'If the drugs don't kill him first.'

Gary listened to the debate but his body refused to respond or allow him to contribute.

'Oh God, we're going to have to carry him.'

'We must be mad!'

'Look, the sooner we do it, the sooner we can get back to enjoying ourselves.'

Gary peered at the young woman but couldn't make out her features. He then looked at her male companion.

'What a fucking loser,' he heard him say again.

Suddenly, there were hands and arms all over his body. Someone began to lift him by his armpits, then by his ankles. His body jolted and twisted, but was then lifted, as if weightless, off the ground.

'He's really heavy,' someone said.

'You weakling,' the young woman responded. 'Come on, let's get him away from here.'

Gary was face down, at most three feet from the ground. He was carried by the arms and legs like a mediaeval battering ram, forcing a path through bemused onlookers. Occasionally, he tried to lift his head, but soon gave up any attempt to see where he was going. For the most part he closed his eyes, and only opened them when he heard a groan of complaint or sensed a change in direction. All he could see in the dark was the reflection of lights in the brown slimy mud and the heels of four wellington boots.

Sometimes the jerking movements made him retch a little, so that acid bile coated his tongue and dribbled out of the side of his mouth. He had lost all sense of movement, as if he was now floating in a void, insensible to all feeling or sound. Am I dying? was the only thought in his now placid mind. Then: am I dead? Gary retched again and spat the vile liquid from his mouth, but still he was unable to answer his questions. His brain was too confused.

The pallbearers, as he now thought of them, began to tire. He heard cursing, recriminations and fading reassurance.

'It's not far now,' the young woman said.

'It's drier here; can't we lie him down and drag him the rest of the way?'

There was laughter. Gary started shivering with cold.

'It must be pretty bad for him now, but can you imagine what he'll feel like in the morning?'

'If he lasts that long.' Gary heard more laughter. 'Perhaps they'll bury him on the farm, who knows?' Someone stumbled and Gary felt himself drop. Before he hit the ground he felt a tightening of arms around his shoulders, lifting him up again. This time, his shoulders were held higher than his legs and he felt a wave of nausea as blood drained from his head. He coughed weakly and passed out.

ELEVEN

Friday, midnight

Gary and Claire began to pick their way through a dense jungle of tents, so tightly packed that campers rubbed shoulders and bottoms through the nylon. Where passable, the valleys in between lay in deep shadow; and Gary cursed as he stumbled over guy-ropes and trod on half-sunken pegs.

Although the sounds of the festival receded as they walked deeper into the camping field, Gary was still acutely aware of the constant booming noise behind his back. How am I ever going to sleep with so much music still playing? he asked himself.

'I hope you know where we're going,' Claire said as she stumbled behind Gary.

'Look out for a fire point with a number forty-four on it, white on red,' Gary replied. 'Just like the one over there.'

'That's a number forty-eight. I hope we haven't gone past it, or we'll be here all night.'

Before he could answer, Gary recognised the sound of Frank's jovial laughter nearby. Once they were close it wasn't difficult to find the tent, as it was lit from the inside by two electric lamps and it glowed a luminous pink. He could see the shadows of the occupants, distorted like elongated aliens, dancing on the outer skin of the tent.

A roar of excitement met their arrival and the girls mobbed Claire to tell her about their adventures. Gary wasn't surprised to hear that boys were involved; and he suspected alcohol also played its part. Marc and Sam were full of the bands they'd seen and a comedian who told rude jokes. Gary listened patiently as Marc repeated 'a couple of the best'.

'Those aren't rude, they're obscene,' Gary said, as he gave Frank a sideways look of disapproval.

'Chill out!' Frank said. 'It was all very light-hearted.' Gary didn't reply, but he was privately appalled. 'Anyway, tell me, how did you two get on?'

Gary avoided his inquisitive stare. Frank had asked the question with a little too much expectation in his voice for Gary's liking. He looked at Claire. She's a cool customer, he thought. If she's noticed the tone of Frank's voice, she's not letting on.

Claire told Frank what they'd done in a very matter-of-fact way, but omitting their moment of semi-passion. Thwarted at the gate by that jobs-worth, Gary fumed silently.

'I'd have thought, with so much time at your disposal, you could have fitted a lot more in,' Frank said, repaying Gary's look of disapproval. Gary shifted uncomfortably and now avoided Claire's eyes. That was unnecessary, Frank, he thought.

Claire mumbled something that he didn't hear properly, before adding in a clear voice: 'Gary wasn't sure what he wanted to do.' She paused before continuing with her eyes firmly on the ground: 'I like a man who knows what he wants.'

Claire raised her head and looked at Gary. It wasn't a hostile or angry stare, he realised, but it expressed a final view. Out of the corner of his eye, he saw Frank watching the two of them closely and smiling thinly.

'Mum, can I sleep with you tonight?' Lucy interrupted.

'And me – I want to see those flush toilets,' Hannah added.

'Hannah, you can't,' Gary said. 'There's a man on the gate who won't let you in without a special pass.' Frank nodded knowingly at this news, with evident sympathy on his face.

'How did Lucy get in this afternoon, then?' she asked.

'I've got a guest pass for her in the tent,' Claire said.

Now it was Gary's turn to stare at Claire, questioning what he had just heard her say. His mouth dropped open slightly, but no words came out. Frank, who was piecing the jigsaw together from the few fragments before him, raised his eyebrows and looked at Claire for some sort of explanation.

'It's a guest pass, but with Lucy's name on it,' she said, glaring back at Gary. 'The company arranged it for me, and Lucy can use it again tonight if she wants to sleep in my tent – but only tonight – and only if Hannah doesn't mind.'

'I do mind,' Hannah said loudly.

'Oh, please, Han, let me go – just for one night.'

Hannah gave her a withering look. 'I thought you were my friend.'

'I am, but I want to sleep with mum – just the one night. Please.'

Ultimately, it was Lucy who decided to go, rather than Hannah who agreed to let her. After Claire and Lucy had left the tent, Frank insisted that Sam spend at least one night with him as well, and took him back to their tent. Marc, who Gary realised was trying to hide his disappointment, said he was going to crash out and vanished into his sleeping compartment.

Gary sat with Hannah in the middle of the tent, amongst the

luggage they had brought with them. He felt wretched in spirit, but even the short rest in the tent had given him more energy. Hannah was silent. She sat on a rucksack opposite her father, pouting. Gary took a swig of cold water from a small plastic bottle. He felt oddly refreshed, but hungry. He unwrapped a chewy breakfast bar – part of the 'supplies' that he had brought onto site for moments like this – and offered it to Hannah.

'I'm not hungry,' she said abruptly.

Gary munched it in silence, but he knew from experience that the peace wouldn't last.

'This tent's driven my friend away,' Hannah said sulkily. Then, in a voice which became increasingly bitter, she added: 'I mean this rotten, smelly tent and the rotten, smelly toilets we have to use – it's no wonder she couldn't stand it anymore.' Tears welled up in her eyes. Her chin scrunched up and pushed her upper lip outwards, in an exaggerated, self-pitying frown.

'Look,' Gary said gently. 'Lucy just wants to see her mum. She knows it's only for tonight – she said so. Lucy wants to come back here and stay with you – and she will, tomorrow night.'

He let the words sink in, though he noticed that they had little appreciable effect on her quivering lip. He looked at his daughter and felt for her. Natalie would have been the same if one of her friends had let her down like that. 'I'm sorry,' he added. 'Why don't you grab some sleep? In no time it'll be breakfast and you'll be seeing Lucy again.'

'I'm not tired, and it's all your fault!'

Gary adjusted his position and scanned Hannah's face for signs of tiredness. 'Really? You've been out in the open all day. All that fresh air – you must be a little…'

'I said, I'm not tired,' Hannah repeated, crossing her arms grumpily.

'Nor am I,' Gary said in a friendly tone. They continued to sit across from each other, but in silence again. Gary knew that he wanted to go out and do something, rather than sleep. He flicked through the festival guide and then suggested to Hannah that he might go out again to watch a display of fire-eating.

'At this time of night?'

'Soon. It starts at half past midnight.'

'And you'll leave me behind, I suppose – looking after him,' Hannah complained instantly, nodding to the inner tent from which Marc's gentle snoring could be heard.

'No, you can come with me, if you want.'

The look of puzzlement on her face showed that Hannah was clearly taken by surprise. 'But how can we leave Marc behind?'

'He's fourteen, he's fast asleep and he won't wake until the morning. There's hundreds of people around if he needs help and… ' Gary paused as he tried to think of another reason why it would be OK to leave Marc alone, '…he's not old enough to go out like you.'

It wasn't quite in the same vein as the other reasons he'd given, but Gary thought it would do. He was sure that nothing would happen to Marc while they were out, but he accepted that it was an act of faith. Anyway, it was a reason that would appeal to Hannah; and Natalie would certainly have approved.

Hannah chewed on the inside of her mouth as she contemplated what Gary had said. 'Alright,' she said after a while. 'If I have to.' Gary wanted to say that no one was forcing her to go; but he knew that if he did, he'd lose the only chance of distracting Hannah from her disappointment.

'We'd better hurry then, or we'll miss it,' he said.

Within a couple of minutes they had donned raincoats and boots. They zipped up the tent quietly behind them, checked the number forty-four above their heads, for reassurance that they would eventually find their way back, and strode down towards the heart of the still-booming festival. They didn't hold hands, but they did occasionally grasp each other and squeeze hands momentarily. These were small gestures, Gary thought, but important ones. They allowed the temporary truce to be maintained and united them in a common venture.

TWELVE

Walking through a big festival after midnight, Gary thought, is a bit like driving in the rush-hour. The only difference is that here no one knows for sure where they'll end up. The place was teeming with people striding purposefully in every direction. Some of them were probably on their way 'home' to a damp and cold tent, but most, he could sense, were just like him: going out in search of more action, anywhere and anyhow.

There were couples arm-in-arm, parents with exhausted children and groups of friends, bouncing off each other's shoulders as they gambolled through the mud. Gary paid particular attention to the singles on their way to meet companions, or standing at tea stalls, lost and with no way of meeting up with anyone they knew. The sky was dark and no stars were visible through the clouds. Despite this, the tracks were well-lit by strings of light bulbs dangling in profusion across the fronts of still-open market stalls. It's like a huge city, Gary thought; one that never sleeps.

He guided Hannah through the crowds, stopping in a café-tent on the way. Gary took a double espresso to reinforce his second wind; he offered Hannah a cola, quietly confident that it would have a similar effect on her.

They didn't talk very much: just a question here about the other's comfort or warmth; a question there asking if the other

84

was tired; or the odd comment about the teeming masses around them. 'It's like being in the middle of an ant's nest,' Hannah exclaimed at one point.

At the circus field, a sizeable group of people had already gathered around a large, unlit performance area. It was encircled by a row of short wooden stakes linked with stout rope. Dozens of expectant children had pushed past adults or crawled through their legs, to sit on plastic sheets spread over the wet grass at the front. Arriving later than most, Gary and Hannah stood at the side of the crowd. When Hannah complained that she couldn't see because of the tall men in front of her, Gary wandered back to one of the nearby food tents and borrowed a heavy-duty milk crate, which he upended for her to stand on.

After only a couple of minutes, a lithe young woman on stilts approached the assembled onlookers. She wore a lustrous one-piece silver suit with double-length legs and a glittering wig. She stood in the middle of the grass and raised a long silver whip above her head.

'Ladies and gentlemen, boys and girls – for your entertainment tonight, I present to you, all the way from the wild Ukrainian steppes, with a stupendous and exciting spectacle of fire, acrobatics and dance, such as you have never seen before, the amazing, the one and only, the incredible, pyrogenic, incandescent, Blazing Cossacks!'

She cracked her whip in the air and then again on the ground, causing most of the children and some of the adults standing closest to the barrier to scream with momentary fear. 'Children – stand well back,' she cried.

As the noise of the second crack faded away, a horde of young people, wearing black clothes and masks, rushed to fill the open space. Haunting music filled the air, creating a psychedelic soundscape. From the darkness, a pair of torchbearers appeared, throwing unruly flames high into the sky and casting deep shadows across the field. Soon, flaming clubs were flying to and fro into the void, twirling and twisting in the air. Burning hoops of flame span wildly around black waists and huge tongues of flame shot out of the mouths of the fire-breathers.

'Impressive,' Hannah said, craning her neck to see more.

The cold air crackled as the flames whooshed ever higher and fanned out, lighting up the heads and shoulders of the onlookers. The smell of methylated spirits and burning hair filled Gary's nostrils, as the visual cacophony of fire made it impossible to concentrate on any one place for more than a second or two. Hannah hugged Gary as the performers created a human tower and began to spin burning torches on tethers between their teeth, creating a wall of flaming Catherine wheels in a pyramid of orange and yellow light.

The audience clapped and roared with excitement and delight. The music came to a climax, when a boom from faraway announced the launch of a rocket. Gary followed its thin trail as it soared into the sky and exploded. Instantly, it formed a perfect white and purple chrysanthemum overhead and lit up the ominous underside of a low cloud lurking unseen and forgotten in the night sky. The upper part of the exploding firework seared into the cloud and vanished, leaving a ghostly glow.

The crowd gasped in appreciation and, as the lights in the sky died away, all eyes looked back at the field: now in darkness and empty of performers, with only white wisps of smoke to remind onlookers that anything had happened at all.

As the clapping and cheering died down, Gary and Hannah disentangled and walked off into the night, in search of more fun.

Gary squeezed Hannah's hand as they walked along in the wet mud. He was keen to build on the success of the fire display, but wasn't very hopeful that she'd accept any other suggestions he might make.

'Why don't we go and find some live music?' he asked tentatively.

'But according to the guide, all the best bands have finished by now.'

'Oh, I expect we'll come across something. Let's go this way.'

As the mud became thicker it started to suck at their wellington boots. With each step their heels rose and became detached from their warm inner soles.

'God, this is hard work,' Hannah said; but Gary was relieved that it was merely an observation and not a complaint. She took another couple of steps but struggled to keep the boot on her foot. She clutched Gary's arm for extra leverage. 'I can't walk in all this mud. It's too sticky.'

She pulled at the upper rim of her boot with the other hand and eased it from the mud. It came free and made a loud plopping sound, as air filled the vacuum left behind. Hannah took a step forward and her boot sank into more mud. 'There again,' she added as an afterthought and with satisfaction in her voice, 'think how toned my thighs will be when I get home. They'll drive the boys wild at school!'

Gary objected to what he'd heard, but Hannah was unrepentant. 'You might not realise it dad, but these things are important for a girl.' Gary wasn't convinced and shook his head. 'Anyway, you're always saying that every cloud has a silver lining; and well-toned muscles are my silver lining. So there.'

Their first taste of live music was in a small, rectangular marquee, where four aging guitarists and a blind drummer were jamming the night away. Gary would have been happy to settle down for a couple of hours to listen to them, but Hannah took a different view.

'You can't dance to this,' she declared, a little too loudly, causing a few heads to turn. Gary winced at Hannah's rudeness, but he only saw sympathetic smiles.

They moved on and in another tent they found a klezmer band with wailing clarinets and fiddles belting out dance tunes. When Gary suggested this music was lively enough to dance to, Hannah disagreed strongly, saying that it was too busy and boisterous.

As they walked deeper into the night, they were assaulted by music from all sides. Hannah declined every opportunity to listen and Gary became exasperated. 'What's wrong with all these tents? It's nearly two o'clock in the morning, there's live music just about everywhere, but you don't want to try any of it. Are you too tired? Do you just want to go to bed?'

Hannah stopped and scowled. 'It's not *my* kind of music, that's all,' she said 'and I think you can hardly call my sleeping bag a 'bed' – so that's not really an attraction, either.'

'Well, what is your kind of music?'

'You know what music I like: rock music; indie rock music.' She put her hands on her hips. 'I like young bands, making lots of noise, with lots of loud guitars. Can't you find me any of those?'

'Frankly, I've no idea. For me, it's enough to be out in the night, without any rain, listening to any music that's going and 'chilling out' as you would say.' He cast around for ideas, uncertain that he'd win this one. 'OK, let's go in that direction,' he said, pointing to three pulsating green lights behind some dark trees, 'and see what we can find there.'

Hannah followed with a loud sigh to show that she was only agreeing reluctantly. Gary could feel the air temperature dropping; he rubbed warmth into his arms and looked over to Hannah to see how she was faring. He saw her stifle a yawn and knew that if something suitable didn't turn up soon, he'd have to take her all the way back to the tent; and, effectively, that would be the end of his night too.

Attracted by short riffs from a growling guitar and snatches of furious drumming, they stepped into a large oval tent. Dozens of dim light bulbs clustered on the central supports like bunches of luminous grapes. They threw a soft and warm light over the blue and yellows stripes of the roof. Garlands of sparkling fairy lights ran around the walls at head-height.

The tent was teeming with young people and on the stage a band in ragged jeans was doing a last minute sound-check. They sound terrible, Gary thought, but they might just do.

He crossed his fingers as Hannah pushed past him to the front of the stage. When she returned, she rattled off the facts, without pausing for breath: she knew the band – that is, she'd of them before – and they came from north London; her friend Laura's elder sister used to go out with the lead singer's cousin; they were really cool; she'd downloaded their single from the Internet; she could hardly believe it; they were great; and – he'd never believe it, but...

Before Hannah could finish, a screeching guitar and a pounding drum beat announced the start of the set. 'I want to dance,' Hannah shouted. Hallelujah, thought Gary. 'Go on then,' he shouted back.

'I can't.'

'Why not?'

'I can't dance in wellies.'

'Yes you can,' Gary said. 'Look at those girls over there.' He pointed at a group of teenagers near to the front of the stage. 'It's so wet outside, everybody's got wellies on.'

'Well, maybe,' Hannah replied, frowning, 'but someone might see me.'

'Who, exactly?'

'Someone I know.'

'Who? Tell me their name.'

'I don't know – someone. I'll look stupid.'

'Look around you, Hannah – do you recognise anyone here?'

'No,' she replied, dropping her head and looking at her boots. 'But that's not the point.' As the band played on with increasing fervour the matted dance floor began to fill up with more young people. Nearby, a group of three girls only slightly older than Hannah were jumping up and down to the music. 'Anyway,' Hannah said, looking both dejected and strangely triumphant at the same time, as if she had found the decisive argument, 'I can't dance on my own.'

'Yes you can,' Gary smiled. 'There are plenty of people your own age and no one will know who you are. Why not join that group of girls? You'll soon make friends.'

Hannah hesitated. Her foot was tapping to the music, the second chorus was just finishing and the band was stepping up the tempo. Gary sensed a tipping point was near and all it needed was a gentle push. He put on an earnest expression and fixed Hannah in his eye. 'Look, I'll dance with you,' he said cheerfully and loudly. Gary stretched out his hand as he spoke.

Hannah looked horrified. 'Oh my God, no,' she whispered in a loud voice. 'Someone will definitely see me then. Sit down – I'll be back soon.' She left his side and disappeared into the now chaotic mob of dancers.

Gary didn't recognise any of the tunes and couldn't hear any of the words, but he appreciated the band's passion and energy: the crashing drums, deep bass line and frenetic guitar work. He searched for somewhere to sit. All of the chairs were taken and he didn't fancy sitting on the damp ground. He moved to the side of the tent, where he spotted a square of thick cardboard tucked away behind a pole. He could tell by the two hemi-spherical indentations that someone had sat on it before. He laid it flat and made himself comfortable. It was a remarkably good fit. He took a swig of cold water from his bottle and, in the midst of the music, his mind wandered.

Claire was wrong to say that I didn't know what I wanted, he thought. I know very well: it's companionship, relief from torment and love. Probably sex, too, if I'm honest, but it's hard to dwell on that with all this noise going on – and I'm not sure Natalie would let me.

I'm fed up with Frank. He was too keen to hitch me up with Claire. What was all that about? He wanted to experience infidelity through me, that's all. I really don't like being used like that. He surely can't have forgotten how much I miss Natalie? I know he was gutted when she died but that should mean he understands the pain I feel. He's an old friend, but I sometimes wonder if I understand him at all.

Poor Marc, I worry about him. Am I giving him enough attention? He seemed so self-sufficient and resilient after his mother died; maybe that's why I've ignored him. Thank God he's been so close to Sam; that must have distracted him from his grief.

Oh, Natalie, where are you? Why aren't you here, now? You were always so plucky and courageous. You were your own woman, determined to do your own thing and go your own way. Our kids are wonderful and you'd love them. You were going to be mine for ever. I was so happy, but I still don't know how I managed to keep such an independent woman all to myself.

Hannah came off the dance floor after the second encore, needing to sit down. Gary looked around but there was no spare seating. As the back of his trousers were now damp, he persuaded her that they should move on.

Tramping across slippery, muddy grass once again, Hannah laid her life plans out before her father. 'I'm going to learn the guitar and have a band of my own. I'm going to play gigs in the middle of the night and travel the world. I'll be famous and rich, everybody will know me and I'll know everybody and…' she paused for breath, '…I'll do whatever I like.'

It was meant as the ultimate aspiration but to Gary it sounded like a reproach. 'What do you mean?' he asked, though he hardly knew why.

'I mean,' Hannah said,' there'll be no one to tell me what to do and no one to stop me doing what I want.'

'Isn't that the case now?'

'You're joking! You're always telling me to do things or, you know, getting in my way.'

'Give me one example.'

'One? I could give you hundreds.'

'I want a list.'

'Well, for starters, I didn't even want to come here, but you made me.'

'That's not fair,' Gary said. 'If I hadn't brought you, you wouldn't have seen that band.'

'Hmmm,' Hannah replied, 'I'd probably have seen them another time, somewhere else.' Gary didn't bother protesting. It still seemed unfair to him and he thought that Hannah was just a bit over-excited and tired. 'And you made me sleep tonight without Lucy.'

'But you're not sleeping: you're out in the open, having fun.'

'But I *am* tired. Can't you find me somewhere to sit down?' Gary shook his head, a gesture lost on Hannah in the dark.

THIRTEEN

They followed the crowds along what seemed to be an old railway embankment and soon found themselves in a long thin field, already heaving with people. Hannah asked where they were; Gary only had a vague idea but felt it best not to admit that he was lost. The field was a riot of noise and lights, with musical acts, shows and other entertainments wherever they looked. It was hard to make any progress through the hordes of people and Gary was worried they might be crushed. He led Hannah to the side of the field, where he thought it would be less congested. In a corner they came across a small marquee advertising itself as a cinema and they dived into it to escape the thronging masses.

Inside, Gary and Hannah found several detached rows of cinema seats in dark crimson velour – a colour so striking that it stood out even in the dark. The seats faced a small portable screen hanging from the far wall. Less than half of the seats were occupied and then mostly by people sleeping. Between the seats, someone had laid carpet tiles, which were now covered in wet earth and crushed grass. There was a counter to the side selling refreshments.

Gary looked at his watch: it was past three o'clock in the morning. Hannah settled down in a seat, while Gary bought hot chocolate and muffins. They sat shoulder to shoulder watching short films: science-fiction fantasies, comedy sketches and surreal animations.

After nearly an hour, the films ended and Hannah's head began to droop. 'Dad, it's really warm and comfortable in here, but I need to go back.'

'That's OK, love. I'm tired too. Let's go.'

In the near pitch black they put on their coats and headed for the thick curtain which served as a door. Gary calculated that they would be back in their tent in about twenty-five to thirty minutes. They pushed the curtain aside and stepped out of the darkness.

To their astonishment, it was considerably lighter outside the tent than in. The sky above was mostly clear of clouds. Overhead, it was a deep purple-blue colour and to the west, purple-black; but in the east the sky was a much paler pastel blue. Apart from one strong bright point of light, the stars had almost vanished.

The scene was completely different to when they had arrived. The crowds had vanished, many of the stalls and tents had closed and much of the music had died down. In the eerie half-light, they could see that the churned-up mud was beginning to dry and a light mist was steaming from yesterday's puddles.

'What is it?' Hannah asked.

Gary was also having trouble comprehending what he could see. 'It's dawn,' he explained eventually. 'Or, at least, dawn is on its way – from over there,' he said, pointing to the east.

'I can't believe it,' Hannah cried, 'that means I've stayed up all night.' Gary pulled the collar of his coat tight around his neck against the cold morning air. 'I've never done that before,' Hannah added. 'I can't wait to tell Lucy!'

'You haven't stayed up all night yet – the sun hasn't risen.'

'When will that be?'

'I don't know. In an hour perhaps; at about five o'clock, I think. Or maybe sooner, I'm not sure. But don't you want to go to bed?'

Hannah hardly paused for thought. 'Can we stay up and watch it?' she asked. Gary smiled. He was impressed that she had such energy, but he had to admit that he also felt re-vitalised and strangely excited by seeing the pre-dawn light. They followed a track leading out of the field and uphill, past hundreds of silent, closed tents. Even as they walked, they could sense the light increasing in strength from their left, as objects around them slowly regained colour and the last of the stars disappeared.

Hannah pointed to the only star which appeared to buck the trend. It was a brilliant, diamond-white point of light set against the pale sky. It was far brighter than any she had seen before; and she asked Gary its name.

'It's called the Morning Star,' he replied.

'What's its real name? It's so beautiful, I love it.'

'Well, it's actually the planet Venus.'

'How can it be a star and a planet at the same time?'

'I didn't say that.'

'Don't you think we learn anything at school? I think you're just making it up. Why don't you admit that you don't know?'

Gary began to explain, but Hannah let go of his hand and marched forward up the hill, stomping her feet as she went.

Near the top of the hill they reached a ring of standing stones, which commanded a breath-taking view of the whole valley. Many thousands of people sat in and around the stone circle and across the grassy slopes, clumped in groups, huddled around small fires or flanked by low-burning candles.

The air was cool and fresh, but impregnated with the smell of wood smoke and sweet cannabis. A primitive rhythmic beating of African drums boomed from the inner circle, together with a regular shake of tambourines, the occasional blast from a trombone and the gentle strumming of guitars. The slopes gave the impression of a huge Iron Age hill fort, full of warriors waiting for battle to commence; and yet there was no tension in the air at all. The atmosphere was like a party, where the partygoers had taken rest, while patiently awaiting the arrival of an important guest.

Gary watched a group of people lighting and launching a pair of Chinese lanterns. They rose sharply with the heat of their flaming wicks, wobbling from side to side and glowing brightly in the mauve-blue morning sky. The first caught fire and plunged burning to the ground. The second continued its ascent to join others already in the sky, until it became a small, distant orange light. Although the lanterns were blown gently away by a weak crosswind, the higher they became the more they seemed just to hang in the air, like a smattering of bright new planets in the firmament.

The focal point of the standing stones was a blazing bonfire, encircled by people perching on cut-off logs. There were friends talking earnestly, young lovers cuddling and lone men with weather-beaten faces gazing into the leaping flames and glowing embers. A young man in baggy shorts and a torn T-shirt approached Gary from the side, his skinny legs rocking on bony knee joints, as if they were about to buckle at any moment.

'Any pills to sell, mate?' he asked.

Gary was taken aback at first, but then felt sad to have heard a young voice with such undisguised desperation. He shuddered when he compared the youth before him with his own children; and he was gripped with a vague fear for the future.

'Please, mate,' the young man begged, but Gary shook his head without saying anything. The young man staggered away, holding onto one of the standing stones to prevent himself falling into the fire.

Gary was thankful that Hannah was looking the other way. He took her hand and they stood behind the people seated around the fire. He felt the heat thrown onto his face, contrasting with the coolness of the air on the back of his neck. They watched a man without shoes swirl around the inner circle, bending and gyrating, and occasionally sitting on the ground in time with the drumming.

'What's he doing?' Hannah asked in a whisper.

Gary thought for a moment that the man was dancing but as he leant over to get a proper look, he saw his hand dart into the fire and a tower of sparks and embers shot into the sky.

'He's keeping the fire going,' Gary replied. 'Pushing the wood from the edges into the middle.'

'Why hasn't he got any shoes on?'

'Maybe because it's so hot near the fire, I don't know.'

Some of the people in front stood up to go. Gary and Hannah took their places, adjusting their bottoms on the knobbly logs, trying to find the least uncomfortable position in which to sit. They sat in silence, gazing at the flames and listening to the drums.

A woman stood up to dance. 'Faster, faster!' she cried at the drummers, and they obliged. Soon several people had left their seats and were beating the ground with their feet and flailing their arms around in a frenzied dance.

Every now and again Gary's thoughts were overwhelmed by a tremendous cheer from groups on the hillside, as more lanterns rose into the sky. They look pretty dangerous to me, he thought; someone ought to ban them.

FOURTEEN

As Gary gazed into the flames, a man approached and asked if he could sit down beside him. He was dressed in an embroidered cotton smock and thin cotton trousers. His neck was decorated with strings of coloured beads and a large shark's tooth on a leather thong. Sun-bleached dreadlocks hung about his shoulders and framed his ruddy face.

'My name's Tyler,' he said, holding out a strong hand for Gary to shake.

'I'm Gary.'

'I've chosen you to talk to,' Tyler said disarmingly, 'because you're wearing smarter clothes than most of the people here, and I thought perhaps you didn't really fit in.' He offered Gary a swig from his can of beer, which Gary declined. 'Do you have any Rizlas?'

'Sorry,' Gary replied, feeling uncomfortable that anyone should think he stood out from the crowd. 'I don't smoke. That is, I've given it up.'

The man lent over to someone else to ask and then sat upright clutching a small wafer-thin piece of paper. He took out a plastic pouch and rolled himself a cigarette.

'Here on your own?' Tyler asked.

'I'm here with my daughter,' Gary said, nodding to his left at Hannah, who was still captivated by the bare foot dancers around the fire. 'I've got two kids here, they're fourteen and fifteen.'

'Sixteen,' Hannah interjected, without moving in any way that suggested she was listening.

'Nearly sixteen,' Gary corrected her.

'I see,' Tyler said, 'but am I right that this is not really your scene?'

Gary was uncertain what Tyler meant. He welcomed the opportunity for some adult conversation, but now felt mildly irritated by this line of questioning. 'Well, I'm here,' Gary said cautiously. 'So I feel OK. I'm just, you know… chilling out.'

'I wonder,' Tyler said, 'if I could ask you what you do.'

'I work in an office,' Gary responded in a rather uninformative way. It was his stock answer when he didn't want to discuss his occupation.

'I wish I could use my brains to earn a living. You must earn a lot.'

'Not really,' Gary replied; 'and life's not cheap when you're on your own with two kids to support.' He waited for a response, but Tyler just sucked on his cigarette. 'Anyway,' Gary added, 'what do you do?'

'I'm a mason; from Wales.' Gary nodded: that explained the soft lilt in Tyler's voice that he hadn't been able to place before. 'I live in a caravan at the moment,' he continued, 'but I'm building my own eco-house on some land I inherited.'

Gary saw that Tyler's fingers were thick and calloused; and he could tell from their shape that he had very muscular arms. 'Must be exhausting work,' he said.

'Yeah, completely; and I'm working far too hard,' Tyler said. 'I've no time for anything else; certainly not for a paid job.'

'What makes it an eco-house?' Gary asked politely.

'I'm using all local materials: granite from an old quarry down the road and timber from the forest. I'm using green sweet cherry wood: it has a beautiful grain and, you know, it's nearly as strong as oak.'

'But won't green wood dry out and shrink?'

'Yeah, and it'll twist too. But if the joint's made well enough, it'll hold fast and be just as strong. The north end's banked up with earth for insulation and it's covered with grass, so the house is practically invisible. Water's from a spring, everything drains into reed beds and there's no cess pit: so it's all in tune with nature, you see.'

'I do. You sound very happy.'

'But what,' Tyler asked, looking pointedly at Gary in the glow of the fire, 'is happiness? Are you any happier in your work than I am in mine? Is a millionaire any happier than either of us? Is money necessary for happiness?'

'No, I agree,' Gary said, 'you don't need money to be happy, but it certainly helps. You can't deny that.'

'Surely you only need your work, your creativity to be happy?'

'True, but without money you couldn't have bought the land on which you're building your house.'

'I inherited the land, as I said.'

'But someone must have bought it at some stage.'

'Yes,' Tyler said, 'but would I be any less happy without the land, if I just lived in the old caravan?'

'You might still be happy living like that, but you'd be frustrated if you wanted to build an eco-house and couldn't.'

Tyler paused. 'You're right, I might be frustrated. Well, it's been nice to talk to you, Gary, but I've got to go now. I need the toilet.' He stood up, shook Gary's hand a second time and left.

'That man was weird,' Hannah said when he had gone.

'Not at all. He was really friendly and interesting.'

'Of course you need money,' Hannah said. 'How could I go shopping without money? That was a pointless conversation. That man was talking rubbish. Sometimes I think that's all grown-ups ever talk about. Who wants an eco-house anyway? It would be damp and cold just like our tent. I've had enough. I want to move away from here now.'

Gary helped her off the log and onto her feet. They walked further up the hillside. Gary spread his coat out on the ground so that they had somewhere dry to sit, and he wondered why he hadn't thought to use it before. They watched the sky become ever lighter in the east and noticed that Venus had started to fade. Hannah clutched her knees and surveyed the horizon, deep in contemplation. Gary felt very close to her. Perhaps the new dawn would mark a turning point in their relationship.

'How long will it be?' Hannah asked.

'Twenty or thirty minutes, I guess' Gary said. 'Are you cold?'

'Yes, but I don't care. It's great up here.'

Gary felt a surge of warmth through his body which compensated for how cold he felt without his coat.

'Mum would've loved this,' Hannah added, 'and just listen to those birds!'

Gary knew, once again, that Natalie had not been forgotten and that she was with them on the chilly hillside. He smiled and stroked Hannah's hair. He had also noticed the dawn chorus and found the birdsong almost overwhelming. The sounds were clear and intense. Explosive trills rolled in the air, accompanied by shrill tweets and rasping clicks. Bright tunes swept back and forth, vying for attention and constantly interfering with each other. They were propelled by a procession of perfect notes peaking and then ebbing away, like waves on choppy water.

The noise was unavoidable and disconcerting; and quite beyond the power of man to affect or control. At times, Gary thought, it was even too loud for comfort. It was a daily avian ritual that would have been recognisable thousands of years ago. Here and now, it was as if the birds were seeking to drown out the noise of the all-night revellers, who huddled for warmth on the damp grass, mocking their cold, tired bodies with their fresh and lively melodies.

Gary was fascinated by the patterns of sound, though at times the repeating notes were so fast that he could barely follow them. His spirits lifted as he absorbed the energy that the birds had released into the air around him. The most surprising thing was that the birds remained hidden in the hedgerows and trees and that, try as he might, he couldn't see a single one anywhere.

'She would have brought a folding chair, several thick blankets and a flask of hot tea,' he said to Hannah.

'I know,' she replied. 'Why didn't you do that?'

Gary shrugged his shoulders. Hannah's comment irked him slightly – and disappointed him rather more – but he just put it down to tiredness. They sat close to each other for warmth, watching the sky becoming lighter and lighter. They tapped their toes to the insistent rhythmic beat of drums, which filled the air with increasing loudness as sunrise approached.

At one point distant low clouds threatened to obscure the horizon, but then they lifted. Gary could make out the shape of trees on a faraway ridge, silhouetted against the bright, creamy light. The sky began to take on a faint yellow hue, slowly replaced by orange tinges, as if ripening like a fruit. The warm colours in the east became stronger. People began to stand in expectation, stretching and stamping the ground for warmth, but never averting their eyes from the line of trees and the bright halos, which had formed around them. The drums beat incessantly and the single, blasted notes of the battered trombone became more urgent.

The air now began to move noticeably at ground level as the temperature dropped. Without thinking, Gary rose to his feet and Hannah followed him. By now, the light grey undersides of the isolated tufts of cloud were splashed with shades of crimson and peach, as if paint had been thrown wildly at them.

'Red sky in the morning…' Gary thought anxiously.

Where before the shapes of the trees on the ridge had been clearly discernible, now they became blurred and distorted by light. Everyone was now on their feet, some standing on tiptoe, as if somehow they might see over the horizon. Suddenly, the music stopped dead; people fell silent and at that precise moment a sliver of radiant golden light edged over the hill, obliterating the trees from sight and flooding the valley below and its cold, damp slopes with glowing warmth and light. A huge cheer arose from the hillside, like the battle-cry of an ancient tribe. As suddenly as they had stopped, the drums restarted their rhythmic sound, though louder and faster, marking the end of night and the beginning of a new day.

The sliver of golden light spread left and right across the

ridge and the curve of the sun rose by barely perceptible fractions, like a wary creature emerging from its lair. Gold gave way to a deep burnt orange, reflecting off Hannah's face and making it look deeply tanned. Light sparkled in her wide, disbelieving eyes.

'It's beautiful,' she whispered. 'It's so beautiful.'

As the sun rose higher and became first an enormous, flattened half-circle, then a burnished orange orb, its rays penetrated Gary's clothes and began to warm his cold body. He hugged Hannah's shoulders and she put her arms around his waist. 'Make the most of this,' he advised her. 'It won't be long until the sun reaches those clouds up there and disappears.'

When Hannah said she wanted to explore the stone circle and see the drummers again, Gary let her go and sat back down on his coat to enjoy the spectacle. Once again, Gary could make out the shape of the trees on the ridge: an expansive wood to the right and, ranging off to the left, single trees, each individually made out by the shape of their boles. He shaded his eyes because, even though it was now only slightly higher above the horizon, the sun had become too strong to look at.

Between the far-off ridge and the nearest tall trees, Gary could now see a number of lesser undulations. These were hard to pick out because a thick white mist filled the valley. Wispy at the edges, a band of low, dense cloud obscured most of the middle ground. It was back-lit by the sun, now pastel yellow rather than orange, which lent the mist a brilliance of its own. Nearby, sunlight broke through the white veil and fanned out in rays.

Gary delighted in the warmth of the sun on his face. He

closed his bleary eyes, shut out the surrounding sounds and prayed silently to the new dawn, like a pagan. Instead of drums, he heard receding birdsong. A fly buzzed in his ear, landed on his cheek and flew off in a second. The skin on his face felt dry and taut, as the heat forcibly extracted moisture from his pores.

As the sun rose inexorably in the sky, the mist in the valley began to recede in equal measure. Gary began to make out the slopes of the fields on the far side of the valley, as they turned from shades of dull grey to a rich and vibrant green.

The sunlight caught a dew-laden cobweb on the ground, its fine strands shimmering in unison and casting the frailest of shadows onto the grass. Gary marvelled at how the spider must have toiled all night to create its trap – and home – amidst the booming party of late-night revellers. What must it have made of the endless vibrations shaking the ground? It probably seemed like a private Armageddon, though the spider must have carried on spinning and weaving regardless, impelled by an irresistible instinct to provide for itself against the odds.

Gary was surprised that the web had survived with so many feet tramping around it. He wondered whether it would survive to the end of the festival, and beyond, when the people had vanished and the fields reverted to farming. In an strange way, Gary envied the simple life of the spider but his thoughts were interrupted when Hannah returned.

Together, they left the standing stones and strolled back to the tent along muddy tracks bound by hundreds of flapping silk flags. The sun struggled to shine through the light grey clouds that now filled the sky. As he kissed Hannah 'goodnight' and then fell into his sleeping bag, Gary felt for the first time in two days that he had turned a corner. He felt confident that things had started to improve. He put the trials of the past behind him and looked forward to later that day, as warmth finally re-entered his bones.

FIFTEEN

The drizzle began to fall soon after Gary had fallen asleep and, by the time he woke near midday, it had been replaced by driving rain. With one ear muffled on a pillow, it sounded as if the tent was on a small island in the middle of a mountain stream. He imagined the water running by on either side, rushing, swirling and gurgling over worn stones and pebbles. The sound seemed to advance, recede, then advance again in a constant rhythmic cycle. It was an oddly reassuring sound that made him feel secure as he lay in his snug sleeping bag.

When he lifted his ear off the pillow, the illusion was dispelled and he could now hear with clarity the pure sound of rainfall on nylon. He opened his eyes and tried to focus on the cotton walls of his sleeping compartment. He felt like he was in a prison cell. He could hear the outside world, but couldn't see beyond the pale white cotton, tinged with pink. His feet felt unbearably hot and it was a struggle to prise off his socks.

The rain subsided and a strange silence fell over the campsite. In only a few moments the inside of the tent became lighter. Gary wondered if there might even be the possibility of direct sunlight soon. He lay on his back enjoying the peace which reigned. He scratched his groin and thought of Claire, then Natalie.

As often happened when he was restless, Gary returned to

the day of the accident. It was a way for his mind to settle down and focus on something important. He had re-lived the incident many times before, so that now even the smallest details were crystal clear.

It had been early in the afternoon. Gary had been sitting in his study at home, shuffling papers. A door had slammed.

'Hurry up,' he heard. 'We'll be late for the kids' concert.'

Gary glanced out of the window over neighbours' gardens. He couldn't really complain how untidy they looked, because he hadn't done any gardening himself for months. Natalie was always nagging him about that. He sipped his tea, but it was now tepid and it gave him no pleasure.

'For God's sake, hurry up.'

The telephone rang. He didn't bother to answer because he knew that Natalie would be unable to resist. It might be one of her friends. That would slow her down, he thought.

He half-listened to the conversation, but it only lasted a minute. He heard hurried footsteps rush past his door. 'What are you doing in there? Can't you come and help me? It's not fair on the children or the school to be late.'

'I'm coming,' he replied. He was reluctant to move until he really had to. Instead, he re-arranged some pens on his desk and sharpened a row of dull pencil tips. There's time, he thought. Anyway, Natalie isn't ready yet.

She thumped on his door and delivered a tirade that he'd heard so often in recent months. He shut the words out of his mind. She didn't really mean what she said.

As he leaned over to put the pencil shavings in his waste basket, he heard an unexpected cry of surprise. It was high-pitched and anguished, and came from the top of the stairs.

He jerked his head towards the door. In an instant, he knew what was about to happen.

Gary heard a loud thud. It was the sound of something soft as it smacked down onto the hard floor. He swivelled in his chair and his hand lunged for the handle of the door.

'Natalie!' he cried at the top of his voice, but it wasn't enough to pull her back from the edge.

The first thud was followed quickly by several others, each noise evenly spaced and equally piercing. The sounds resonated through the joists and echoed ominously in the hollow floor. As Gary swung around the door frame onto the landing, Natalie had already vanished down the stairs, clattering against the bannister spindles. It might have sounded like a xylophone, but for the whip crack of splitting dry wood and the wrenching of nails from their tight, hundred-year-old holes.

He heard Natalie rolling over and over the stair treads and then her head as it cracked against the wall. The sounds became more urgent and accelerated into a deafening climax. Before he reached the top of the stairs Gary heard a final, tremendous crash, louder and longer than all the other sounds; and then there was silence.

The peaceful afternoon had been disturbed for only a few seconds, but Gary could still feel the after-shocks swirling in the air around him. He stood at the top of the stairs in disbelief.

I'm not to blame for this, he thought as he rushed down the stairs towards the mangled body at the bottom. He was shaking as he fell to his knees at her side, horrified by the smears of blood on the wall and the unnatural slant of her neck.

'Natalie, what have you done?' he asked aloud.

He touched her cheek. It was still warm, hot even. He fumbled for her wrist, but he was trembling so much that he couldn't find a pulse. He bent over her to listen for breathing, but he couldn't keep still long enough to hear. It can't be true, he thought.

He stepped over her body and picked up the telephone in the hall. He called an ambulance. 'Yes,' he said, 'the police too,' but he didn't really know why. 'Fifteen minutes? Can't you come sooner?'

He put the phone down and ran back to Natalie. She hadn't moved at all. Her eyes were bulging with terror. Not a single blink. Oh, Natalie, he thought as he held her limp hand. What am I going to do? How will I cope? He broke down and sobbed for several minutes, hunched over her body. 'You can't leave me,' he cried. 'You can't leave me.'

Eventually, he let go of Natalie and sat on the step next to her. He wiped his eyes with his shirt sleeve and surveyed the carnage. Among the debris of twisted body and spikes of wood, he noticed a book. Its spine had split and the pages were torn and bloodied. The shiny cover was blue, white and red; a school book. How many times had he said not to leave things at the top of the stairs? This was definitely not his fault.

Gary picked up the tattered pages and decided he'd throw them away. He'd keep the truth to himself and no one else need ever know; it would be his secret.

He heard a distant siren and felt a sense of panic. Don't act as if you've done something wrong, he told himself. You're blameless.

He kissed Natalie's cold lips and said a last farewell. When the ambulance arrived, he knew they would take her away. He wondered what he should do next. He was thinking about the longer term, about the children. They would be devastated too. How would they cope with all this? The strains would be unbearable.

He left the body and dropped the school book into the swing bin in the kitchen. He heard urgent knocking on the front door and went to open it. As he did so, he realised what he must do.

He stopped for a moment and made a silent vow: I'll remain loyal to you, Natalie, for the rest of my life… I'll preserve your memory to the end… Nothing will ever change the love I feel for you and no one will come between us.

Gary listened to the sound of children playing outside. He could also make out the occasional roar of camping gas on a small stove. No doubt, he thought uncharitably, it came from some diehard campers, who preferred their tea under-heated, scummy from tannin and tasting of metal, rather than buy a freshly brewed cuppa in a marquee not a hundred yards away.

Somewhere nearby he also heard the tentative strumming of a cheap ukulele. Gary thought of the poor parents. They had probably bought it the night before to placate a child cooped up by the rain. Gary wondered how long it would be before the child lost interest and sank into the inevitable misery of being unable to play even a simple tune.

Gary had just finished dressing when he heard Frank's cheerful booming voice outside the tent.

'Wakey, wakey, campers! Time to shake a leg! The rain has stopped you know and it's quite bright out here.' Frank grabbed one of the ridge poles of the tent and shook it vigorously. 'But you'll still need your wellies,' he added, 'because the ground's like a swamp.'

'I'm up,' Gary called, but Hannah and Marc just grunted, being the least effort required to acknowledge that they had heard the message.

'Look what I've got for you, my friend,' Frank grinned as Gary stepped out of the tent. 'It's the perfect breakfast.' Frank pointed at a bulging shopping bag at his feet. 'Would you like to start the day with a Bloody Mary?' he beamed.

'I'm not sure.'

'Oh, come on man, it'll definitely kick-start your day.'

'Have you got enough?' Gary said, trying to stall for time.

'Sure. I've brought a carton of tomato juice – the organic stuff, mind you – and there's vodka aplenty. Or white rum if you prefer.'

Gary grimaced at the last suggestion, but in no time Frank was squatting on the ground mixing vodka and juice into clear plastic beakers. He offered one to Gary and then fished a small red bottle out of the bag.

'This, Gary, is the real McCoy,' he said enthusiastically. 'You just have to try my old woman's hot pepper sauce.' He put a few drops into each beaker. 'Really,' he added dismissively, 'it's the only thing she's good for.'

'That's a bit harsh,' Gary replied, taking the beaker and sipping the fiery concoction. He felt it flow down his gullet and react with his gastric juices, generating, so it seemed to him, quite volcanic amounts of internal heat. 'No ice?' he asked with a smile. 'No, really, I'm joking; it's delicious,' he added quickly when he saw Frank's face drop.

'Cheers then, my good friend. Down the hatch!' Frank

replied, as he tipped back his head and emptied the beaker in one gulp.

Gary stepped back into the tent and called on the teenagers to get up for a late breakfast. He heard Marc groan that he couldn't face getting out of his sleeping bag because he was too warm and dry. He was only able to persuade him by saying that Sam was outside waiting. Gary then leant towards Hannah's sleeping quarters and called out her name a couple of times in a loud and cheerful voice. Hannah told him she was tired and to leave her alone.

'But we're going to meet Lucy, too.'

'So what?'

'I thought you wanted to tell her all about last night.'

'Yeah, obviously, but I've got a whole day to do that.'

'Aren't you hungry?'

'You're always trying to make me do things that I don't want to do. Why don't you just leave me alone?'

'Sorry,' Gary replied, frustrated by her response. 'As I recall you came out last night of your own accord. We just want your company, so there's no need to be tetchy.'

'Tetchy? Tetchy?' Hannah cried. 'That's what you used to say to mum. It made her miserable, so don't start on me.' Gary was stunned. He decided to withdraw and to leave her in the tent if she wanted, but Hannah was warming to her theme. 'Anyway, why can't I be tetchy? I'm cold and tired, there's water in the tent, my back hurts and instead of letting me sleep, you bang on and on, trying to get me to do this, to do that.'

'Hannah, please calm down and stop being so irrational.'

'Irrational?' she shouted back. 'First you tried to control

115

mum, now you're trying to control me. So, just fuck off and leave me alone! OK?'

Gary reeled out of the tent, where Frank and Sam were standing open-mouthed. Gary couldn't see Hannah but he imagined her sitting up in her sleeping bag, her face contorted with rage and her fists clenched. He heard a thump like a sack of potatoes falling to the ground and realised that he'd been right, at least about her sitting up.

'Wow,' Frank and Sam said together.

'Oh, don't mind her,' Gary said unconvincingly. 'We stayed up all night and watched sunrise. She's just tired and possibly hormonal. It's my fault because I was pushing her.'

'Don't blame yourself, old friend, she just has her mother's fiery genes, that's all,' Frank said, in a voice which sounded oddly admiring.

'I don't know where she got all that control stuff from,' Gary said. 'In our relationship, it was definitely Natalie who wore the trousers.'

'I know,' Frank agreed.

'How do you know?' Gary snapped.

'I knew you both for years,' Frank said defensively. 'Natalie was the most headstrong woman I've known: that was her attraction.'

'That's not the same thing.'

'Look,' Frank said, 'you always used to complain that she bossed you around: that's all I'm saying. You even told me that you didn't think Natalie respected you anymore. I'm sure that was rubbish, but those were your words, mate, not mine.' Frank paused. Gary was no longer looking at him, but was staring at the wet grass, as if deep in thought. 'The bottom line,' Frank continued, 'is that Natalie was a strong-willed, independent-minded, feisty woman and…'

Gary lifted his head suddenly and looked into Frank's eyes.

'And we all know how you like feisty women, Frank.'

'I don't know what you're trying to say, Gary, but this isn't about me,' Frank replied carefully. 'I was just going to say that Hannah is feisty too, like her mother was – that's all.'

The two friends stared at each other. After a moment Gary shook his head. 'Oh God, I don't know what to think. I'm sorry I was so short with you. Hannah's taken me a bit by surprise this morning and she's really wound me up. We had such a lovely time last night, I really didn't expect all that.'

Gary heard the swish of nylon as Marc stepped out of the tent. Sam let out a cry of delight and ran to embrace him. Frank laughed and Gary smiled. It was good, he thought, to see such a strong and happy friendship amongst all this strife. He asked Marc to tell Hannah where they were going, so that she wouldn't feel abandoned and lonely. He picked up the bag containing the vodka and tomato juice, handing it to Frank as a peace-offering. With Frank's arm coupled in his in a comradely way, and with Marc and Sam shoulder to shoulder, the four of them set off in search of food.

SIXTEEN

They walked briskly along the wet gravel track which led from the campsite to the market, joining a line of people in ill-fitting cagoules and cheap plastic ponchos.

'This isn't a rock festival,' Gary said to Frank, who was striding along beside him, 'it's more like one of those terrible refugee camps you see on the telly.'

'With one major difference,' Frank said. 'At least here you can buy a mean cappuccino 24/7; and fresh doughnuts in five flavours!'

When they arrived at the breakfast tent, they found that half of the interior had been flooded by the morning's downpour. A couple of white plastic chairs were floating in the far corner, along with an assortment of bottles, polystyrene cups and, inexplicably, a rubber ring. The caterer had erected a temporary awning to cover the front entrance – 'until the monsoon stops and the waters drain away,' she said grimly – and had set up tables and the remainder of the chairs under it.

Before they had finished eating, Hannah arrived, looking drowsy and very unhappy. 'This place is almost as wet as my bedroom,' she grumbled, as she re-launched one of the plastic chairs that had become beached on the edge of the pond.

'How was last night?' Frank asked her.

'It was OK, I suppose,' she replied grudgingly, avoiding Gary's eyes. 'Where's Lucy? I want to tell her about it.'

'Tell us.'

'No. I'll end up repeating myself. Anyway, we didn't do much: just saw a few short films and then watched the sunrise. Nothing special.' Hannah would not be drawn further. Gary felt that she had rather short-changed the others with her limited response, so he decided that he'd recount the tale of the previous night himself.

Before he had a chance to say anything, Sam called out to say that he could see some blue sky. 'It looks like there's an ice-breaker, making a great big crack right through the clouds.'

'What?' Hannah said. 'That doesn't make sense.'

'And that's like the blue sea behind it,' Marc added to support his friend.

'It certainly feels cold enough,' Hannah said, gripping both sides of her body with her hands and simulating a shiver.

Gary went to buy Hannah some food and by the time he returned to the table, Claire and Lucy had arrived. They were both captivated by Hannah's animated blow-by-blow account of the previous night. Even from far away, Gary could hear the excitement in her voice.

'You wouldn't believe how many people stay up all night,' Hannah said. 'It was like a huge party on the hillside, with a massive bonfire, loads of drumming, people dancing everywhere... And we met this really cool man who's building his own eco-house... And you should have seen the sun rise, over there...' she pointed vaguely eastwards. 'Yeah, it was five in the morning. Can you believe? It was *so* beautiful, Lucy, I can't even begin to describe it. You'd have really loved it!'

'It sounds cold and boring to me,' Marc said.

'I wasn't talking to you.'

'Well, we could all hear you.'

'Just don't listen, if you don't want to.'

'Oh, sorry,' Marc replied, poking his sister in the back.

Hannah swung round and swiped at him with her hand, missing as he ducked. 'Why don't you just piss off and leave me alone?' she said with frustration. Marc waggled his tongue before her eyes; Hannah grabbed his ears and hair and started shaking his head; and then Marc began to pummel her with his fists. Gary put down the food he was carrying but before he could step in and separate them, their chairs had collapsed and they fell onto the ground. They were still kicking and punching each other as Gary and Frank pulled them apart.

'That's enough, you two,' Gary shouted. 'Your behaviour is unacceptable.'

'She started it,' Marc protested.

'I did not,' Hannah yelled indignantly. 'He poked me in the back.'

'But she was being horrible to me.'

'Stop it now, both of you,' Gary said firmly, the anger in his voice rising in order to make the teenagers listen. 'You have to understand, Marc, that Hannah is just a bit tired and tetch…' His voice died away. 'Let's just say she's tired from last night. She'll be better when she eats something.' He put the food in front of Hannah and held onto the plate. 'And as for you, young lady, there's absolutely no need for that kind of language.'

Hannah looked at him defiantly, lifting her shoulders and raising her chin in an exaggerated frown. After a moment, she snorted air loudly through her nostrils, as if in disgust, turning so that she no longer had to look at him. She picked up a fork and began to toss baked beans into her mouth, chewing them as noisily as she could.

'Was it wise to keep Hannah up all night?' Claire asked.

Gary could hardly believe his ears. He could feel his anger rise again. 'So, I'm at fault, am I?'

'No, I didn't say that,' Claire replied briskly. 'I just wondered if she was really old enough for that kind of thing. I mean – look how tired she is.'

'I'll be the judge of that,' Gary said coldly. 'She's only missed out on a bit of sleep and, after all, she had a wonderful time – she's told you all about it.'

'I mean, when Hannah gets tired, she gets so bad tempered.'

'Try telling her that.'

'It's OK, Claire,' Hannah interrupted, looking over her shoulder. 'I do get a bit cross sometimes when I'm tired. I'm sorry if I upset you.'

'You haven't upset me, Hannah,' Claire said, 'but I think you've upset your father.'

'He'll survive,' she muttered between mouthfuls. 'He always survives.'

'Anyway, mum,' Lucy said, tugging at Claire's sleeve. 'Can I go out with Hannah tonight and watch the sunrise too?' Claire hesitated. 'Please, oh, please,' Lucy begged. 'Pretty please, with a cherry on top. Hannah knows exactly where to go and what to do, and we'll be very safe together.'

'What do you think, Frank?' Claire asked. He had remained silent, sipping his coffee and moving his attention from person to person, as if watching a tennis match. Frank's eyes met Claire's and he held them there in a fixed gaze for several seconds without blinking. Gary watched them both, trying to understand what was going through their minds.

'It's a difficult one,' Frank said in a leisurely way. 'I'm sure it'll be perfectly safe, especially if they stay together. If they take raincoats, a torch and a mobile phone they'll be prepared for almost anything. So, I can't see why not.'

Claire wavered and looked at Frank again for reassurance. Gary was no longer angry, but he felt a growing sense of incredulity as he listened to their conversation. He looked from Frank to Claire and then back again. They appeared to be looking at each other in wonder, with a kind of fascination from which neither could break free.

'After all, if the girls are self-sufficient,' Frank added, 'that'll give you time to do what you want tonight.'

'Well,' Claire said after a few more seconds of mental calculation, 'I don't see why not.' Then, as an after-thought she added: 'That is, if you don't mind, Gary.'

Gary's mouth had dropped wide open. He struggled to find the right words. 'I don't believe what I'm hearing,' he said quietly. 'One minute, I'm the ogre for allowing my daughter out all night, and the next you two have more or less agreed that she and Lucy can do exactly the same, tonight.'

'It's not like that, Gary,' Frank interjected.

'I don't get it.'

'Gary, it takes time to think these things through.'

'All of a minute-and-a-half,' Gary replied with irritation in his voice. 'Well you tell me, Claire – is it wise to let the girls stay up all night?'

Claire blushed and bit her lip. 'I'm sorry, Gary. Please forgive me. I spoke too soon and I didn't mean it to come out the way it did. Hannah clearly had a great time and, if you think it's safe, I'd love Lucy to share the experience.'

They stood in silence. Gary could feel Lucy's eyes burning in the back of his head. Frank also seemed to be pleading with him and Gary felt puzzled and uneasy. He scratched his head and wondered whether perhaps his reaction had been a bit hasty. Was he being unreasonable? Had he just misunderstood what everyone had been saying, because Hannah had wound him up again?

He looked at Frank and Claire, standing, and at Hannah and Lucy, who were now sitting. They were all imploring him to give his blessing to the plan. Gary felt removed from the scene unfolding before him. It was like he was in a silent film: Claire started speaking but he couldn't hear anything that she said. He felt as though he was in a huge bubble, where normal life was temporarily suspended; and he would remain there until he made his decision.

Gary felt manipulated by adult and teenager alike. He wanted to resist, but he couldn't express his thoughts clearly. More importantly, he was unable to pinpoint where his anxieties and suspicions lay. Without grasping the various forces and influences acting upon him, Gary's defences failed. He sighed then shrugged, spreading out the palms of his hands in an act of surrender, as an outward sign of agreement. He let out a quiet 'I suppose so,' with such a suppressed tone of resentment that only he could notice it. But it was enough for the bubble to burst and for normality to return or, at least, a version of it.

Lucy screamed with delight and threw her arms around Hannah. Frank and Claire let out laughs of relief and stood there, Gary thought, grinning like two Cheshire cats. Frank patted Gary on the shoulder and said something to him in a warm, congratulatory tone, which again Gary didn't hear.

The only other person to set himself against the prevailing euphoria was Marc, who muttered unhappily that 'she always gets her own way.'

They left for the main stage, with the teenagers forging ahead along the muddy track and the adults struggling to keep up. Hannah and Lucy held hands, swinging their arms, laughing and skipping. Marc and Sam were arm-in-arm, marching along united and deep in conversation. Frank and Claire walked side-by-side, occasionally rubbing shoulders. From time to time, Frank would gallantly take hold of Claire's elbow and forearm to guide her round a muddy puddle.

Gary observed all of these things as he trudged along behind them. He was still uneasy about the decision to let the girls stay out all night. He tried to shrug off his anxiety, accepting reluctantly that the die was cast.

Looking at the others, he wondered at the way people's moods could alter so rapidly, so unpredictably, like shifting air currents. Gary ascribed the change of mood to the appearance of the yellow sun, now overhead in a vast blue sea chequered with fluffy white icebergs. He felt better in himself but at the same time, deep down, he feared it was only because he was alone once again.

Natalie would have understood, he thought. She would have wanted him to continue holding a candle for her, even after so long a time.

SEVENTEEN

The bottom of the pyramid field had suffered badly from the rain. Two great pools of water lay on either side of the stage. The central area, where several thousand people had now congregated, was firm but covered in sticky brown mud. Gary was pleased that the boys were leading them to the upper slope, which still sported some green grass. They picked their way through the waiting spectators sitting in rows of camping chairs, lying on plastic sheets or just standing in small groups, chatting, smoking and drinking.

The boys found a clearing that they could call their own and stopped as a huge roar welcomed the band on stage. The lead singer welcomed the festival goers with a hearty 'Hello Glastonbury!' and a loud 'Are you having fun?' both of which produced a deafening response. Gary asked himself if he was having fun and answered that yes, he was, despite the obvious hardships and Hannah's mood swings. He wondered if Hannah and Marc were enjoying themselves, but didn't really doubt it when the teenagers started to dance, clap and sing along with the band.

Frank and Claire were also dancing but in a strange circular fashion, rather like African villagers, Gary thought. He watched their hips twist and turn in time to the music, with their rumps slightly protruding and their backs arched, heads lowered and arms raised to shoulder height. They each held a paper cup in their right hand and were trying hard not to spill too much of their drinks. Their dancing seemed to pivot around the cups, which were practically stationary in the air, as if they were fixed points on an invisible post.

When Gary recognised a song, he tapped along with his feet, but he didn't feel that he was getting as much out of it as the others were. He put it down to tiredness; and simply thinking about the lack of sleep made him yawn.

As Gary's attention wandered, his eyes were drawn to a young woman walking up the slope, with her back to the stage. She was tall and slender and wore a mauve smock over faded black jeans. Long, straggly curls spilled out of a purple knitted hat and onto her shoulders. She wore a fine silver ring through the side of one nostril and had a dark crimson spot on her forehead. Gary saw that she was carrying a tray in her hand and on it stood maybe two dozen small plastic beakers filled with something pink.

'Vodka jellies, vodka jellies!' she chanted.

As she approached, Frank let out a whoop of delight. 'Oh yes,' he said with glee. 'We'll have some of those.' Gary looked with suspicion at the beakers and their translucent contents. Jelly made with vodka seemed a strange combination to him. 'Let's buy some for us and some for the girls,' Frank suggested as he searched his wallet for money.

'For the girls?' Gary said. 'Surely we don't want to encourage that?'

But it was too late: Hannah and Lucy had heard and now completed the circle which surrounded the young woman. 'We want to try them,' they called out together. 'They look so pretty.'

'They're alcoholic,' Gary said.

'Come on, dad,' Hannah replied. 'They're absolutely tiny and can't possibly do any harm.'

Gary realised this was probably true, but taking vodka jellies from a stranger carried its own risk. Gary wasn't sure that he wanted to consume one himself. He peered at the little beakers and tried to divine their contents. 'Are they alright?' he asked the young woman, immediately recognising the naivety of his question.

She gave him a broad, reassuring smile of tombstone white teeth. Her blue eyes blazed and her clothes glowed in the sunlight. 'Of course, I made them myself.' Her eyes twinkled flirtatiously. Gary peered into the depths of her pupils. His mind began to swirl as if he were being hypnotised. He had to raise his hand to his face to break the connection.

'Where did you make them?'

'In my tipi,' she replied immediately. Gary needed something more than this: who was she and could she be trusted? Gary opened his mouth to ask a further question but she raised a finger to her lips, gently silencing him. He felt as if he were under a spell. His objection, his caution, had been rational and reasonable, but they had been neutralised by a persuasive force beyond his understanding.

'Don't be so uptight,' Frank said, as if from far away. 'It's just a bit of harmless fun.'

Gary tried to explain that everyone should be more careful about what they ate, but his words fell on deaf ears.

'Well, I'd like one,' Claire said, throwing her weight behind Frank. 'There's no harm in them – it's only jelly.'

It's not 'only jelly' Gary thought, but his tongue felt inexplicably tied and mute.

'Gary, what's wrong with you?' Frank hissed as he produced a banknote and bought five beakers.

It seemed to Gary that the young woman just vanished into

thin air, but he knew that could only be his imagination. He looked about him, but she was nowhere to be seen. As he emerged from her spell, he realised that the band was still playing songs, the teenagers were still dancing and his foot was still tapping the soggy ground. Frank handed round the vodka jellies. Gary watched the girls lick the beakers clean with their tongues. He tested his, but quickly spat out the sickly goo which melted in his mouth. He threw the little beaker to the ground.

'You knew I didn't want Hannah to have one of those,' Gary remonstrated with Frank a little later.

'Get a life!' Frank responded. 'You can't go on moping around like this forever.'

Gary felt helpless and disempowered. Hannah was his daughter and he was responsible for her. Was this too small an issue to make a fuss about? Probably, he concluded; but he remained unsettled and had an overwhelming feeling that Frank had usurped him once again.

The sky began to fill with seagulls, circling in air currents created by the driving heat of the sun. Gary wondered what had brought them to this field. It couldn't have been music, he smiled, but it didn't really matter why. He welcomed their presence as a visible reminder of another world outside the confines of the festival.

He imagined their journey from the blue-green expanse of the sea, perhaps twenty or thirty miles away. He watched them soaring, diving and rolling like waves over the glorious English countryside, until they arrived above this noisy valley choked with people. Gary longed to be free like the gulls and fly with them to the coast; though he worried a little that they may prefer landfill sites.

The gulls played with each other. They appeared to crumple together like screwed up balls of paper and fall towards the ground, before spreading their wings and gliding smoothly back up into the sky. They soared in a vaguely circular motion pecking at each other's beaks as they nearly collided. Then they span away, before plunging once again towards the ground. The gulls were blown gently away from the field by a wind that Gary couldn't feel. Soon, their high-pitched cries were gone too. He followed the fast-diminishing grey and white specks with envy.

The gulls were replaced by a single large crow, which began to fly over the crowded field from the other direction. It was much closer than the gulls had been. It flew with purpose straight across the masses below, determined not to be deflected by the wind. Unlike the gulls which came from the coast, Gary knew that the crow must be local. He watched the bird increase in speed, as if suddenly pushed along by the amplified music.

Gary noticed that several heads around him were also following the bird fly overhead. While the seagulls had offered him a vision of freedom and given him hope, the crow seemed to present a bad omen. He snorted when he reflected what a preposterous thought that was. However, he couldn't keep his eyes from the bird and he found himself twisting his whole body to follow its flight.

The crow reached the end of the field, having traversed tens of thousands of heads in under a minute. As if realising that this vision of humanity was truly exceptional, it wheeled round in a wide arc, dropping lower and lower, surveying the scene below. Then, suddenly, it shot upwards and flew off to the right. It's loud 'caw' coincided with a momentary lull in the music and was carried the length and breadth of the field, apparently magnified by the speakers. Many people now looked upwards, released temporarily from the artifice of the music, to watch the black wings sail effortlessly across an azure sky and disappear over the trees.

The band performed for about forty minutes: less than half a normal gig, Gary thought. He was pleased to have seen them, because they were pretty good. There was no time for an encore: the stage hands had started to remove the band's kit before the musicians had even left the stage. Gary followed Frank, Claire and the teenagers as they wandered from the pyramid field in search of more entertainment in the now bright, mid-afternoon sunshine.

As they walked along the group split up and then reformed so that, at different times, Gary had the company of adults or teenagers, or both. He kept to himself and, as much as he could, he didn't take part in any of the conversation. He thought Hannah sounded chirpy, as she continued to talk about the previous night in gratifyingly positive tones. Several times Marc repeated that he wanted to tell him something important, but he kept being interrupted by the others.

As he sauntered along Gary began to feel relaxed and, he supposed, relatively happy. He hoped that his boots would soon become superfluous, as he felt the ground gradually harden underfoot. At the end of the market stalls he found himself at the back of the group, smiling and with his hands in his pockets. He looked ahead and noticed that the others were out of sight. He was rather enjoying being on his own, when he saw Marc marching towards him, looking miserable.

'I've lost Sam,' he said gloomily.

'When did you last see him?' Gary asked.

'About ten minutes ago, by the dancing caterpillars.'

Gary looked back but could only see a thick mass of people and two willow giants towering above them. 'Does he know where we're going?'

'I don't even know where we're going; I'm following you.'

'I see,' Gary said. 'I was following… well, nobody really. We were all just going along in this general direction.'

Gary felt sorry for Marc; he understood that he'd have more fun with someone of his own age. All he could do was commiserate. Then he recalled that Marc had wanted to tell him something important, so he asked what it was.

'Later; I'm not in the mood right now,' Marc replied. 'Anyway, where *are* we going, dad?'

Gary wanted to repeat that he had no idea; but something in Marc's voice made him hesitate. It then dawned on him that Marc was looking for more than simple directions; what he really needed was some parental guidance and leadership. 'We'll go this way,' Gary said decisively, pointing ahead in the direction they had been walking. 'And I'm sure we'll bump into the others soon.'

Whenever the track divided, Gary and Marc took the least busy path and they soon found themselves in quieter pastures. Marc had been glum and uncommunicative as they progressed; Gary on the other hand became more cheerful as the last remaining clouds began to break apart and fray at the edges, clearing huge expanses of blue sky. His steps seemed to lighten and he was comfortable being lost in his own thoughts.

They bought kebabs and sat on a wooden bench wolfing them down. They didn't talk; all Gary could hear were grunts of delight, the smacking of lips and the occasional long, drawn-out hum of satisfaction. In fairness, Gary realised, the sounds didn't only emanate from Marc. Gary pulled a piece of fat from between his teeth and wiped his fingers on a tissue.

'That was delicious,' Marc said, 'but my mouth's burning from all that red stuff.' Gary offered him water. Marc took a swig and then leant against his father's back with his eyes closed. 'This sun is great,' he yawned. 'I think I could sleep.'

Gary closed his eyes as well. He felt the sun's warmth on his cheeks. When he opened his eyelids he squinted in the bright light and everything, near and far, was thrown into focus. He closed his eyelids and began to feel drowsy. 'So could I,' he said.

Gary's lips began to dry out and he worried that the tip of his nose might burn. The sounds around him deadened. Through his eyelids he could see a bright red sea, pulsating with ever-shifting patterns and dark maroon filaments. He felt as if he were floating in a huge globe of hot blood, which slowly resolved from red to gold as he became accustomed to the sensation.

He opened his eyes again and saw several vertical strands of hair, dangling in front of his face. Even squinting in the light, they were too close and too fine for his eyes to focus on; but somehow they made him feel hemmed in, like the bars of a cage. He brushed the hair aside and looked out over the nearby field; and it seemed that all colour had been bleached out by the sun.

Gary rubbed his eyes for relief and, as his fists cut out the light, he saw new circular patterns of gold and green, etched on a black background. The patterns remained in sight when he opened his eyes again, as if they were floating above the grass. Although Gary found it all very surreal, he enjoyed the spectacle; it was his own private entertainment.

'Dad, what are you doing?' Marc asked.

'Sun-worship,' Gary replied. He saw a quizzical look on Marc's face.

'Dad, can I ask you something?'

'Of course.'

'Do you believe that mum's in heaven?'

'Yes,' Gary replied without hesitation.

'Do you believe in God, then?'

'Not really.'

'How can you believe in one, but not the other?'

Gary looked again at his son and saw shadows from some nearby bunting playing on his face. 'It's up to you what you want to believe,' he said. 'Do you think your mum's in heaven?'

'I hope so. That way I might see her again.'

Gary smiled. 'Yes, I want to see your mum again, too. It's just that…' Gary stopped abruptly; a lump had appeared in his throat and he found he couldn't continue. He tried to take a breath, but his chest felt hollow and empty.

'… It's just that…' he said again, but a surging feeling of loss overwhelmed him. He tried to pull himself together; this wasn't the fatherly leadership that Marc was expecting.

'…I don't know when it'll be.'

He gulped and tears flowed from his sun-kissed eyes. Marc put his arms around his father and held his head to his chest. Gary lent against his son and wept uncontrollably. He tried to say 'I'm sorry' but the words couldn't break through the sobbing.

'It's OK dad, it's OK,' Marc reassured him. 'If it helps dad, when the sun shines I often think it's mum up there, shining down on us. If you thought that too, maybe it would help you get back to normal sooner.'

He waited for his father to control his tears. Gary rubbed his eyes with the back of his arm and sniffed hard, to stem his running nose.

'You see, dad,' Marc continued after a while, 'I sun-worship, too.'

EIGHTEEN

Sunday morning, 4.00 a.m.

Gary snapped back into consciousness, to find eight hands gripping tightly on his wrists and ankles. The smell of damp earth filled his nostrils and the ground rose and fell beneath his eyes like the sea. A mocking call of 'Bring out your dead!' announced their arrival at the medical tent. There was more laughter tinged with relief. Gary's brain was engulfed by waves of nausea.

'What's wrong with him?' asked a new female voice.

'No idea. We just saw him face down in the mud and picked him up.'

'He's not one of your group?'

'No. He's a stranger.'

'OK, sit him down there and we'll take a look.'

'Do you think he'll be alright?'

'Oh, I'm sure he'll live. I'll get a doctor to see him soon. You did well to bring him here.'

'It was the least we could do,' a male voice said, obviously basking in the praise. 'Anyone would do the same.'

'I thought you said he was a loser and we should leave him.'

'Get off – anyone could see he needed help. But he *is* a fucking loser – just look at him.'

'Is he conscious?'

Gary wanted to answer, but didn't know how.

Gary sat shaking with cold on a metal fold-up chair, just inside the door of the medical tent. Someone draped two thick grey blankets over his shoulders. He thought he knew where he was but, at the same time, he really had no idea. The euphoria of the dance field had disappeared. Kareena was a name in his head, but he couldn't conjure up any image of her face. His recollection of the night was a blur.

A woman was speaking to him, asking questions that he didn't understand. He gave a grunt in response.

'Get him onto the floor,' he heard her say.

Hands from nowhere lifted him off the chair and laid him onto a mat, rolling him onto his side with his arms bent at the elbow. His limbs ached as he shivered uncontrollably, but he felt comfort from the weight of the blankets over his body. Without warning his stomach contracted and he vomited several times.

He felt something being wrapped firmly around his upper arm; a hand squeezed his wrist and a hand touched his forehead. A bright light shone into his eyes; he tried to close them, but determined fingers held the lids open; and while the intrusion of light was painful, it was only fleeting. His head was lowered onto the mat and he could smell the vomit for the first time, filling his nostrils with a pungent sourness.

'A bit dilated, but both pupils are reacting. He doesn't look too bad. Can you get someone to wash him down?'

More hands carried him the length of the brightly lit medical tent, past aluminium struts, white plastic chairs and pastel-coloured cubicle screens. Two men in white clothes held him upright, while someone removed his shirt and sprayed his upper body clean with warm water from a shower head. The warmth coaxed Gary out of his stupor and, feebly, he tried to brush wet hair out of his eyes.

'Feeling better?' someone asked.

One of the men towelled him down and gave him a clean T-shirt to wear. 'Is this yours?' he asked, handing Gary a creased photograph. 'It was in your shirt pocket.'

With their help, Gary stumbled slowly back to the entrance of the tent. He sat back down on the fold-up chair, pulling more blankets over his shoulders. A young woman sat behind a small camping table to his side, tapping details into a laptop. She gave him a sympathetic look and smiled.

'Hi,' she said with a soft Scottish accent that he recognised from earlier. 'My name's Rosie and I'm a volunteer nurse. How are you feeling?'

Gary nodded.

'Can I take your name?'

Gary frowned. Words wouldn't come out of his mouth.

'Don't worry, there's time,' she said. 'Have you been drinking?'

Gary rocked his head from side to side.

'A little, perhaps?'

He nodded. It was only a little, at least during the night.

'Have you taken any drugs?'

Gary frowned again. It was a simple question, asked for a genuine medical reason, but he found himself reluctant to answer it. Could he really admit that he'd taken drugs? What on earth would she think of him? How could he face her, if he told the truth?

'I think you might have taken something, from the way

your eyes looked in the light,' Rosie said, encouraging him to reply. 'Have you smoked any cannabis?'

Gary thought of the joint that he'd been given and he nodded.

'Have you taken any tablets, any ecstasy?'

Gary lifted a single finger in front of his face.

'Just one E?'

He nodded.

'Anything else?'

Gary shook his head. There didn't need to be, as the shame was complete.

'I see. Sit still please. I'm just going to check your eyes and take your pulse and blood pressure again.'

She came around the table and carried out the checks. She touched a bruise on his forehead and Gary recoiled slightly.

'You're going to be alright,' she reassured him. 'But I'm a little worried that you might have had a minor head injury when you fell, so I'll get the doctor to look at you soon. Meanwhile, I'd like you to wear this yellow wrist band. It's to ask people to get help if you become ill later.'

Gary looked at her, but his eyes wouldn't focus. He wanted to say thank you, but he felt too light-headed to concentrate. The tent began to spin and he felt someone catch him, as he fell forward slowly off the chair. The lights went out.

NINETEEN

Saturday, 3.00 p.m.

The sound of rolling drums and a tune from a bugle drew Gary and Marc to somewhere new. They joined a crowd which had collected around a large open-sided gazebo. The frame was decked with garlands of white flowers and coloured balloons bounced against the corners. Inside, Gary could see a man dressed in a flowing black robe and white dog-collar.

'We are gathered here today,' he began, 'to witness the joining together of two people who, until recently, were hardly known to each other.' He raised his hand to subdue a drunken cheer. 'Anthea, please bring in the happy couple.'

A dinner-suited man beat a fast, rhythmic drum roll on a snare drum which hung around his neck. A woman in a white tuxedo and fairy-wings led the couple in from the side. Gary laughed when he saw them: he was a giant in a leopard-skin leotard with dreadlocks and tattoos; and she was petite, in a bright green veil, white T-shirt and tutu. She carried a small bouquet of brightly-coloured plastic flowers in one hand and a can of lager in the other.

'What's going on?' Marc asked.

'It's some kind of wedding, I think.'

A mariachi band in wide sombreros broke into a furious song and the crowd clapped and stamped their feet. The bride took a swig of lager and handed the can to her groom to finish.

'He looks like Tarzan,' Marc whispered.

The parson stepped forward with an open book in his hands. If they're having second thoughts, Gary mused, there's no escape now.

'Do you, Tony,' the parson began, 'take this woman to be your unlawful wedded wife?'

'I do,' Tony said with a wet grin.

'And do you, Jane, take this man to be your unlawful wedded husband?'

Jane giggled and blushed. 'I do,' she shouted joyously.

'Is there any reason why,' the parson asked the assembled well-wishers, 'these two should not be joined in unholy matrimony?' Gary heard several lewd suggestions doubting Tarzan's manhood, but the parson was undeterred. He raised his hand and announced solemnly: 'I hereby pronounce you man and wife.' A huge cheer rose from the crowd and fistfuls of broken teabags rained down on the happy couple. The bride threw the bouquet over her shoulder, as she and her husband beat a hasty retreat, followed closely by the musicians and the parson.

The bouquet flew far too close to Gary for his comfort and was caught by the outstretched hands of the woman standing next to him. 'Let's go,' he said urgently to Marc, 'before one of us is sucked into marriage with a stranger.'

When they were at a safe distance, Gary stopped to buy straw hats to protect them from the now fierce sun. Puddles were steaming and shrinking and, for once, Gary felt too hot in his wellington boots.

'What was your wedding like, dad?' Marc asked as they continued to wander.

'Nothing like that.'

'But it wasn't a church wedding, was it?'

'No. Your mother and I didn't believe in that sort of thing.'

'Why did you get married at all, then?'

'What a funny question. Because we loved each other, of course.'

'Sam told me that his mum and dad were there.'

'Yeah, that's right. They got married before us, just after we all left college.'

'Why did you wait before getting married?'

'You're asking a lot of questions for someone who hasn't shown any interest in this subject before.'

'Sam says he didn't think mum was ready to marry at the same time as his parents.'

Gary stopped and looked at his son. He was very surprised that Marc was pursuing this line of questioning and even more surprised that Sam had any any view about him and Natalie. He wasn't quite sure how much detail he wanted to go into.

'Did Sam say why your mum wasn't ready?'

'Not really. Only that she wasn't very happy beforehand.'

'And who told Sam that? Was it his father?'

'Or his mum, I don't know.'

Gary was upset now. This was personal information and it shouldn't have been discussed with Sam, or passed on to Marc. Natalie hadn't been happy for months before they married, not since her miscarriage. In fact, before he proposed to her, she'd been pretty depressed as he recalled; but he really didn't want to discuss that with Marc now, or at all. Maybe Frank and Joyce had discussed it and Sam had overheard them; but why would they do so after all these years and why hadn't they been more discreet?

'Well, your mum was a bit low after leaving college,' Gary explained, 'but I think that was all to do with leaving friends behind. She cheered up a lot though when I proposed to her and she was really happy the day we got married.'

'So were Sam's parents your witnesses?'

'Yep, that's right: Frank and Joyce were the obvious choice. In fact, your mum was desperate they should be there, because we'd all been such close friends.'

'Why did it matter who the witnesses were?'

'I suppose it didn't, but ideally you'd want someone there you knew really well and liked. Who would you have as your witnesses?' Gary asked, hoping to divert the conversation. 'Would you prefer a small affair like us, or do you think you'd like a church wedding with a Mexican band and tea leaves for confetti?'

'Neither, thanks. It all sounds far too weird for me. I don't think I'll be getting married at all.'

They took a break to listen for a few minutes to a folk singer who sang in Acadian French, accompanied by harp and banjo. On a nearby stage Marc became excited and enraptured by an unreconstructed punk band, until he realised with horror that the drummer was wearing no clothes. He hadn't noticed at first and it came as a real shock when the drummer left his seat and harangued the docile audience from the front of the stage, in the apparent belief that a naked man throwing abuse would encourage them to dance.

Marc was still talking about the man's body piercings, 'rude bits' and sagging bottom, when they saw Hannah and Lucy walking towards them in animated discussion, with Frank, Claire and Sam not far behind.

As the teenagers exchanged stories, Claire told Gary about the stand-up comedian they had seen in the cabaret tent.

'It was pretty graphic stuff,' Frank added, 'and I was a little worried about poor old Sam for a while. But Claire didn't mind, did you?' He winked and nodded at her, making sure that Gary noticed. Claire looked away and Gary detected a slight colouration of her cheeks. 'It didn't leave much to the imagination,' she said quietly.

'Amazingly, Sam didn't appear that interested,' Frank said. 'I thought all teenage boys were into that sort of thing but, mostly, he just whinged about missing Marc.'

'The girls were quite different,' Claire added, having regained her composure. 'They complained that it was all smutty and disgusting, but they still watched it through their fingers and laughed at all the jokes.'

'A real education for them all,' Frank chuckled.

'I don't think those girls are safe with you, Frank,' Gary said, alarmed at what his daughter must have seen and heard.

'Oh, don't be so prudish – it was comedy. If you can't laugh at sex, I don't know what you can laugh at.'

Gary was still not happy, but he knew it was too late to do anything about it now. 'I give up,' he sighed. Maybe education through comedy was OK; maybe he was being over-protective. After all, it wasn't as if Hannah had seen real sex on stage, not even a simulation. It was probably healthy to laugh at these things, given that the whole sex routine was – so far as he could remember it – ludicrous.

How many times had he and Natalie fallen about laughing, when they'd tried to spice up their sex lives with new positions? And what about all those hysterical sex toys? But as a father of pubescent teenagers, he couldn't just treat it all as a joke. The sexual act might be funny – especially in the hands of a skilful comedian on stage – but the emotions that went with it, and the potential consequences, were all serious. No: at best, Frank was missing the point; at worst, he was shirking his responsibility to the young to gratify his own interest in sex; and Claire wasn't much better.

The boys announced that they were off to explore on their own and the girls soon followed suit. When they had gone the adults made a beeline for a refreshment tent.

Gary sprawled out in an old armchair and was pleased to note that the smears of mud on the crinkled leather had now all dried. Frank placed three mugs of filter coffee on the low table before Gary's feet and sat opposite him, next to Claire on a sofa. Gary didn't intend to raise the subject again, but found himself unable to keep silent.

'Did you know what that comedian was like when you took the girls to see him?'

Frank looked disappointed for a moment and then frowned with irritation. 'No, I didn't,' he replied firmly. 'But please let's not go over all that again.'

'Why didn't you leave when you saw it was unsuitable?' Gary continued, almost involuntarily.

'It wasn't that bad,' Claire said.

'Oh, really? Now you say so.'

'Relax, old man,' Frank said in a friendly drawl. 'You know what these places are like. They get very crowded and there are people sitting around you on all sides. It's just not that easy to get up and go, even if you want to.'

'Rubbish. If it was half as bad as you implied there was nothing to stop you leaving.'

'The girls were laughing like mad, Gary. They would have made a scene if I'd tried to make them go. It would've been plain rude to leave in the middle of a performance.'

'This isn't a posh theatre we're talking about. No one's bought tickets to see the comedian. This is a music and arts festival, in a field, in the rain, where half the audience is wearing wellington boots. The same etiquette just doesn't apply.'

Gary knew his voice was too loud but he was frustrated that he wasn't making any headway. Frank and Claire sat quite still, as if frozen: only the steam rising from the three mugs betrayed any movement. Why did this matter to him so much? Was it that Hannah was growing up and he was losing control? Was it the duty he owed to Natalie to protect and nurture their child in her absence? Or did he just resent seeing Frank and Claire sitting together on the sofa – thigh by thigh – when he felt so all alone?

Claire spoke first: 'Maybe it's my fault. I was OK about Lucy watching the show and I just assumed Hannah would be fine. Sam didn't seem much interested and so it didn't occur to us to leave. I'm sorry.' Gary turned to Frank with a look that said: And what have you got to say?

'I'm sorry too,' Frank said with resignation. 'I really am. I didn't think you'd mind for one minute – I just didn't think.'

Gary tapped his mug with his fingernails. Now he was angry with himself for creating a scene. After all, he thought a little belatedly, there was probably nothing on stage that Hannah hadn't learned about at school – from her friends if not from her teachers. 'I'm sorry, guys,' Gary said, grasping the handle of his mug. 'I'm sorry that I made such a fuss. I think I'm just a bit tired from last night.'

Once again he had surrendered with hardly a fight; Gary was disgusted with himself. Frank and Claire looked relieved and Gary saw their cheeks brush, as if they were congratulating each other for having diffused the situation. Gary banged his mug down on the table, immediately spilling coffee over his hand.

'Ouch,' he exclaimed, shaking it vigorously. Claire asked if he was OK but Gary just grimaced and blew on the scald.

'Oh dear, I hope your hand isn't completely out of action,' Frank said with mock concern. 'You never know what you might need it for.'

Gary squirmed and tried to avoid Claire's eyes. Frank burst out laughing at his own joke and rocked forward in the sofa, nearly propelling Claire onto the ground. He grabbed the edge of the table to steady himself, pulling it over with the three mugs. Now Gary laughed, releasing the tension which faded away as quickly as the hot coffee soaked into the ground.

'Let's get out of here,' Gary said. 'It was lousy coffee, anyway.'

TWENTY

As Gary emerged from the marquee he felt the full blast of the late afternoon sun, still radiating heat as it began its slow descent. He looked up at the blue sky with satisfaction. Yesterday's dark rainclouds had blown off to the west and he could see their white cousins billowing on the skyline, like a row of misshapen giants. He also noticed a few wispy clouds coming in from the east. Thank God, he thought; they must mean that high pressure and better weather are on their way.

'I wonder who's playing,' Claire said as they came across a large stage with a wide silver canopy.

'An American, I guess,' Gary said, looking at the energetic guitarist fronting the band; 'but I don't recognise her or the music she's playing.'

Frank reached for his pocket guide. He ran his fingers vertically then horizontally down the programme until their tips reached a name. 'It's Joan Martell,' he said with surprise. 'She's British, isn't she? I didn't know she was still going strong.'

'Blimey,' Gary said. 'Let's stay and watch her for a bit; she used to be one of Natalie's favourites, you know.'

'Yeah, I remember.'

Gary looked again at the stage, but his eyes were dazzled by sunlight reflected off the canopy. He raised his hand to shield them. 'She sang ballads in those days, but this music's much rockier.'

'That's not rock music, mate, that's the blues.'

'I thought all music was the same to you.'

'The blues speak to the soul, man. I just love the blues.'

'I love the blues too,' Claire said as she exchanged glances with Frank. 'It's so moving.'

'Hello, Glastonbury!' Joan Martell shouted into the microphone. 'Are you having a great time?' The audience returned a tumultuous affirmation. 'This afternoon we're going to play some songs from our new album, but don't worry – we'll mix them up with plenty of familiar tunes.' A cheer rose into the air. 'Some of you may know this one,' she cried, as she strummed her guitar briskly and launched into one of her old hits.

Gary listened closely to her melodious vocals, which quivered with feeling and occasionally soared to intense heights. He was immediately transported back twenty years. Goose-pimples sprang up all over his body and the hairs on his arms stood on end. He began to sing words that he didn't realise he knew. He tapped his feet, not in the present in a field, but in the past on a beach, with a beautiful young woman by his side.

He imagined Natalie's feet twisting in the sand as she danced to the very same song on her radio. He smiled as he recalled her lively bronzed thighs, her short cotton skirt swishing from side to side, her flat stomach flexing as her hips lifted and dropped to the beat. He could see her tantalising breasts bouncing in a plunging bikini top, her waving brown arms and long, slender neck. He followed the shape of her mouth as she mimed the words of the song. Most striking of all, her eyes were filled with tears of delight and emotion, which spilled down over her glowing cheeks, glistening and sparkling as they dropped onto the golden sand.

If only she could be here now, on his arm. What excitement and joy she would have from listening once again to the songs of their youth. They had been so carefree and so in love: safe, secure and happy for the rest of their lives.

Gary's simple swaying had now become a lively dance. He smiled at Claire, who was also dancing and seemed lost in memories of her own. She smiled back and Gary noticed her moist, red eyes. I know how she feels, he thought: it's bitter-sweet remembering a life that has passed and can never be repeated.

Gary hugged Claire, who hugged him back. Frank joined them and soon all three were dancing closely, more subdued and reflective. They listened attentively to the words of the old songs, one after the other, smiling, laughing, crying and singing together.

They left the field at the end of the set, arm in arm, gushing with emotion and reminiscing about the past. They walked in step with Claire in the middle, and Gary and Frank on either side. They agreed that Joan Martell was a blues goddess; that it was the best gig they had ever seen; that they were best friends; and that this wonderful camaraderie would last for ever.

It was after five o'clock in the afternoon when Gary arrived back at his tent, exhausted. He and Frank had parted from Claire by the rainbow peace flag, which marked the corner of the camping field. Claire wanted to return to the crew camping area to have a hot shower and put on some clean clothes for the evening. Gary and Frank had strolled up to the campsite, before Frank too had broken off to go back to his own tent, 'for a nap.'

There was no sign of Hannah or Marc, so Gary pulled one of the sleeping mats out of the tent and sat on it, to enjoy the afternoon sun. Although it was peaceful in the campsite, with little local noise, Gary was aware of the constant hum of music coming from elsewhere on site. It didn't bother him, because it seemed remote and he was still in a state of elation from the rekindled friendship with Frank and Claire; especially with Frank, with whom he had crossed swords several times over the previous couple of days.

Frank's all right, Gary told himself. He's been a really good friend for many years. Remember how supportive he was when Natalie died. He'd been so understanding, so genuinely upset himself at the loss of someone who was dear to them both. Gary clasped his knees tightly with his arms. How could he have allowed such friction to arise between them? Frank's such a loyal and trusted friend and you don't find one of those every day. No, he must blame himself for the recent misunderstandings. He shook his head, as if to remove any residual doubt in his mind, and he looked again at the sky.

Gary frowned instinctively. Something's not quite right, he thought. Fair weather clouds overhead were to be expected, but the clouds to the west had turned gunmetal grey, and there were many more of them. Surely they should have blown away by now?

He turned his head a half-circle. The dark clouds had spread around the curved horizon, as if they had hit a barrier and could go no further. It's like I'm in a giant fish bowl, he thought. I'm surrounded on all sides and can't escape, and nor can the rain clouds. But why am I so uneasy? After all, they're probably fifty miles away. No, it must be something closer.

His eyes were drawn to the flags and pennants fluttering over the campsite. There was no discernable pattern, as they flapped in different directions, changing at will in the undisciplined air currents eddying around the field. Stillness descended, flags drooped and long pennants wrapped themselves around their poles.

Gary saw a neighbour also look up, with a puzzled expression on his face. What's going on? Gary wondered. Why have the clouds stopped moving? He shuddered as the breeze picked up the flags and pennants again, pointing them all to the east. Immediately, he understood that the wind had gone into reverse: the storm clouds were on the march again, back towards the festival.

Gary closed his eyes and turned his face towards what remained of the sunlight. I must grab it while I can, he thought. He crossed his legs and straightened his back; he really ought to do more yoga. As he listened to the sounds of the campsite, he heard voices he recognised, in a state of excitement: Marc and Sam were approaching. Some way behind them, more indistinct, came Hannah and Lucy. A warm glow filled his heart: he'd enjoyed the time on his own, but now he wanted company. The boys fell silent as they cleared the guy rope at the corner of the tent. They stopped a few feet before him. Gary smiled and opened his eyes.

It took a few moments for Gary to adjust to the light and to focus on Marc and Sam. At first, all he could see were two broad grins looking down on him but, as he began to make out their features, the grins took on a mix of defiance, guilt and uncertainty. The boys stood completely still as if waiting for a reaction.

Gary glanced briefly at their clothes but he could see nothing out of place. His attention moved quickly to Sam's face, seeking a clue. His fixed, inane grin was giving nothing away. Then he turned to look at Marc's face; and he was shocked by what he saw.

'What the hell have you done?' Gary cried as he jumped to his feet. 'Where's all your hair gone? You've been shorn to within an inch of your life.'

Gary ran his hand over the patterned bristles above Marc's ear and then along the wedge of thicker hair – dyed blue – which tumbled from the crown of his head to the nape of his neck.

'Do you like it?' Marc grinned.

'It's *terrible*!'

'I told you he wouldn't like it.'

'What will they say at school?'

'Oh, I didn't think of that, but it'll be OK.'

'No it won't,' Gary said, his voice rising in equal measure to his sense of frustration and helplessness. 'For God's sake, Marc, it looks like there's a ferret on your head!'

'Told you,' Sam muttered, as Hannah and Lucy arrived at the tent.

'Cool new haircut, don't you think dad?' Hannah asked, with a glint in her eye.

'No, I bloody don't. And I don't see what's so funny,' Gary said angrily. The girls started giggling. They tried to suppress their mirth, but it was as hopeless as trying to stop bubbles gushing from a bottle of champagne. They burst into fits of uncontrollable laughter.

'It's just a bit of fun,' Marc said, having regained confidence by the arrival of his sister.

'But your hair was so beautiful – all those curly locks…'

'It was baby hair!'

'You had no right to do that,' Gary said, the anger in his voice catching the teenagers by surprise. They stopped laughing and their grins contracted.

What sanction could he impose? He could threaten to withdraw Marc's pocket money, but that would be a delayed response, which would feel petty when the time came to enforce it. 'You had no right,' he repeated.

Gary could sense his own weakness and he felt sure that Marc and the others were aware of it too. They remained silent, waiting for sentence to be passed. Gary opened his mouth, not yet sure what he was going to say. Marc was looking down at the ground, but Gary could feel Hannah's eyes fixed on his. It was as if she were trying to read his mind, as if she were calculating his reaction to the situation which presented itself.

'Marc…' Gary said with as much authority as he could muster, but he hesitated too long. Marc raised his eyes and looked at his father. 'It's not terrible,' he said clearly. 'It's my hair and I like it.' His eyes blazed with pride and defiance.

Gary looked at Sam, gripping the top of Marc's arm in an act of fraternal support. The haircut wasn't the whole picture, Gary knew that. It wasn't even the symptom of a problem. No, it was a statement of intent, a symbol of something as yet unspoken; something had changed in their relationship, but Gary didn't understand what it was. 'But Marc…' he pleaded.

'Dad, get over it,' Marc said. 'You know it'll grow back.'

Gary gave up: the damage was done and he knew that a

showdown was futile. He was surprised to see that he had clenched his fist and he quickly released the tension in his hand. 'You'll regret it,' he said with dejection in his voice. 'I really hope you do. Maybe that'll be a sufficient punishment.'

It would also be a valuable learning experience, he thought. Marc had stepped over the line but, after all, there was no going back now. Why bother to try and re-establish the boundaries? Marc was getting to the age where he had to start to make decisions for himself and to make his own mistakes.

'Sorry dad,' Marc said unexpectedly. 'I didn't know that you'd be so upset. I won't do it again, I promise.'

Gary wasn't sure whether he was being sincere or not, but he was grateful to hear the words. He saw a smirk on Hannah's face and puzzled over the calculating look in her eyes. He sat back down, landing heavily on the mat.

'So,' he asked with little enthusiasm, to anyone who might still listen to him, 'what are we going to do this evening?'

TWENTY-ONE

Gary hardly registered Frank's arrival at the tent, followed by Claire moments later. He didn't hear their comments about Marc's haircut, but he could tell by his reaction that they weren't exactly complimentary. Sam said something to his father, which earned him a sharp rebuke. Lucy made a sarcastic comment to Hannah, which Claire heard and which made both Marc and Sam snigger. Voices and tensions began to rise, drawing Gary from his self-imposed isolation, so that he found himself in the midst of an angry, squabbling rabble.

He cleared his throat loudly, but no one paid any attention. He stepped forward causing a momentary lull, as the others acknowledged his attempt to intervene, but then the recriminations and threats continued. He raised his hand and stood in silence, as if he were in school waiting for a chance to speak. Gradually, an awkward silence fell.

Gary suggested that they all go and eat; and the effect was immediate, as if a switch had been thrown: anger and annoyance gave way to feelings of hunger and a mutual desire to feed the body. When it was clear everyone wanted to eat different kinds of food, they agreed to split up and meet again in forty minutes.

Frank grabbed a couple of ready-made rolls and pulled Gary into a nearby beer tent. It took twenty minutes of small talk and a second pint of cider before Gary raised the subject of Natalie.

'You know, I still expect to see her every time I open the front door,' he said. 'I still hear her voice when I go into the living room. I even make cups of tea for her from time to time. The kids are always complaining and pouring them away.'

'We don't need to talk about Natalie now,' Frank said.

'Why not? She's always on my mind.'

'Alright, but what can I say?' Frank sighed wearily. 'It's just taking it's time to work through. What does your doctor say?'

'That I should be better by now. What would you expect? She tells me that bereavement usually takes one or two years, and that three years is too long. But, Frank, I can't see any sign that I'm getting over her.' He sipped his drink as he contemplated his next sentence. 'And why should I? I ask myself. It would be a betrayal.'

'You should see a therapist.'

'I am seeing one.'

'And it's not helping?'

'Who knows? He thinks I can't dwell on Natalie's death for ever, just like everyone else. On the one hand he's right, it's just a matter of time but – what no one seems to realise – it's also a matter of *timing*, and it's my right to choose the timing. Don't you agree?'

'Well, yes I would, if it wasn't interfering with normal life.'

'It's only interfering with my life, so it's no one's business but mine.'

'What about the kids?'

'They seem to be coping fine.'

'Yeah, kids are more resilient than you think.'

'The worst is that it was such a senseless death.'

'Anyone can trip and fall down the stairs,' Frank said sympathetically. 'But you know, we should be getting back to the others.'

'I know, I know. But the *way* it happened, that's what gets me.'

'She just tripped, Gary, that's all. It was no one's fault.'

'But it was, Frank, and that's the hardest part.'

Frank creased his forehead. 'What do you mean?'

'Oh God, I miss her so much,' Gary said, swigging another mouthful of cider. 'I know it's the drink talking, but she was so loving, so loyal, so devoted to me and the kids. It just came out of the blue and they were devastated. It was so completely out of their experience. None of us had a chance to say goodbye. We all wondered if we could have done anything to save her, or to prevent it happening.' Tears began to well up in his eyes. 'Frank, I loved her so much. She meant everything to me.'

'I know, mate, I know,' Frank said softly, extending his hand, 'but you just can't go on like this for ever. You need to think about yourself a bit more. Please, Gary, look on the bright side. We're at Glastonbury and you should be enjoying yourself without dwelling on the past.'

Gary nodded, but withdrew his hand.

'Natalie meant a lot to everyone,' Frank added. 'We all miss her.'

'Especially the kids,' Gary said, wiping his eyes with the back of his hand. 'Especially the kids – and that's the problem.'

'What's the problem? It was just an accident, Gary. Come on, pull yourself together. We've been over this so many times.'

'No, Frank, it wasn't just an accident,' Gary said, looking

pointedly at his friend. 'Natalie… she… she slipped on one of Hannah's school books at the top of the stairs.'

Frank lifted his eyebrows in surprise. 'Just an accident, mate,' he repeated. 'The coroner said so.'

'*Not* just an accident,' Gary said bitterly. 'Hannah put the book there… *she* did it… I'd told her a thousand times not to leave things at the top of the stairs – precisely because people might slip on them.' Gary's eyes drilled into Frank's.

'We shouldn't have had that second pint,' Frank said. 'I didn't realise how tired you were. Let's stop and go back to meet the others.'

'Hannah was to blame; don't you see?' Gary continued. 'She knew not to put books there. She was too wilful, or too lazy or disobedient, to take notice. It was *her* fault that Natalie died.'

Frank sat impassively. He picked up his pint and downed the last inch of cider. He placed the empty cup down on the table. Gary didn't move and his eyes glazed over, as if he was looking straight through his friend.

'Have you said anything to her?' Frank said quietly. 'Does she know anything?'

'Of course not,' Gary said, as his shoulders slumped. 'How could I say anything to her? I just repeat the mantra 'it was an accident, it was no one's fault' and I'm sure she has no idea. I don't know how she'd cope, if she knew. I threw the book away when I found it.' He paused and ran a fingernail along a crack in the table. 'As you know, the official version is that she just tripped and fell. That's the truth as far as the kids are concerned.'

Gary finished his drink and slotted his paper cup inside Frank's. 'I haven't told anyone else, Frank, not even my therapist.' His voice was barely a whisper. 'I had to keep it a secret, for Hannah's sake. I'm sorry to burden you with it too, but inside I'm so angry – so angry *with her* – and I'm so empty and sad without Natalie.' His voice petered out. Frank reached out again and Gary gripped his hand tightly. 'I'm sorry, Frank, if I've over-reacted about all this,' he continued, 'but all this thinking about Natalie has been more emotional than I expected.'

'I know how you feel, mate,' Frank replied sympathetically. 'It's going to be OK, you know.'

'Frank, you won't tell anyone, will you, and definitely not Hannah?'

'No, that would be quite wrong,' Frank said. 'You did the right thing to get rid of the book, Gary. It's best that Hannah never knows. Natalie would have approved of that.'

'Yes, she would,' Gary whispered, as tears rolled down his cheeks.

Hannah was furious that they had arrived late at the main stage. She shouted at the adults to hurry up and, despite Gary's protests, led them all much closer to the front than they wanted to be. She said it would make up for missing the beginning of the band.

'I blame *you* for the delay,' Hannah said angrily to her father. 'You just couldn't tear yourself away from the booze, could you?'

'It wasn't me, it was the crowds,' Gary said lamely. 'Normally, we'd have had enough time.'

'But you took for ever and we needed to leave sooner. Why don't you ever listen to me?'

Gary looked to Frank for support, but he was deep in

conversation with Claire. 'Can I get anything right with you?' he asked, but Hannah was already too far ahead to hear.

Shortly before the end of the set, Frank went to fetch some more drinks in the hope of avoiding the inevitable crush that would soon follow. As the band left the stage, the setting sun dropped below the lower edge of the thick grey clouds. A huge glowing disc filled the sky, framed between the clouds and the western horizon; and bright rays of orange light filled the valley.

'Marc,' Gary shouted. 'It's time for sun-worship: now or never!' Marc glanced at Sam and rolled his eyes with exaggerated embarrassment.

As it slowly sank, the sun grew wider and redder. At last, only an extended sliver of bronze light topped the distant hill and lingered tantalisingly, before vanishing with an unexpected flash of bright turquoise. The light dropped noticeably and with the gathering dusk the temperature began to fall. Gary zipped up his jacket against the rising breeze. He moved his weight from foot to foot in an effort to keep warm.

After a while another band took to the stage, but Gary was more interested in looking at his surroundings. A shaft of white light now beamed like a beacon from the apex of the pyramid, cutting into the dense clouds above. The remaining patches of clear sky were deep purple but the stars still struggled to be seen. The valley had been transformed into a compact blazing city, by hundreds of thousands of twinkling lights. If it weren't for them, Gary thought, we'd be in total darkness now.

The last band of the night was due to come on stage at about eleven o'clock. While waiting, Gary felt a spray of fine rain as it traversed the field. People everywhere pulled hoods over their heads and opened umbrellas. They huddled together for warmth and shared blankets and plastic sheets.

Gary longed for the clouds to pass and leave them alone, but one glance skywards told him that they were here to stay. There was a collective grumble from the mass of disappointed music fans when a second wave of rain doused the field. As a persistent drizzle became established, the band came on stage. The cheers of the crowd were overwhelmed by the rumble of distant thunder.

Within minutes raindrops began to splatter on hats, coats and trousers, trying to find any breach in the spectators' defences. There was more thunder, closer still. A flash of lightning forked in the distance. Anyone who missed it was left in no doubt of its existence by the vicious crackle which followed a second later. Steady rain now began to fall, in unrelenting sheets. Gary noticed people nearby packing bags and leaving for the shelter of their tents.

Hannah wailed with disappointment. 'What are we going to do? I wanted to see this band so badly, but I'm getting too cold and wet.' Lucy opened an umbrella and held it over their heads. 'When's it going to stop?' she asked.

'I don't know,' Frank replied, 'but I don't think this band's worth getting soaked to the skin for.'

'But they're one of the reasons we've come here,' Lucy said.

'Let's find some temporary shelter,' Gary suggested. 'We've only got one umbrella and the coats are only shower proof, not rain proof.'

'But then we'll miss the band,' Hannah said.

'If the rain doesn't stop, we can go back to the campsite. You'll still be able to hear the band from there.'

'Why didn't you tell us that before?' Hannah asked; 'Instead of dragging us all out here to get wet.'

It had rarely been the case that Gary welcomed more rain, but a sudden heavy downpour brought the argument swiftly to an end. They joined the sea of disappointed faces streaming away from the field, leaving behind only diehard fans still willing to brave the elements. Near the campsite they stepped into a large marquee, which was heaving with steaming bodies.

Lucy wiped the rain from Hannah's face and Sam hugged Marc for warmth. 'Oh, the joys of music festivals,' Frank muttered.

'Hot chocolate, all round,' Claire said as cheerfully as she could. 'I'll get them and it's my treat.' Frank offered to join her and help carry.

Gary turned to the teenagers. Marc and Sam had disengaged but still looked cold and miserable.

'We want to go back to the tent,' Marc said.

'So do we,' Hannah added. 'It's terrible out there.'

'The rain will pass,' Gary replied. 'It's too early to go to sleep, isn't it?'

'This rain is never going to stop,' Sam said, pointing to the water cascading over the edge of the door flap. 'And did you hear that thunder?'

The general mood improved after the communal rite of drinking hot chocolate had been completed, but the constant battery of rain on the canvas roof persuaded them all that their night had ended. Only Gary was restless to do more.

'Don't go back to the tents,' he pleaded. 'This weather won't last and, even if it does, there's plenty going on out there, under cover. You'll miss out if you call it a day now.'

'Oh, Gary,' Claire said, touching his arm. 'You're so enthusiastic and full of energy. I don't know how you keep going.'

'The night's still young,' Gary protested.

'*Night* is the operative word,' Marc said loudly.

'And we're tired,' Lucy added.

'What? You're teenagers, you're the future. It's us oldies that are supposed to be tired – not you lot!'

Frank looked at Claire. She raised her eyebrows and the corners of her mouth turned up slightly in the beginning of a smile. She brushed the back of his hand and a frisson of electrical excitement shot up each of their arms.

'You know, Gary,' Frank began, with a dreamy smile, 'you're right to say that the night's still young and there's lots to do out there, but it's been a long day and…' he glanced at Claire, '… and there comes a time when a man just needs to lay his hat.' He grinned broadly and slapped Gary on the shoulder. 'Go and enjoy yourself, mate. I've had all the vertical exercise I need for today.'

Gary frowned with disappointment and turned to the teenagers. 'We're definitely going back to the tents, dad,' Hannah said solemnly. 'Lucy's going to stay overnight with me and we're going to listen to the band in our sleeping bags. We'll talk to dawn if we want to, but not in the rain.'

Gary looked at Marc, who shook his head. 'Sam's invited me to stay in his small tent tonight. I can go, can't I?'

'What does Frank say?'

'Frank says that's fine,' Frank interjected. 'Sam needs someone to keep him company tonight. I've already moved the luggage into the big tent.'

Gary felt dejected. For a moment he wondered if he should throw in the towel and head back to the tent too. As if blowing itself out with a series of thunderclaps, the storm subsided and the rain began to ease. Gary looked expectantly for the others to change their minds, but they all took it as a chance to dash back to the tents before the rain started up again. Hannah and Lucy sprinted in one direction, Marc and Sam in another.

'Keep dry, old man,' Frank said, as he took Claire's arm in his. 'I'm just going to walk Claire back to her tent. Have fun and don't stay out too late.' Gary watched them walk off into the murky night. 'And don't do anything I wouldn't do,' Frank called back as an afterthought with a big knowing wink.

As he watched them disappear, Gary saw Claire slide her arm around Frank's backside. He shuddered as he saw her playfully insert her thumb inside the waistband of his trousers. He crushed the empty cup he was holding and slung it in disgust at the dustbin in the corner. 'You make me sick,' he seethed out loud. 'The whole bloody lot of you!'

Gary was determined to go and enjoy himself and yet he hesitated. It wouldn't be so easy on his own, especially in a festival full of hedonistic fun-seekers. He asked himself repeatedly: what are you trying to prove, and to whom? He thought of Natalie. Strange, he hadn't thought of her all night. Surely he wasn't trying to impress her, to show her that he was still capable of doing things independently? He was quite sure that he didn't need to prove anything in that department.

The rain had now all but stopped. The air was cool and the ground was soft and mushy underfoot. It'll be worse lower down the hill, he thought. Wasn't that another reason just to give up and go to sleep? He stepped into a nearby urinal and, as he spat into the trough, a sticker pasted on the metal frame caught his eye. 'It's better to die on your feet,' he read, 'than to live on your knees.'

What sense should he make of that? Did it mean that he should stand up for himself, be more selfish and do what *he* wanted to do? He groaned when he thought of Claire and his ineffectual fumbling last night. Had he really given up so easily? Was that living on his knees? Or was it the fact that he was still in thrall to Natalie; still a slave to his past?

No, he decided, I've got nothing to prove to Natalie or to Claire – or to Frank and the teenagers, for that matter. I only have something to prove to myself. It's simple, really: I'm not bound to the past for ever, but I'm a free man, with a will of my own and a future.

TWENTY-TWO

The slackening rain persuaded many people to return to the main stage. Booming vibrations from the last act of the night shook droplets off guy ropes and drooping leaves. Gary watched the flow of determined humanity surge back along the muddy tracks with a sense of urgency, like desperate exiles seeking salvation in a promised land.

He resisted the temptation to join them and set off in the opposite direction. It wasn't as easy as he thought: the pressure of bodies was so great that he was jostled to the edge of the track, and then shouldered into the slushy mud at the side. People looked at him with surprise and puzzlement, as if his decision not to go back and see the band was irrational folly.

This is hard going, he thought, as he stumbled into a pothole and liquid mud splashed the rim of his boots. He veered off and headed down another path, which took him into the bright, burning heart of the festival.

Gary wandered for several minutes like a moth flitting in the dark, disorientated by too many lights. He was glad to be free from the demands of the teenagers and from the irritation of watching Frank's shameless flirting with Claire. He was surprised that neither Hannah nor Lucy had commented on such brazen conduct. Hannah, in particular, would not usually let such inappropriate adult behaviour go by, without a withering look or disapproving comment.

As he walked further from the main stage, the music began to wane until all that he could hear was the distant thud of drums. With the other instruments and the singer stripped away, the remaining beat was a hollow, primal sound. No doubt other people found it magnetic, Gary thought, but he needed to break away and to escape.

He dived into a tent and ordered a mug of tea at the counter. In place of drumming, his ears were soothed by the gentle plucking of a mandolin. Clutching his steaming drink, Gary went to find somewhere to sit. This is awkward, he thought. I don't like being on my own and I've got no one to talk to. Everyone's busy with their own friends and they won't welcome my intrusion.

He cut across to the far side of the tent, passing by three older women in camping seats. They were deep in conversation and didn't glance up at him. A few steps further along, Gary found an empty seat and it wasn't immediately clear if it was free. Gary went to sit on it, when one of the women turned towards him, as if she had a sixth sense.

'Sorry, that's taken,' she said in a friendly voice. 'It's Clive's chair and he's just gone to the toilet. He'll be back in a minute.' She smiled and returned to her conversation. Gary wasn't entirely surprised, but he was a little disappointed.

'No worries,' he mumbled. 'I'll sit down over here.' He waved at a nearby patch of grass, which he eyed unenthusiastically. It looked damp and sloped at an uncomfortable-looking angle. He retrieved a plastic sheet from his backpack, folded it in two and laid it on the ground. Taking care to land on target, he sat on the sheet, with his back resting on a rigid support pole. He tucked up his knees and placed the pack between his legs.

Gary sat in silence. He held his mug tightly, as if it had become his companion, and stared into the swirling, milky brown liquid. He wished Natalie had been there with him, but wondered if she'd have been happy sitting on a sheet of plastic, being steadily drained of warmth and looking forward to little more than a night of rain and mud.

He watched a young woman with a guitar step up onto the small stage in the corner of the tent. She sat on a stool and checked the tuning of her strings. It had started raining again and drops were falling through a tear in the roof, creating a watery veil between the performer and her audience. She moved the microphone stand out of the way and a helper placed a plastic bowl at her feet to catch the water.

Unperturbed, she introduced herself quietly and then filled the tent with mournful songs of unrequited love, betrayal and death. Gary's foot tapped slowly in time with the music. It helped him blend in and take part in the communal experience; but it also masked his now intense loneliness.

Natalie would have said to give up and go back to the tent. Gary certainly felt the allure of a warm and dry sleeping bag; but a more fundamental force prevented him moving from his chosen place on Earth: it was the vitality of live, unmediated music. The young woman's musical talent quite simply astounded him. He was completely in awe of her gifted fingers, her harmonious vocal chords and her wonderful ability to narrate a tale through song. I'm not going anywhere, he heard himself say back to Natalie. I may be alone, but I want to be here.

A man in baggy brown trousers and a creased jacket sat heavily on the camping seat next to Gary's plastic domain.

'Hi there,' the man said cheerfully.

Gary turned to examine his new neighbour. 'Hi,' he replied.

The man wore a peaked cap, which made him look like a steam train driver in an old Wild West film. Silver-grey hairs sprouted from underneath the hat and flowed exuberantly over his ears, neck and shoulders. His face was creviced with age. The man must have read the look of surprise on Gary's face and chuckled.

'Good, isn't she?' he said, nodding towards the singer.

'Yeah, she's got a beautiful voice.'

'I saw her last year,' the old man continued, 'on her debut performance. She's improved quite a lot since then.'

'Do you come here often, then?' Gary asked with bemusement. He knew the festival attracted people of all ages, but he hadn't expected to meet someone quite so old, quite so late at night.

'Oh yes,' his new companion chuckled again. 'I've been coming here for years.'

'With those ladies?' Gary asked, pointing to the three women still talking in a huddle.

'No, no – they're just old friends I meet up with every year. I come on my own to soak up the atmosphere, to meet people and to drink cider.' He laughed and patted Gary on the shoulders. 'What about you, are you alone, me old hearty?' he asked.

Gary paused momentarily; there was something familiar about the man that he couldn't put his finger on. He then explained about the teenagers and his friends having all gone back to their tents. The old man nodded, as if he understood Gary's situation perfectly. He laughed again, baring his yellowed teeth.

'I'm Clive, but they sometimes call me the Captain' he said, extending a warm and callused hand for Gary to shake. 'It's difficult sometimes, being out on your own,' he added sympathetically.

Gary reached over to shake his hand.

'I'm Gary. And yes, I admit, it's nice to have someone to talk to.'

Gary was genuinely relieved that he no longer had to pretend to be bonding with his mug of tea. He gulped down the last mouthful, now tepid and swirling with stray tea leaves. He choked briefly and his body fought back against the small black flecks of tea, which had attached themselves to the back of his throat like an unwelcome swarm of insects. An intense burst of dry tannin added to the distaste.

'Where are you camping?' the Captain asked.

Gary cleared his throat of obstacles. 'We're in the family field, by the acoustic tent.'

'Quiet in there,' the Captain said, nodding his head. 'And the toilets aren't bad, either.'

'Try telling that to my daughter. You'd think I'd scarred her for life, the fuss she made about the plastic loos.'

'Oh dear,' the Captain replied. 'You shouldn't use those things. The metal khazis are much better. They're open to the air, so there's no smell and you hardly ever have to queue.' He smiled broadly. 'On the other hand, it doesn't pay to look down into the pit below – that could put her off just as much, I suppose.' He slapped his knees with mirth. 'Aye, aye!'

'You seem to be an expert on the toilet situation,' Gary grinned.

'It's worth knowing about these things. But for an old-timer like me, the toilets here are nothing compared to what we had to put up with in the army.'

Gary raised his eyebrows. 'When was that?'

'A long, long time ago,' the Captain laughed. He looked at Gary as if reading his mind. 'I'm eighty-three years young,' he added with a wink. 'Would you believe it?'

'I'm amazed,' Gary said. 'So why do you come to Glastonbury, with all the people and the noise?'

'Well it's not for the cocoa and slippers, I can tell you that.'

Gary had an even stronger sense that he'd met the Captain before, but still couldn't place him.

'Did you have any trouble getting tickets?' he asked.

'Oh, I don't bother with tickets anymore,' the Captain replied, with obvious delight at the look of amazement on Gary's face. 'It became far too difficult to get my hands on them – I haven't got a computer and I could never get through on the phone.'

'So,' Gary pressed him, 'how come you're here?'

'I got a job as a steward. If you can't beat them, join them,' he laughed loudly. 'I work about six hours a day, sometimes in the morning, sometimes in the evening. The rest of the time is my own, to wander about, meet friends and listen to music. You don't get paid, mind, but you do get in for free, and there's great camping and cheap food.'

'And what sort of things do you do as a steward?'

'Everything: ticket control, the car parks, bands, comedy shows, the cinema tent, the kids' field. You name it, I'm there. I was stewarding this tent about an hour ago, but then my friends came' – he signalled to the three women at his side – 'and I've stayed on to see the next act. Great isn't she?'

They talked about the bands that Clive had seen, the

weather, troublesome teenagers, Natalie, the variety of food you could buy, watching sunrise from the standing stones, Gary's cold backside, the relationship between damp air and stiff joints, the army, global warming, Zen Buddhism and more. Gary fuelled the conversation with hot tea and extended his friendship to Clive's three female acquaintances, all pensioners working to earn their right to be at the festival.

The nearest was called Winifred; a thin woman with tousled grey hair. She was very lively and always cracking jokes to make the others laugh.

'Do you want some hash?' Winifred asked Gary sweetly.

The question was so unexpected that Gary didn't understand her at first. He thought she was offering him some food, but as he went to question her, the penny dropped.

'It's been a long time,' he said with an embarrassed laugh. 'I almost didn't know what you were talking about.'

Winifred didn't say anything but waited patiently for his answer.

'Go on, Gary,' the Captain urged with a wide grin. 'It's good stuff, you know.'

Gary hesitated. It really had been many years since he had smoked cannabis. He and Natalie had decided to give it up for an extended Lent, which had then lasted for most of Hannah's and all of Marc's childhood. They hadn't wanted to set a bad example, but now Gary was tempted to try it once again, to savour the sweet taste and to fill his feet with air.

'I'd love to,' Gary replied, 'but I haven't got any gear – I couldn't do anything with it.'

'That's no problem, I'll roll you a joint if you like.'

'Well, OK then. That'd be great; but how much?'

Winifred waved his question away. She pulled at the tartan

blanket covering her knees to make it flat and laid some thin cigarette papers on top. She then lifted them to her lips with her mildly arthritic fingers, licked the edges carefully and gently pressed the sheets together. Gary watched with fascination as she took some tobacco from a plastic pouch and crumbled it along the length of the paper, before rubbing and crushing a tiny block of compressed hashish over the top. With a satisfied flourish she rolled the paper together to make a long joint, thin at one end and spreading out like a trumpet at the other.

'Here you are,' she smiled, handing over her artwork to Gary. 'It's on me. Keep it for later.'

Eventually, Gary's bladder was full and he decided the time had come to take his leave. He stood up and stretched his limbs, before folding his plastic sheet and packing it away.

'Well,' he said to the Captain, shaking his hand, 'you've really made me feel welcome and lifted my spirits – thanks. I feel fit for anything now.'

'It's been a pleasure meeting you, Gary,' he replied, standing up and patting him on the back.

'Any hot tips where I should go next?' Gary asked.

Clive looked at his watch.

'Oh, it's late,' he said. Then, with a sparkle in his eye and a playful grin he lent over close to Gary's ear.

'There's only one place to go at this time, me old hearty,' he whispered loudly, 'and that's to a rave in the dance field!'

TWENTY-THREE

Gary tracked towards the dance field, steering past laughing and singing crowds. The heavy rain had stopped and the air was fresh. Underfoot, he waded through sloppy mud, without lifting his boots clear.

He played with Winifred's gift in his pocket. He liked the feel of the crisp, dry paper between his fingers. The joint represented danger, adventure and nostalgia, all rolled into one compact object. For a moment, he thought about throwing it away. He didn't smoke any more, after all, and somehow even accepting it had constituted a betrayal of his pact with Natalie. But, as he tramped along in the liquefied mud and began to regress into a sense of isolation, he decided that he could afford this little luxury.

He put the joint in his mouth and immediately picked up Winifred's scent mingling with the coarse tobacco and sweet cannabis. Need he light it at all? he asked himself. He already knew the answer and approached a stranger for a match. The man agreed readily, in return for a quick puff.

When the joint was back between his nervous lips, Gary sucked on it gently, causing the bell end to blaze in a fury of red and yellow embers. As he inhaled the smoke, the first taste was of strong tobacco, which seared the back of his throat. It was considerably stronger than he remembered from the past. He filled his lungs and held his breath, feeling an unpleasant pressure inside his chest. He suppressed an urge to cough and then slowly let out a steady stream of smoke with undisguised relief. What a disgusting habit, he reflected, as he wheezed and beat his chest with the flat of his hand. No wonder he'd given it up.

He felt no elation yet from the cannabis, just an overwhelming rush of nicotine up his spine. It surged like a bullet train curving on its tracks and shooting into the back of his brain. That's the real drug, Gary thought, as the nicotine spread into every part of his body, making the veins tingle and the heart palpitate. He dragged again on the joint, and a third time, until he could smell the sweetness of cannabis in his nostrils.

The effect of the second, illicit drug was much softer than the nicotine. At first he noticed lightness in his limbs, then a strange numbness, which started in his toes and worked its way up his body, as if he were a vessel being filled with an anaesthetising fluid. He lost feeling in his fingers and a soothing sensation began to roll gently up his spinal column.

The sensation was unassuming and benign at first but soon it became more intense and more thrilling. Gary pulled again on the joint. He experienced blissful agony as he struggled to contain the mounting feeling of pleasure, but this time it passed the point of no return. Despite his efforts, its ascent was unstoppable. This was no speeding train crashing into his brain, Gary thought, this was a firework rocket launching him into heavenly oblivion in a shower of sparks.

Gary continued along the track, which was illuminated by a series of lamps on posts. As the peaks of the marquees in the dance field loomed ahead, Gary found himself following in the wake of a pair of flower-patterned boots. Whenever they caught the light, the yellow, pink and blue petals came to life and seem to dance before his eyes. It made him happy to see them and he smiled.

He reached the entrance to the field and stopped, uncertain where to go next. He waited for inspiration, looking expectantly at a number of other people also standing close by. One of them was a woman in her late twenties; Gary thought that she looked familiar, but he couldn't be sure in the dark. He waited for a gap in the procession of people walking past before he crossed the track and approached her.

'Excuse me,' he said. 'Don't I know you?'

The young woman looked at him and shook her head without speaking. Gary was disappointed; he could have done with some company right then. As he turned to go, the woman reached out and touched his shoulder.

'Maybe,' she said.

Gary was confused and excited: did he know her? He scanned her face, taking in her large eyes, slender nose and dark, flowing hair. His gaze wandered down her swan-like neck and over her beautiful, curving breasts, snug beneath a tightly-fitting rainproof jacket. He gasped and was transfixed.

Their eyes met again. 'I thought so,' Gary said, 'but I can't remember where we met before.'

'You gave me a lift in your car when I ran out of gas,' she said, smiling. She placed her hands on her hips. Gary followed them and gazed longingly at the tiny triangle of light that filtered through her jeans, where her thighs met her pelvis.

'Kareena,' he breathed.

'Wow – you've got a great memory!'

Gary pinched himself, trying to regain some control of his mind. 'It's such an unusual name,' he said.

'But where are your kids?' she asked.

'I don't know. In bed I think, or out somewhere.' He shook his head; he'd forgotten that he even had children.

'Well, I've lost my friends hours ago and no one's picking up my calls.'

'Is your boyfriend with them?' Gary asked, guessing that she wouldn't be alone at the festival.

'What boyfriend?' she said with resignation. 'That's part of the problem too.' She groaned with mixed frustration and anger. 'Anyway, where are you going?'

Gary pointed towards the dance field. 'What about you?'

'Well, I'm just wandering around in the mud and feeling sorry for myself. I ought to go back to my tent, but it feels so wrong.'

A wild idea crossed Gary's mind. 'If it's any help…' he said, confidently at first but then with hesitation in his voice, '…you can come with me if you like.' His voice had reduced to a hoarse whisper, not because he had effectively asked Kareena for a date – although he had – but because as he spoke, the fingers of his right hand had begun involuntarily to ease off the wedding ring on his left. Gary stood there bewildered and breathless, toying with the ring in his hand, wondering what he was doing and what it all meant. He slipped the ring into his trouser pocket. 'We could keep each other company,' he added unnecessarily.

Kareena wavered and seemed uncertain. Gary watched her look him up and down slowly and deliberately. She had an expression of curiosity on her face, as if she was weighing up the options. Gary ached for her to say yes. At first, she appeared stern; then her features softened and she gave Gary a knowing smile.

'Why not,' she said firmly. 'That'd be cool; but don't you want to do your own thing tonight?'

'This *is* my own thing.'

'Well, if you're sure you don't mind, I'd rather be with you, than wander round on my own.' She turned in the direction of the dance field and Gary stepped by her side, his heart racing. 'You will say,' Kareena added, 'if you decide you want to go off on your own.'

Gary was touched by her consideration, but alarmed that she clearly didn't share the exhilaration that was coursing through his veins and filling him to almost bursting. He steadied himself as they walked side-by-side, trying to exert equal control on his emotions and the spaced-out feeling caused by the cannabis. Come on, pull yourself together, he told himself. And get real – you're far too old for her.

As an aid to control Gary stopped swinging his arms as he walked but held the hems of his coat with his fists. He then relaxed and started to spread out his fingers on either side. He breathed steadily and deeply. Platonic forces in his mind began a counter-assault on the feelings of passion that had been unleashed by meeting Kareena. He began to calm down. After all, he told himself, this was merely a temporary expediency, an ad hoc friendship to pass away an hour or two during the night. He sighed with disappointment, as the reality of his situation became clear.

As they approached one of the marquees in the dance field, a group of people pushed past them, laughing and shouting. Gary felt surprise as Kareena's hand grabbed his. They looked at each other.

'Sorry,' she apologised. 'I hope you don't mind. If we get separated, we'll never find each other again in this place.'

Her innocent explanation was insufficient to hold back the combat troops of passion, which no longer retreated in his mind, but now set upon and overwhelmed all opposition.

The marquee was a massive, conical structure of wood and steel poles, taut red canvas and thick rope. It towered above the trees that lined the field. Some of the side panels had been stripped away, leaving wooden poles to support the rim of the canvas roof, so that the tent had the appearance of standing on stilts.

As they approached, the tent lost its shape. It became like a huge spaceship looming above them, an impression heightened by throbbing music from within and by lights, which flashed and changed colour with bewildering rapidity. The light show intensified and subsided in intricate patterns, responding directly to the music.

Gary brought two cans of lager from a man at the edge of the tent, who pulled them out of what seemed to Gary to be a magic dustbin, filled with an inexhaustible supply of beer and ice. Kareena tried to decline, saying she'd had enough to drink already, but Gary pressed the can on her. Clutching hands and drinks, Gary and Kareena entered the tent, in awe at what they saw around them.

Above their heads the tent was festooned with giant curved shapes, brightly lit in psychedelic colours. The shapes spun around slowly and gracefully in the gentle flow of air which swirled through the open sides. There were cone-shaped sea-shells, enormous spiral galaxies and cigar-shaped torpedoes, revolving around each other in what appeared to be perpetual slow motion.

Gary stared at the iridescent colours. The shapes seemed

so low and close, that he reached up to see whether he might touch them, and giggled quietly to himself when he couldn't. Kareena pulled Gary's hand and led him deeper into the tent, towards the stage. Waves of electronic noise grew louder and washed over the excited audience waiting for the final live act.

Gary watched men dressed in black swarming like ants on the stage, assembling two drum kits, fitting microphones to stands, tuning guitars, taping down electrical cables and testing the volume of the speakers. Behind them, bright images danced to the music: giant yellow discs with inanely smiling faces, interchanging with flashing symbols of arrows, birds and aeroplanes, then second-long strips of film: faces, speeding steam trains, divers doing somersaults and marching soldiers. Gary tried but was unable to break the hypnotic spell of repeating images and insistent music. He was mesmerised.

'It's great in here,' was all that Gary could manage.

'Yes,' she replied. 'What's the name of the band we've come to see?'

'I don't know,' Gary said. 'Clive just told me to come to the dance field.'

'Who's Clive?'

'I don't know; just a man I met.'

Gary looked at Kareena: she was as beautiful as he remembered a couple of minutes before. He grinned and laughed at himself: because of the cannabis he had trouble remembering anything at all. Certainly, Clive's face was a blank. Gary also forgot his name the instant he mentioned it to Kareena. He wasn't even sure where he was; nor could he recall how he arrived there, or how he and Kareena had met.

But it doesn't matter, he told himself, because I've got the girl; and nothing can go wrong now.

Kareena asked how long they'd have to wait for the band, but Gary didn't know. She pecked his cheek and they both laughed nervously. Gary held her around the waist; after a moment she pulled away, but he didn't mind: he'd touched her skin and the sensation lingered on his fingertips. People pressed in from behind forcing them closer, but now Gary hesitated and he kept his arm by his side. He noticed a man approaching steadily from his left; not moving towards the stage as he expected, but working his way along the rows of people in front of him.

'E's? Tabs?' the man hissed as he shouldered his way through the gaps. When he reached Gary he stopped and stared at him, with bemused curiosity in his eyes. Gary felt uneasy; he didn't like being scrutinised like that. The man turned his head to look at Kareena and he furrowed his brow, as if trying to work something out. An unlikely couple, he seemed to be thinking.

The man was older than the rest of the audience, but still not as old as Gary. He wore cut-off jeans and a faded yellow T-shirt. His neck and shoulders were a riot of flashing lights from the brightly-coloured glow sticks wrapped around them. The tops of his cheeks were cratered with pock marks and a thin scar curved down the right side and into his mouth. The man gave a knowing smile, as if he'd cracked the puzzle, and it curled slowly into a sneer.

'E's? Tabs?' he repeated, almost mockingly.

Gary shook his head, but Kareena reached out and touched his tattooed arm. 'How much?' she asked. Gary didn't catch the answer but heard Kareena complain.

'It's the market price,' the man replied. Then he looked again at Gary, as if making a calculation. He leaned towards

Kareena and grinned, revealing a row of crooked teeth. 'You're a real beauty,' he said and then he whispered something in her ear that Gary couldn't catch. 'And I'll give you a special price,' he added.

'Just give me the tabs,' Kareena replied sharply.

The man shrugged his shoulders. 'Your choice,' he said.

Kareena eased a tightly folded bank note out of her trouser pocket as the man reached into the leather pouch around his waist. He produced a clear plastic sachet and exchanged it for the money.

'It's pure stuff, so go easy,' he said as he slid in front of a group of people nearby and vanished.

The sachet contained three small white tablets and Gary watched Kareena drop one of them into the palm of his hand. It looked so simple, so perfect, so fragile. 'What is it?' he asked.

'Ecstasy,' she replied.

'I've never had one before.'

'Don't worry. If you're not used to it, only take half.'

Gary tried to bite the tablet with his front teeth. He already felt high from the cannabis he'd smoked earlier and wondered if he should take even half. He was vaguely aware that he didn't approve of drugs, especially because of the children, but his thoughts were disordered and he couldn't be certain. He looked at Kareena and was reassured by her smile. He watched her put a tablet on her tongue and wash it down with lager. He looked for a reaction and when he saw nothing, he bit again on the tablet she'd given him.

Both halves fell into his mouth. Faraway in the recesses of his mind an alarm rang urgently, warning him to spit them both out. He knew he ought to and deep down he wanted to.

He retracted his tongue to where the half-tablets now lay, and filled the front of his mouth with saliva. He turned his head to find space to rid himself of the alien objects, when his face met Kareena's. She reached her arms around his shoulders and gently slipped her tongue between his lips. He swallowed and cleared his mouth, before engaging and pressing and tasting her tongue with his.

A siren sounded, lights began flashing all around the marquee and the band came on stage to the cheers of adoring fans.

Still coupled, mouth to mouth, Gary and Kareena were carried forward as the excited crowd surged towards the stage. Bright yellow lights flashed in front of them and billowing white mist tumbled over their heads. A deep electronic bassline reverberated through their bodies, increasing in volume in gradual steps.

People began to rise and fall to the rhythm, like a swelling sea. A drum beat joined in, followed by a dreamy keyboard and undulating guitar riffs; and together they built up steadily to a climax. Kareena's tongue thrust and gyrated inside Gary's mouth, stimulating every surface.

The instruments screamed at each other, the lead singer screamed at the microphone and the audience screamed back. Everywhere, heads shook and arms flailed. A thunderous sound assaulted the spectators, who absorbed the rhythmic energy and transferred it into a furious, repetitive, hypnotic dance. Feet stamped, hips crashed and arms flexed.

Kareena's tongue was forcibly ejected from Gary's mouth by the irresistible twisting and rolling of bodies; her face radiated happiness as she took up the feverish dance around her. Gary was overwhelmed by intense sensations of sexual desire and communal frenzy. It was as if his body had been plugged into a high voltage electrical supply, causing his nerves to spark and his muscles to convulse.

Gary danced and sang and waved his arms. He pulled Kareena's body closer and began to kiss her hungrily. He filled his lungs with the sharp, fresh scent of her perspiration. Balls of sweat rolled down his back and soaked his shirt, so that it clung to the contours of his steaming torso. He felt strong, youthful and alive once again; and invincible, too.

Suddenly, he saw a drumstick fly from the stage and shoot over the sweaty heads in front of him. 'It's mine!' he yelled, leaping into the air.

TWENTY-FOUR

Sunday morning, 4.30 a.m.

Clutching the grey blanket that had been draped over his shoulders, Gary sat on the edge of a mat waiting for the doctor. Someone brought him a mug of hot sugared tea. Gary let it cool, inhaling its familiar and refreshing aroma. When the heat had passed, he gulped it down and filled his body with a rush of glorious, internal warmth. For a moment he felt invigorated but then he choked slightly and, without warning, the liquid in his stomach flew with force out of his mouth onto the ground. Gary coughed and spluttered. Rosie returned with a roll of tissue and cleaned his face.

'It's not a good sign if you can't tolerate liquids,' she said with some concern in her voice. Gary then heard Rosie talking to a doctor further inside the tent. 'I'm not sure how serious it is. He could just be dehydrated,' he heard her say. 'He might just need to stay here for observation, but his heart rate's a bit high and his blood pressure's a bit low.'

'I think he'll be OK,' he heard an older woman say, 'but we'd better call the field ambulance to take him up to the medical centre. They can decide if he just needs a drip and observation, or if he should go to hospital.'

Gary panicked. Hospital? Surely not?

'No,' Gary mumbled when Rosie came back, 'I don't need a… '

'Well, at least that's got you talking,' she beamed. 'But you don't need to worry. It's routine, just to check you're OK. The ambulance will be here in ten minutes and they'll probably just keep you at the medical centre for a few hours.'

'My ki…' Gary began, before stopping in his tracks. He had suddenly remembered his children but a deep instinct stifled his words. It was as if the memory of Hannah and Marc had kick-started the conscious side of his brain. Don't mention the kids, he thought. It'll take too much explaining.

'Your what?' Rosie asked, leaning closer; but Gary just shook his head.

Gary felt miserable. His shame had become a profound guilt. What had been he thinking of? He was still a little uncertain what had brought him to the medical tent but, as events began to re-form in his mind, like a broken jigsaw piecing itself together, he understood that his predicament was all of his own making.

He saw a couple of legs encased in dirty green wellington boots poking out from underneath the curtain of one of the cubicles. Perhaps he could just stay here and lie on a mat like that, he thought. Surely that would be better than going off to the medical centre or, worse still, to hospital. Weren't they being over-cautious? Wasn't the night nearly over, anyway? He looked out to see the sky was beginning to lighten. Another dawn? He must be mad!

A man walked past him to the reception desk. A nurse took details before cleaning and dressing his cut knee. He watched a girl leave a cubicle with her arm in a sling, with instructions to walk to the medical centre with her friends and a note requesting an x-ray. It was still very busy and Gary despaired that they had ordered an ambulance to take him across the festival to the same place.

He decided quickly that he couldn't leave the children on site without him. If the ambulance came, who knew when – or if – he would return? Everyone would be worried sick and he'd have a lot of uncomfortable explaining to do. He knew Frank would be supportive, whatever happened – he was the eternal good friend. Hannah and Marc needed him there to support and guide them. It was bad enough losing their mother, without losing the second adult in their lives. No, he thought, it wouldn't do to go in the ambulance. Anyway, he realised, as distant blue flashing lights began to reflect on nearby tree tops, Sunday would be their last day and he didn't want to miss it for anything.

As Rosie approached, a young woman came into the medical tent complaining that the sole had come away from her leather sandal and could she have some surgical tape to fix it? Rosie was distracted for a moment. Gary shuffled the blanket off his shoulders as he stood unsteadily on his feet. Then he lunged out of the tent, staggering back onto the pathway by which he had arrived, like an awkwardly-designed mechanical robot. He dodged other people on the path and, in doing so, caught the guy-rope of a tent with his foot and tripped. He fell to his knees, swore and pulled himself up stiffly. He struggled forward again and regained the path. He couldn't read any of the signposts because of the tears now pouring from his eyes, so he just headed down hill, hoping to find his bearings at the bottom of the valley.

He suppressed an urge to retch again. He plodded on, determined to reach his tent, with one recurring thought playing in an endless loop in his mind: Sunday would be better; tomorrow – today – would be the best day of all.

TWENTY-FIVE

Gary was asleep as Hannah and Lucy approached the tent, arm in arm, singing with exhausted joy. The sky was a lustrous blue, as if clouds had yet to be invented. The bright yellow sun had an unimpeded view of the festival site. Flagpoles and tents threw long shadows over puddles that were shrinking before their eyes. Steam rose from the ground into the morning air, as mud dried and became firm underfoot. Troupes of late night revellers traipsed back to their sleeping bags, sated with pleasure.

Gary stirred. He stretched his aching body, still half-asleep. He declined to wake, preferring to delay the inevitable coming to terms with reality. Anyway, he was desperate to finish a dream that was only part-way through.

He was running in a field, through tall green grass towards a house he knew. He was calling Natalie's name and waving his arms urgently. He was trying to reach the house. He had important information for her but, however fast he ran, he approached the house only very slowly. Time was running out.

He jumped across a brook, but it expanded beneath his feet even as he flew, until it was a wide, shallow river. He fell into the water and tried to raise his head, but some force kept his face submerged. He held his breath and struggled, again and again, but it was no use. He gasped for air but instead he inhaled water. He had drowned and he awoke with a start. He gasped again for air, realised it was only a dream and slowly lowered his head into the damp, spongy morass of his pillow.

Hannah pointed out two squirrels chasing each other around the trunk of a side-lit tree. They watched the animals freeze and become alert, waiting for the girls to pass by safely, before continuing their game. All around them was a stillness that only early morning on a summer's day could bring. The silence was punctuated by sporadic bird calls and the distant sound of a barely visible jet liner high in the sky: a sole reminder of the normal world outside the confines of the fence.

A couple of enterprising stall holders were brewing coffee and unstacking plastic tables and chairs. Another pulled down the shutter on a mobile trailer, having sold out of doughnuts and bagels the previous night. Warmed by the sun, Hannah and Lucy looked forward to sleep, as the ridge of the pink tent came into sight.

Gary had re-entered the dream and was now in the back garden of his house. An imaginary wall of decrepit ivy-covered bricks surrounded the garden on all sides, separating him from the house itself. Only the roof tiles and the tops of the first-floor windows were visible over the wall. Gary could hear Natalie's voice in the house, talking and laughing. He called her name, but she didn't hear.

He knew he had to escape the garden and reach Natalie in the house. He started to walk around the garden wall, feeling and pressing the bricks as he went. He turned at each corner until he had completed the full square. 'Natalie,' he called, 'watch out!' But there was no change to the sounds coming from the house. He walked as far away from it as he could and stood on tiptoe, trying to peer into the windows over the garden wall. He imagined that he saw Natalie's hair, swinging from one window to another and he called out her name again, loudly and urgently.

Gary became agitated. He started to run along the walls, pushing and fumbling at the bricks, tugging the ivy and trying to climb wherever gaps in the pointing appeared. He listened to Natalie's voice, but it had become softer and less distinct. He started scratching at the bricks and running in random directions until, from nowhere, he came across a cracked and weathered wooden door in an archway.

He looked over his shoulder at the house, as if he had a choice to make. Natalie's laughter became louder and Gary's heart ached to be with her. He looked at the door. Slowly, he twisted the rusted handle and eased the door open. He hesitated. He looked back at the house. He thought he heard Natalie's voice call his name, but there was no longer anything he could do. He walked through the door and out of the walled garden. As he did so, he heard a muffled scream, then a much louder scream and then, inexplicably, the plaintive cry of 'Dad!'

'Oh my God,' Hannah screamed. 'Dad!'

'Oh my God,' Lucy repeated.

'Look at him – dad, are you all right?'

Gary opened his eyes and lifted his head. Hannah was open-mouthed at the unzipped door of his inner tent. Lucy stood next to her, with her hand covering her mouth. 'I'm OK,' he croaked, as his forehead slammed into a wall of pain.

'Aaaggghhh!' he groaned, raising a hand to soothe his brow. The back of his throat felt raw. The taste of stale tobacco and cannabis filled his dry mouth, adding to an already terrible sense of nausea, and his nostrils were filled with a fetid stench.

'You've been sick everywhere,' Hannah cried, shocked out of sleepiness.

Holding his head, Gary took stock of the pool of sticky vomit all over his sleeping bag and clothes. With his hand he felt his damp, matted hair and, there, a few inches beneath him, he could see the imprint left by his head on the sodden pillow. His stomach tried to retch again at the overpowering smell, but it was completely empty and a spasm of pain clutched him from inside.

He gave Hannah a look that said: 'Sorry', 'Don't worry' and 'Help me' all at the same time. 'I'll be all right,' he whispered. He tried to lever himself up but couldn't raise his body beyond the elbows.

'Oh, dad,' Hannah said with a voice full of sympathy.

'What are we going to do?' Lucy asked. 'Shall I get mum?'

'No, definitely not.'

'What then?'

'It's obvious – we'll have to clean him up.' Gary tried to protest but any movement sent his head spinning. 'First,' Hannah said, 'let's get some water to clean out his mouth. I can smell it from here.'

Hannah pulled away the soiled sleeping bag and dumped it outside the tent. Holding her nose against the stench, Lucy reached into the sleeping compartment and handed Gary a beaker of water. Hannah rummaged in her wash bag and produced two tablets, which she offered to Gary.

'Take these,' she said. 'They're powerful painkillers. I need them for my periods and they're my last ones – so you'll have to buy me some more later.' Gary tried to refuse the tablets. 'Get them down you,' Hannah insisted. 'I can see you've got a headache and these'll sort it out.'

As Gary opened his fingers to accept the tablets he felt something sticking to the palm of his hand. With a groan, he peeled away the crumpled photograph of Natalie that had been returned to him at the medical tent. It was creased and smeared with mud and sweat. The picture was almost unrecognisable as a good part of it had become detached from the paper and remained on his hand, like a pale mirror image of the original. He screwed it up and tossed it away, before swallowing the tablets with a slurp of water from the beaker. He grimaced and whimpered.

'Men!' Hannah said contemptuously. 'They don't know what pain is.' She produced a flannel and towel. 'Get me the water bottle by the door,' she said to Lucy.

Hannah was soon on her knees, pouring water onto Gary's face and washing the mud and vomit from his eyes. 'Keep still!' she commanded as she poured water through his hair. 'We can't have you going out looking like a tramp.'

'I don't think I'll go anywhere today,' Gary groaned.

'What do you mean?' Hannah replied. 'As soon as you're decent, you're going to have a shower down by the kids' field, before the queues start.'

'But…'

'No buts – I'm in charge here, until you sort yourself out or…' She paused to look at Lucy before continuing: '… or until you can behave like an adult.' Lucy giggled and even Gary smiled despite the resulting hammer blow on his crown.

'Lean forward,' Hannah said, reaching over Gary's back and pulling the soiled T-shirt over his head and shoulders. She looked with curiosity at the yellow band on his wrist. She asked Gary where it'd come from, but he didn't reply. Hannah used a baby wipe to clean the small wound on Gary's forehead and he winced with pain. 'I haven't got any plasters, but it'll get better quicker if it's exposed to the air.'

She searched in his rucksack and found a fresh T-shirt and a clean pair of jeans. 'Put these on and I'll get Lucy to fetch some sweet tea for you.'

'I don't take sugar,' Gary mumbled.

'You'll take what I say. Sweet tea's good for invalids.'

She gave some money to Lucy who was hovering by the entrance of the tent. 'And get me a strong coffee too,' she added.

'I thought you hated coffee.'

'Desperate times call for desperate measures.'

The morning sun quickly turned the site into a vast field of greenhouses, driving campers out of their sleeping bags into the fresh morning air.

Gary shuffled past slowly with a bright yellow towel slung over his shoulder. A wash bag dangled from his fingertips and his open-toed sandals made satisfying slapping noises on the drying ground. He greeted other campers with an imaginary nod, trying not to shake his delicate brain against the inside of his skull. Every step had to be negotiated with the utmost care.

The bags under his eyes weighed Gary down, making him stoop as he progressed along the path. He was tired, but felt beyond sleep. His body was in shock and he had to squint to stop sunlight blasting his retinas.

The shower hut was hidden behind some trees at the end of the track. It was a dilapidated wooden structure, resembling a wide railway carriage without wheels. The curved roof had been painted inexpertly in primary colours. A central opening housed the boiler, set above a roaring fire of spitting logs. Sweet-smelling smoke curled gently into the sky through a small metal chimney pot.

Gary saw that there were two entrances and two queues. The queue to the left was long: about forty campers stood patiently, drinking tea and coffee from paper cups and chatting in subdued tones. The queue to the right was much shorter: maybe a dozen people, who appeared to be moving quite quickly through the open door, replacing campers who came out equally quickly, with wet and tousled hair.

I wonder what the difference is, Gary asked himself before joining the shorter queue. He removed his shoes and stepped inside. It took a moment for his eyes to adjust, and then he recoiled in horror as he realised it was a communal, mixed-sex shower. I've got to get out of here, he thought. He turned and made to leave, but found his exit blocked by a large woman already removing her dirty T-shirt. Gary gasped as she revealed a sweat-stained bra and a chest generously tattooed with red and turquoise skulls, serpents and snarling lions.

The woman stretched her flabby arms behind her back to unfasten the clasp. So mundane and automatic was this task, that she closed her eyes and yawned as she did so. Gary peeped into the cavernous mouth, with its missing and brown-stained teeth and pale, furred tongue. His stomach churned. Oh please, no, he thought, as the woman pushed her voluptuous breasts into his face, forming the deepest cleavage that he'd ever seen. He was appalled at the prospect of their imminent liberation, but it was the smell of old sweat which forced him around on his heels and propelled him deeper into the hut.

He trembled as he undressed. He tried but failed to ignore his temporary companions: a young, athletically-built man, joyously soaping his dangling penis in full view of everyone; the bare back of a shapely young woman bending as she pulled down her trousers and knickers before his eyes; a wizened old man; fathers and pre-pubescent sons; mothers and daughters; and the tattooed behemoth approaching the unused shower head next to where he stood.

This can't be right, he thought. Some of these girls are only Hannah's age. He turned his back to them and faced the wall of the hut, trying to neutralise the unwelcome sexual stimuli. He closed his eyes as an extra safeguard. Gingerly, he washed his hair in the jet of hot water, finding that if he could direct it to a particular point on the nape of his neck, it massaged his spine and reduced the pain in his head.

Clean and somewhat refreshed, Gary headed back up the field. He brought three cups of tea and three small bacon rolls. He scowled in disbelief at the sight of his soiled sleeping bag, lying outside the tent. He was about to unzip the door, when he heard a mobile phone ring inside.

'Hi Hayley,' he heard Hannah say in a tired voice. 'Great to hear from you. How are things going?'

Gary stood still. Hayley was one of Hannah's close friends, whose parents couldn't afford a ticket. He understood the importance of the call: Hannah had mentioned several times that she wished Hayley could be there too. He decided it was best not to interrupt. He would let Hannah have space to talk, while he sat on the grass sipping his tea and nibbling his roll in the sun.

'Yeah, there's so much to do here,' Hannah said more brightly. 'You'd love it.' Gary smiled and chewed delicately on the bacon. 'There's about a dozen different stages – big ones and little ones – and you wouldn't believe which bands I've seen.' She reeled off several names and Gary was pleased.

'I even went on one stage and danced with the band, but then this vicious security guard pushed me off and I landed on my back.' Gary stopped chewing. When was that? Last night? She hadn't mentioned that before. He stared in the direction of her voice, beginning to feel concerned.

'And we've eaten all types of food: you know, chow mein, Mexican, stuff I don't even know what it was.' There was a pause before Hannah continued: 'Well, the toilets are only disgusting. Yeah, there are showers, but the queues are too long. I'm so dirty, I'll need a bath *and* a shower when I get home.'

There was a long pause as Hannah took another question. Gary smiled again: nothing too bad, he thought; and yet there was something in Hannah's voice that worried him.

'Nah, I don't go round with dad much. He always does what *he* wants, anyway. He never thinks of me, or does what I want to do.' Another pause. 'Yeah, parents are so selfish. And do you know what? Last night my dad got really drunk. I mean, really, really pissed and he was sick everywhere.' Gary nearly choked on his roll and he had to fight to hold down a noisy cough.

'Yeah – and you know who had to clear it all up? Yours truly – yeah – and he never said thank you, or anything.' Another pause. 'The weather? It's been lousy – rain and wind all the time. It's so depressing, you know. Nothing's ever dry; and there's mud everywhere. If it wasn't for Lucy being here, I'd come home early.'

Gary shuffled with discomfort. He wanted to move, to stop eavesdropping, but he was gripped by the frankness of Hannah's revelations.

'Oh yeah, I saw her,' Hannah's voice continued. 'But she's skanky and a whore, and she can't even sing.' Another brief pause. 'No, I wanted to – they're awesome – but dad doesn't like them and he dragged me off to see some boring old hippies, who couldn't sing either. It was so embarrassing.' Gary frowned. He didn't recognise what Hannah was saying at all. Had he dragged her anywhere? He didn't think so, but it hurt his head when he tried to delve into his short-term memory.

'I couldn't wait to get away last night,' Hannah continued. 'Yeah, from dad and his weird friend Frank, who's always eyeing me and Lucy up. He's totally disgusting – even more than my dad.'

Gary started, but the sudden movement triggered an explosion in his brain that stopped him jumping to his feet. His hand moved automatically to hold his head in place. He touched the wound on his forehead, which started to throb. He had to leave or interrupt, or something.

'We must be eating six meals a day and I've put on so much weight. Seriously, I'm so ill. But last night was really great – no, really.' Gary went to clear his throat loudly, but changed his mind at the last moment: he desperately wanted to hear Hannah say something good about the festival.

'We met these really nice Italian guys. Yeah, me and Lucy. Oh I can't remember their names; one of them was called Stefano. Twenty or twenty-one, I think. They were really good looking. One of them's got a Ferrari. Yeah, must be loaded. They were so funny and we had a great night out…' Hannah's voice became softer, as if she was aware that her voice might carry and other people might hear. 'You know, dancing and drinking. Yeah, of course we snogged...'

Gary could hardly hear Hannah now. She was speaking more urgently, as if she knew that her time would be up soon, but her voice became quieter and quieter. 'Yeah... yeah... their tent... Lucy too... yeah, really... don't be silly...' and then all Gary could hear was a soft cooing, like a dove. It was more of a murmur than distinct speech, and it was conveying a message so secretively he doubted even Hayley could hear it.

This is terrible, Gary thought; I've heard enough. He slurped the last of his tea, then coughed and shuffled noisily towards the entrance of the tent.

'Oh my God,' he heard Hannah say breathlessly. 'Dad's back – I've got to go. I might call you later, if my battery doesn't run out – you have to queue for like three hours to charge anything here. Speak to you later.'

Gary unzipped the door of the tent in a deliberately noisy and ham-fisted fashion. 'Hi Hannah, I'm back,' he called, a little too loudly. 'I've got you and Lucy some tea and some bacon rolls.'

Hannah pulled back the nylon door and stood in his way. Gary understood she wanted to know how much of her conversation he'd heard, but she didn't say anything. To sidestep her unspoken question he said innocently: 'Sorry I've been so long; the queues...'

Hannah stared at him, trying to read his puffy red eyes. 'You look terrible,' she said quietly.

'I'll survive,' Gary grinned.

'You ought to get some more sleep. Use Marc's sleeping bag – he's still with Sam. I'm going back to sleep, too, but we have to leave the door open or it'll get too hot.'

'But I bought you these,' Gary said, offering her a cardboard tray.

'Lucy's asleep,' Hannah replied reaching for one of the cups. She took a sip. 'This is nearly cold. What's taken you so long?' Then, as if a sudden suspicion entered her mind: 'What have you been doing for the last ten minutes?'

Gary looked at his shoes, searching for an answer. What explanation could he offer that would convince her? He looked at her sheepishly and said simply: 'I got lost.' Hannah looked at his grey face and bleary eyes and whispered: 'You loser', before disappearing into her inner tent.

TWENTY-SIX

Gary slept fitfully on top of Marc's sleeping bag. He dreamed about Hannah's telephone conversation and his imagination filled in the parts he hadn't overheard. Over and again, he tried to picture the events of the previous night through Hannah's eyes. He could create a scene of kissing in a tent, with an exciting fumbling of hands and clothes, but no more.

Maybe his mind wouldn't let him imagine the intimate details, he thought. He just hoped that Hannah was exaggerating and showing off on the phone; and that in Lucy's company she'd been safe from the amorous young Italians. If only I knew, he thought, I could rest.

Not long after midday Gary woke again, thirsty and hungry. His headache had subsided, but his back ached from lying on the rough ground. He could hear soft snoring and air whistling between teeth. Although it was uncomfortably hot in the tent, he guessed that the sky had clouded over, because he could no longer see patterns of sunlight playing on the walls of the tent. His hunch proved right as he poked his head out of the inner tent and looked out of the open door. Thick grey clouds stretched in all directions, being pushed along by an unseen weather front. He heard the girls stir.

'Hannah, are you awake?' he called gently. His question was met with a growl of exhausted complaint. 'If you're hungry, I'm going to the food tent to try and find the others and to get something to eat.' He heard a non-committal grunt, which suggested that he'd struck a chord.

The sun broke through the clouds as Gary's lunch arrived: poached egg on toast. Perfect invalid food, he thought. The yolk blazed gold, like a medal in praise of his culinary choice. He loved the sharpness of salt, the tang and fire of ground pepper, the hot, thick liquid coating his tongue, the soft inside of the barely-toasted bread and the sweet ooze of melted butter. They all made Gary hum with pleasure. He recoiled only momentarily when he crunched on a tiny piece of broken shell. His tongue set to the task of probing every corner of his mouth, to find and then expel the offending particle.

Gary scraped the remains of the yolk from his knife onto his fork. He then sucked the fork and pulled it between his teeth and closed lips. As he ended the meal the sun disappeared and he wondered if he'd see it again that day.

He looked up and recognised a familiar figure approaching, scratching her dishevelled head and stifling a yawn. 'No one else here yet?' Hannah asked, as she sat down opposite him. She stretched out for his mug of tea and helped herself to a mouthful.

'Just me.'

'How are you feeling now?' she asked, raising her eyebrows.

'Not too bad, considering.'

'You're joking,' Hannah said. 'I can only imagine how much you must've drunk last night. You still look awful.'

'I really didn't drink that much,' Gary said, sounding faintly aggrieved.

'Well, it must've been something else then, eh?'

'I don't know what you mean.'

'You were smoking last night, weren't you?' Hannah said, wagging her finger at him as if he were a naughty schoolboy.

'Absolutely not.'

'Liar. I could smell it all over your clothes and your breath stinks – even now.' Hannah grimaced and held her nose with her fingers, as she averted her head. Gary sat in silence. When he opened his mouth to reply he could feel fumes of tobacco rise from his lungs and he closed his mouth at once.

'Where did you go, anyway?'

Gary hesitated but not before he'd mentioned meeting Kareena. He told her briefly about the dance field and how, having parted from Kareena, he had slipped in the mud on the way back to the tent. Hannah sat in amused silence until he had finished.

'You're a bit old for her, don't you think?'

'Don't be daft – nothing like that happened,' Gary protested weakly. 'We probably only spent an hour or so together, before she went off to find her friends.' He fiddled with a teaspoon as he spoke.

'Liar,' Hannah whispered again. 'You men are all the same.'

It was now Gary's turn to raise his eyebrows. 'What do you know about all men being the same?' Hannah's eyes flashed a severe warning at him. Oh dear, he thought, danger lies ahead.

'It's well known,' she replied carefully. 'Anyway, are you going to see her again?' Gary laughed and pulled a face, thinking to himself: if only you knew. He shook his head and said out loud: 'I can't see why, and I wouldn't know where she was anyway.'

Hannah smirked and gave him a look that said: 'I bet.'

Gary waited for her to say something, but she remained silent. 'So what did you do last night?' he asked eventually. 'I thought you and Lucy had turned in for the night, but now I realise you stayed out.'

Hannah picked her dirty fingernails for a moment, then looked up at her father. 'Nothing much,' she said.

'Come on, you must have done something.'

'We hung about, listened to a bit of music, sat around a bonfire, met some friends.'

'Oh yeah, who?'

Hannah glared at him: 'Some friends,' she repeated with emphasis.

'Anyone I'd know?'

'Do I have to tell you about everyone I meet; and everything I do?' Hannah sighed. Gary shrugged his shoulders. 'Adults always seem to do nothing, so why can't I? I'm practically an adult, so why do I have to answer all these questions? It's like the Inquisition.'

She banged her fist on the table, making Gary's cutlery jump and fall with a fierce metallic crash. A sharp pain jabbed inside Gary's skull and he raised his hand to his temple. 'Sorry,' Hannah said, holding her own head. 'I know what it's like. I'm going to have an alcohol-free day, too.'

Gary stared at her, amazed. He knew that she drank vodka when she could get her hands on it, but to the extent that she needed an 'alcohol-free day'? What had come over her?

'Have you got a hangover too? How much did you drink last night? You know, Hannah, I'm really worried about you.'

'Oh, don't give me that,' Hannah said. 'How can you worry about me, when you came back last night in the state you were in? I don't know what's wrong with you, dad:

chasing young women, smoking, drinking, getting completely paralytic and sick everywhere. Dad – *you* worry *me* – but you know, I just can't go on investing all my energy in you and your problems.'

They sat in silence as Hannah ate the food that Gary bought her. He drank water, swishing it around with his tongue and forcing it between his teeth, as he tried to purge his mouth of the taste of stale tobacco. He felt miserable. Hannah watched him from the corner of her eye, with a look of disdain, tinged with pity.

'Hello!' a familiar voice boomed from nowhere, as a large flat hand landed unexpectedly on Gary's shoulder.

'For God's sake,' Gary spluttered, 'I nearly jumped out of my skin.' He turned to see Frank beaming at him, with his white teeth exposed to the fullest possible extent and his brown eyes gleaming with joy.

'How are we today?' Frank asked rhetorically. 'Me? I'm on top of the world. But you…' he added with a pause and a look of genuine surprise, '…you look awful. What happened to you last night?'

'Don't mind me,' Gary said slowly. 'Tell me about your night.'

'Oh, *we* had a wonderful time last night,' Frank guffawed. He winked at Gary and indicated towards Claire behind him, by a single throw of the head over his left shoulder. She was studying her feet with unusual intensity.

'Why am I not surprised?' Gary asked. He felt a pang of jealousy, mixed with resentment and frustration, but at the same time his brain was not clear enough or sufficiently sharp, to justify his feelings. He stared at Claire.

'And what, my good friend, do you mean by that remark?' There was an awkward silence. Gary looked into Frank's eyes, trying to read his mind, as if telepathic thoughts really could jump the three yards between them.

'It's hardly a state secret that you two were joined at the hip last night, when you left that tent together.'

Frank laughed and threw back his head. 'What? Two friends walking along, keeping each other warm in the drizzle? You're out of order, Gary.'

'I'm not the one breaking the established order,' Gary snapped back, in a voice which sounded more like a snarl.

'I've done something wrong, have I? Don't speak in riddles, mate. Speak your mind.'

Claire stepped forward. 'For God's sake,' she muttered, 'you're acting like a couple of schoolboys.' She pushed past Frank and disappeared into the tent to buy coffee. Hannah, who had been half-listening turned to her father.

'What's going on?' she asked. 'I don't understand.'

Gary and Frank looked at each other once again and agreed telepathically to a mutual cease-fire. Gary smiled weakly at Hannah. 'Nothing,' he said.

'Oh I see, that adult 'nothing' again.'

Gary looked at Frank, daring him to speak. Frank stood open-mouthed, eyes fixed on Hannah, but he remained silent. 'Well, I still don't understand,' Hannah said in the absence of an explanation. 'Adults are weird; I hope I don't turn into one – well, at least, not one like either of you.'

Frank excused himself to fetch the boys and Hannah returned to the tent to find Lucy, so that Gary was alone when Claire returned.

'You're like a bear with a sore head today,' she said, as she sat opposite Gary with her mug of coffee.

'Are you surprised?'

'Yes, very surprised. What have I done that's so wrong?'

'You hardly need me to tell you,' Gary sulked.

'Well, if you're not able to say it to my face, I suggest you forget it – and start acting like a nice human being again.'

Gary ran his fingers through his hair; if only he could straighten his thoughts in the same way. He looked at Claire through tired eyes. Although she'd hurt him, deep down he knew it was Frank who had betrayed him. He tried to find the courage to say sorry and to say that it didn't matter. He pleaded silently for her to understand.

'Don't pity me,' Claire said, misreading the look on his face. 'You're not even brave enough to say what you think.' Gary tried to hold them back, but the words 'you and Frank' burst out before he could stop them.

'Oh, give me a break,' Claire said harshly. 'Old lover boy is hardly in a position to complain about Frank and me. Anyway, who are you to tell me what I can and can't do?'

Gary shifted uneasily in his seat. 'Frank's married.'

'But it's not the happiest of relationships, I think even you'll admit.'

'Frank's easily-led.'

'Oh, and you're not? Or is it just that you think I'm loose and on the make?'

'I never said that; I never would.'

'It's what you meant.'

'No, it isn't. Not at all.'

'So why all the concern about Frank? What about me and *my* needs, or don't they count?'

'It's just that Frank…'

'Sod Frank – what about me?' Claire's cheeks reddened and angrily she swept a stray hair from her eyes. She waited for a moment for a reply, but Gary was at a loss for words. He wanted to hug her and say that she'd got it all wrong; but the words wouldn't come out.

'You think I'm an easy lay, don't you?' Claire said coolly.

'What? No! That's not true.'

'Well, you didn't mind groping me the other night, so you must have thought something along those lines…'

'Claire, please, you've got it all wrong. I like you… I respect you… We had fun…' He hesitated as he looked over Claire's shoulder and saw Frank return. '… you must understand… you… you turned me on.'

'Did I? Did I?' Claire hissed. 'Well that's very nice, isn't it? So I'm just an object – something to touch that'll turn you on when you feel like it.'

'That's not what I meant at all,' Gary said, sounding desperate. 'I just wanted to say: you weren't the problem – it was *me*.'

Frank was now very close; and both Gary and Claire could hear him whistling cheerfully. Claire's face was pale.

'As I told you,' she said icily under her breath, 'I like a man who knows what he wants, and it seems to me that you don't have the faintest clue.' In the couple of seconds before Frank arrived Claire added a barely audible 'Poor Natalie', and watched Gary wince.

TWENTY-SEVEN

Gary was still reeling from Claire's words, when Frank sat down next to him, having failed to find the boys.

'I hope nothing's happened,' he muttered.

'Don't be daft. They've just gone out somewhere,' Claire said.

'Maybe,' Frank said, scratching his head. 'At least they're together, I suppose. You know, those two have hardly been out of each other's pockets all weekend.'

'You sound as if you're complaining,' Gary said. 'I say it's a good thing that they've been keeping each other occupied.' Then he added knowingly: 'After all, think of the freedom it's given you.' Frank ignored the comment but asked in an innocent voice whether Gary and Claire had made up.

'We'd never fallen out,' Gary grunted.

'Things are fine,' Claire added. 'Let's move on and talk about what we're doing this afternoon.'

Frank sat at the table. He bent his head nearer to Gary's and said in a low voice: 'She's got a great campsite, there.'

'Piss off,' Gary replied, moving away from him. 'Anyway,' he said, looking at Claire, 'how did you get into the compound?'

'Oh,' Frank said, 'that was easy. Tell him, Claire.'

Claire shuffled awkwardly in her seat. 'I borrowed a pass from one of the catering staff,' she whispered.

'Don't they have names on them?' Gary asked incredulously. Claire fell silent.

'It was busy and dark and it was raining, so no one really looked,' Frank chuckled. 'Good luck, wasn't it?' He beat the palm of his hand on the table to emphasise his point. 'You know, Gary, I *really* like a woman who knows what she wants.'

Claire shot up from her seat. 'I've got to do some shopping with the girls,' she said quickly. 'Let's meet again in the jazz tent at five.'

'If you see the boys,' Frank beamed, 'tell them to join us in the beer tent over there.'

'I don't want another drink in my life,' Gary said.

'Nonsense,' Frank said as he pulled Gary out of his seat. 'What you need is a hair of the dog that bit you.'

'Can't you tell that I'm really fed up with you and Claire, and that I'm not in the mood for a drink?'

'Oh, Gary,' Frank said, putting his arm around his shoulder. 'How long have we been friends? Since before Natalie came on the scene, that's how long. We're best mates. Claire's a late arrival. You can't let a little thing like Claire come between us. You always come first, before these women. Let me buy you a drink and then you can tell me what you did last night. By the look of you, you had one hell of an adventure.'

Gary sighed. He still felt dejected but he welcomed the warmth of Frank's words.

Oh God, he thought, as they walked towards the open awning of the beer tent, I'm acting like a complete idiot. What do I care about Claire? If I'd slept with her, I'd only feel guilty and if Hannah ever found out, I'd never hear the end of it. Maybe I've had a lucky escape.

'OK, you can buy me a drink,' he said to Frank, with a more optimistic tone to his voice. 'You dirty dog,' he added loudly, as if drawing a line under the recent past.

'Aha!' Frank cried, squeezing his arm. 'That's the Gary Cochrane I know and love.'

Even as they walked the short distance to the beer tent, Gary could feel his spirits lifting. His body no longer slouched like a depressed, unemployed stick figure in a Lowry painting. Instead his spine straightened, he held his head up and pulled his shoulders back. He knew that heavy drinking was out of the question, but his mouth was already moist at the prospect of half a pint of hoppy bitter. He also craved an urgent remedy for his throbbing headache. Gary smacked his lips and swirled his tongue in anticipation. Things, he thought, would be looking up soon.

A clap of thunder burst overhead like an artillery shell, causing both Gary and Frank to stop dead at the entrance of the beer tent. They looked up into the weary, grey sky. The wall of sound grew louder, expanding to fill the whole valley. A second explosion brought thousands of conversations to an end, in mid-sentence. Gary wondered how much brain power would be needed to pick up all the broken threads.

After a few seconds of silence, the hubbub of voices rose again, only to be slapped back down again by another peal of thunder. From faraway another faint sound reached Gary's ears. It was unfamiliar at first, like the hiss of rice being poured it into a saucepan. But the sound grew louder and came nearer and ever more urgent: the sound of rain sweeping over thousands of hollow tents.

'They call it 'Flaming June', don't they?' Frank muttered

as he led Gary into the beer tent. 'That's a fucking joke, if I ever heard one.'

Gary was thrilled by the first sip of warm beer. It was sweet with a bitter finish and a fresh flowery bouquet; an elixir with instant rejuvenating properties. It felt as if the beer and his mouth became one, the moment the liquid had passed his lips. He gulped it down and took another sip straightaway, with a loud satisfied slurp.

'You know, I only asked for a half,' he said to Frank. 'I'll never be able to drink a whole pint.'

'We'll see.'

For a while they stood and chatted, but they sat at the first opportunity.

'I hope Marc's not leading my Sam astray,' Frank said cheerfully.

'More likely the other way round.'

'Well, Marc's older and Sam's always been very impressionable.'

'Sam's old enough to look after himself,' Gary said. 'Anyway, Marc isn't like that.'

'What isn't he like, Gary?' Frank asked pointedly.

Gary looked at him, surprised at the question. 'I meant,' he replied slowly, 'Marc's a sensible boy.'

'Maybe they've met a couple of nice girls.'

'At lunchtime on a rainy Sunday, in a field? I don't think so.'

'Well, something's going on. They're not in their sleeping bags and they're nowhere to be seen.'

'They'll be fine,' Gary replied, beginning to worry about what might have happened to them.

Frank had soon finished his pint when Gary's cup was still

more than half full. Gary bought him another and they sat across the table listening to the rain, which was now torrential.

'I'm thinking of leaving early,' Frank said unexpectedly.

'What do you mean, early?'

'This rain, the mud, the cold – it's not worth it.'

'You can't go before Beachy Head play – they're the whole reason we came.'

'Not the whole reason, not even really part of it,' Frank replied, tapping his fingers on the table. 'I only said that they were probably the best thing on all weekend, but I was never much of a fan.'

'What time is early?'

'I don't know yet – I haven't discussed it with Sam. That's why I want to find him. Maybe five or six o'clock.'

'But that's really early, in fact it's only a few hours away. You're joking, aren't you? You'll miss loads of other bands too – I mean some really great ones.'

'My dear friend,' Frank smiled, 'it's the rain – I've just had enough.'

'What are you going to say to Joyce?'

'The same. She'll understand.'

'No, I meant about Claire.'

Frank snorted loudly and with incredulity he replied: 'Don't be stupid – I'm not going to say anything about Claire to Joyce. Why the hell would I?'

'Well... I... I don't know,' Gary stammered. 'I suppose not.'

'You're really not yourself this weekend, are you mate?'

'I don't know. I thought I was fine, but lots of stuff has happened.' He paused. 'It's all to do with Natalie. You know, it's all still there in the background.'

'For Christ's sake, Gary, you're going to have to come to

terms with it some time. I thought this weekend was going to be a fresh start for you and the kids. What's happened?'

'I can't get her out of my head. Why did it happen like that? Why did she have to die?'

'Gary, Gary, Gary – we've been over this a hundred times, a thousand times before. It's not your fault and it's not the kids' fault. She'd had a bit to drink and she stumbled. Maybe there was a book where it shouldn't have been, but it was still an accident.' He patted Gary's shoulder and his eyes implored him to see sense.

'You *know* it was an accident and you have to accept that, for Hannah's sake – for both the kids' sake.'

'I suppose you're right,' Gary replied reluctantly. 'It could've happened at any time.'

'Drink up, then,' Frank urged.

'This beer makes me feel better,' Gary said, taking another sip, 'but I just wanted to take the edge off my hangover, not replace it with another.'

Frank pressed him to explain and so Gary gave him an abbreviated version of the previous night's events. Frank giggled like a boy as he heard the tale unfold. 'Excellent news,' Frank said approvingly. 'After some nookie at last; that's a very good sign.'

'No I wasn't. It just happened that way.'

'I see,' Frank said with a look of exaggerated solemnity. 'That explains it.'

'At least I didn't go out to create a situation.'

'What? Like me and Claire?' Frank retorted. 'That wasn't 'a situation' I created, that 'just happened' too. The only difference being, I knew how to handle it, mate, and you didn't.' A note of slight annoyance sounded in his voice.

'You've got a wife and kids,' Gary said, 'so what were you doing fooling around with someone else?'

'Don't preach at me about being married,' Frank said sharply. 'Your marriage may have been 'oh so perfect', but mine's a life sentence.' Frank's smile vanished and he frowned. 'For God's sake, Gary, what's got into you?'

Gary shrugged.

'Claire's not the first,' Frank continued, 'and if I've got anything to do with it, she won't be the last.'

Gary was shocked. 'How could you?' he asked.

'Don't tell me I didn't give you first bite of the apple,' Frank said crossly. 'I gave you every encouragement a man needs. I took your son away for the night and the rest, mate, was up to you.'

'What about all that stuff about 'my dear wife' that you always say?'

'Oh, please don't mock me and please don't get on your high horse either. You were married for years to Natalie, so don't tell me you never strayed.'

Gary was flabbergasted. He wanted to shake his head, but a vague doubt prevented him. He trawled through the years of his relationship with Natalie, but his brain was tired and befuddled. There was no instant recall of memories: he was operating less like a fast computer than someone flicking through a box of index cards. He stopped at those which contained the names of female friends and acquaintances, to analyse whether any extra-marital experiences could be associated with them; and at cards that contained details of the few nights he had spent away from Natalie, the few trips abroad.

There was of course the awkward incident with Suzanne,

but he'd known her before he met Natalie, so she didn't really count. Anyway, Natalie had got the wrong end of the stick about her. No, when he reviewed the past, he found nothing – there was absolutely nothing there.

Gary felt vindicated: of course there was nothing. He knew that he'd been faithful to Natalie in body and soul.

'No,' he said definitively, dispelling any remaining doubt. 'I never strayed.'

Frank looked surprised. His forehead knotted with a pained expression and he shook his head in apparent despair. Slowly, he finished his second pint of beer. 'You poor sod,' he exhaled. 'I need another drink.'

'Not for me,' Gary replied, as Frank went off to the bar.

When Frank returned he put his pint and wallet on the table. 'You're a sad bastard,' he said.

'What's sad about fidelity? I loved Natalie and she loved me. We were happy and the kids were happy. I had no need to be unfaithful.'

'Maybe I should have said that you're a lucky bastard then,' Frank said grudgingly. 'Let's drop it. I want to talk about going away in the summer.'

'This *is* the summer.' Gary raised his arms at the rain lashing the roof of the tent.

'I mean the summer where you're guaranteed some sun. Why don't we take the kids to Spain or Greece in August and dry out? A few days in the sun and we'll all forget this nightmare. How about it?'

'You're a great friend, Frank. I don't know what I'd do without you.'

As they stood up to go, Frank knocked his wallet off the table and Gary picked it up from the ground. It fell open and he passed it to Frank. Both men froze at the point where the leather became a link in a chain between them: a link held by two hands, thumbs uppermost on either side.

There, protruding from one of the pockets meant for credit cards, was a small photograph of Natalie. Not a photograph with straight sides, but one cut out around her head, excising, Gary realised, his own that had once been next to hers. The friends pulled on the wallet. Gary's eyes met Frank's.

'Why have you got a photograph of Natalie in your wallet?' The words came out automatically, toneless.

'Let go of it, Gary,' Frank replied slowly and deliberately.

'Answer my question. And don't give me 'she was a friend of mine too' or any bullshit like that.'

'It's not important, Gary, let it go.'

'Why would Frank have a photo of Natalie in his wallet?' Gary asked out loud, as if posing the question to himself. He gripped the wallet harder.

'It's nothing. Forget it.'

'It's everything. She's everything. What does it mean?'

'It doesn't mean anything.'

Gary's wild eyes stared into Frank's. Then, slowly, their gaze moved back down to Natalie's smiling face in the wallet. Gary felt sick as he realised he'd uncovered another of Frank's affairs.

'I want to know.'

'You don't want to know. Forget it, I said.'

'Tell me how you came to have it there.'

'She's an old friend of mine too…'

'Leave it out, Frank. You know that won't wash. And who cut off my head from the photo? You or her?' Frank jerked the wallet out of Gary's hand and put it into his back pocket.

'What does it matter? You know, you're such a bloody martyr,' he sneered.

'How long?'

'Long enough. What does it matter now?'

'You double-crossing bastard!'

'Oh, yeah?' Frank said defensively. 'Which one of us made her give up her career and then did fuck all in the house, or to help out with the kids? You just did your own selfish thing, as usual. And it was the same with Claire: you just thought of number one and then blamed her for your own pathetic cowardice. You know, Gary Cochrane, I've just about had enough of you.'

Gary was speechless and held his hand to his head.

'You were no better last night,' Frank continued. 'Chasing a woman half your age, getting blind drunk, puking up everywhere and expecting your own daughter to clear up the mess. And now you act as if you're surprised Natalie had a drink problem and went elsewhere, for love and affection.'

Gary tried to speak but found himself only able to clear his throat. He hadn't expected to hear such a tirade and tears welled up in his eyes.

'You fucking bastard,' he said, as he rose with fists clenched. Frank jumped up more quickly and pushed him back down onto his seat.

'Do you want to know the reason why?' Frank asked. Gary shook his head, which was raging with pain and anguish. 'Only when,' he replied.

'When? What does that matter?' Frank shouted angrily. 'It's

the *why* that matters. I'll tell you if you want – you really should know.'

'I don't want to know. Haven't you done enough damage?'

'Me? Oh, that's rich, coming from you, from what Natalie told me.'

Gary shuddered. 'When?' he repeated.

'Didn't you hear me, Gary? It's the 'why' you need to be concerned about, the 'why'. You've been avoiding the truth for far too long and now it's time to face the music, Gary.'

'Tell me when.'

'When? 'When' was the year you went off for two weeks to do poncy yoga, leaving her to cope all on her own, after the disastrous fucking Christmas with your parents. That's 'when' if you need to know. But now, Gary, the 'why'…'

'Don't tell me!'

'Gary, you sad git; this is your only chance. If you don't let me tell you now, I'll never tell you.'

'Go away,' Gary said weakly. He rose slowly to his feet and glowered at Frank. 'Go away,' he yelled as took a sudden swipe at Frank's head. Frank took a step back and avoided the blow.

'Natalie was about to split up from you, Gary,' he said, turning from the table. 'You ought to know that, at least.' He began to walk away; but then he hesitated and turned back. 'You should be grateful, Gary. It was only because of her relationship with me, that you two continued for as long as you did.' He paused, as if uncertain whether he should carry on. 'If she hadn't died, Gary, she would have told you all this herself. I'm sorry for your loss – I really am – but my old mate, your loss is nothing compared to mine. The truth is, Gary, you're nothing but a fucking loser – and you know it.'

TWENTY-EIGHT

Gary reeled backwards, his head spinning and his heart racing. He grasped a wooden support to keep his balance. He watched Frank leave the beer tent and disappear into the rain. Gary didn't know where to turn or what to do. He wanted to sit down again but his seat had been taken. Gradually, as his heart beat slowed down, he noticed that the people at the nearest table had frozen and were silent. Five faces were looking at him, their eyes full of pity mixed with horror at what they had obviously overheard.

Gary felt sick again and wanted to retch, but he could only manage a dry cough. The man sitting nearest to him swung his legs around the end of the bench and stood up.

'I don't know who you were talking to,' he said to Gary, 'but it sounds like you've had some pretty hard news, pal.' He smiled and he put a friendly, reassuring hand on Gary's shoulder. 'So come and join us for a while.'

Gary looked at the stranger and tried to decline the offer, but the man's friends immediately rearranged themselves, so that there was room for him at the table. Drained of any strength to resist, Gary sat down.

'Hi, I'm Allie,' said a young woman in a bright yellow cardigan. She stretched out her hand for him to shake. 'And I'm Joe,' said her rather older partner.

'We live close by,' a third friend explained. 'We're here on a free day-ticket for locals.'

'I didn't know they existed,' Gary replied, still shell-shocked. 'I had real trouble getting mine.'

He declined an offer of beer, citing his delicate state, but gratefully accepted a pint of orange juice and lemonade. The clink of ice cubes was the most pleasing sound he'd heard all weekend.

They talked music, farming, beer and cider, relationships, politics, film and sport. Another drink arrived and Gary was shouted down when he tried to contribute to the cost. 'Don't forget you had to buy your ticket and we didn't,' was all he heard.

Allie presented an inexhaustible supply of smutty jokes that made the table fall about laughing. Tears rolled down Gary's cheeks. He wasn't sure if they came from laughter or from sadness, but it didn't matter, either to him or to his new-found companions. The tears flowed into his mouth and mixed with the juice; the resulting sweet and salty flavour reminding him of the wake after Natalie's funeral. The recollection made Gary cry even harder.

It's like I'm in a Greek tragedy, he thought, but somehow I'm wearing the happy and sad masks both at the same time.

Maybe he was laughing because now he knew the truth – or, at least, that part of it he'd let Frank tell him. Maybe he'd been released from the suffocating myth of Natalie-past. Even calling it a myth was progress; his therapist would be proud. He began to feel that his sadness at losing Natalie was tempered now by a certain relief: a sense that the time for grieving was over and that he had to look forwards, not backwards.

In truth, his mind was a jumble of barely coherent thoughts, but he did have an over-powering feeling that, perhaps, this was the real turning point, and that things *would* get better from now on. He didn't really believe it, but still he crossed his fingers.

Suddenly, Gary snapped out of the dream world which had engulfed him. He surveyed the scene of jollity around him and, all at once, felt a stranger and out of place. What am I doing here with all these drunk people? he thought. He declined a third drink and said that he really must go. He stood up and saw the same five faces looking up at him, as before, but the pity and the horror had vanished.

'Thanks for taking me under your wing,' he said.

Bob, the man who had first invited him to join the group, rose from his seat and offered him his hand. 'I understand you've got to go,' he said with a tipsy and jovial smile, 'but I want you to know that we've enjoyed your company very much.'

Gary was astounded and for a moment at a loss for words. He shook his head and mumbled: 'No... It's me that should thank you for being so friendly, for...'

'Rubbish,' Bob exclaimed. 'We're all here to have some fun and whatever it was that that bloke said to you, well, you needed a distraction.'

'Thanks,' Gary said. 'I certainly agree with that. I feel a lot better now. So – thanks, again.'

Bob shook his hand vigorously. 'We're not going anywhere in this rain – we're just going to drink and chat right here. You can come back any time you want, pal. We'd be pleased to see you again. Chin up!'

Gary could feel the tears welling up in his eyes once again. He mumbled another thanks and left the tent, his breast burning with gratitude and resolve.

Gary was glad of the fresh air. The rain had now changed into a light drizzle and people were walking about under umbrellas and with hoods pulled over their heads. The ground was saturated again and the paths were awash with water and mud. Not for the first time that weekend, Gary thought that the festival site resembled the Somme.

Music was still being played all around him. Although the fields in front of some of the stages were waterlogged, bands struggled on bashing out their tunes. Gary wasn't bothered to know their names; he simply wandered from field to field, taking in whatever entertainment there was. The audiences for the outdoor events were depleted, but the marquees were crammed full.

Gary bought himself a can of cola, hoping to benefit from the caffeine. From a distance he saw Marc walking towards him deep in thought and looking worried. He waved to attract his attention and Marc jumped when he saw his father.

'You startled me,' Marc said, 'but I hoped you'd be around here.'

'You sound desperate,' Gary replied. 'Let's find some shelter.'

'Dad, I want to tell you something.'

'Yes, yes, when we find some shelter.'

'I have to speak to you *now*, dad.'

'Can't it wait?' Gary asked.

'No, it can't,' Marc said with all the assertiveness he could muster. 'You never have time for me, but I have to talk to you right now. Even in the rain.'

They stood facing each other in the drizzle, heads covered with nylon hoods. 'Here?' Gary asked.

'Here.'

Gary sipped his cola. 'It had better be good.'

'For Christ's sake,' Marc cried. 'Don't you understand?' Gary could see terror in his son's face and there was earnestness in his voice that he'd never heard before.

'Fire away,' he said. 'I'm all yours.'

Marc stood still for several seconds, trying to formulate the correct words. He opened his mouth to say something, but faltered. He looked at his feet, then again at his father.

'Dad,' he began, shuffling his feet. Gary stood impassively and waited. 'You know I spent last night in Sam's tent?' There was a long pause. 'Well…' he continued, '…Sam's gay.' He spoke very softly and Gary only just caught his words.

'Are you sure?' he asked quietly.

'Definitely.'

'Does Frank know?'

'Are you joking? He'd go berserk. Sam could never tell him.'

'So why are you telling me?' Marc stood before him in silence. Gary shook raindrops from his hood. 'Can't this wait, Marc?' he asked, but he said no more when he saw the panic in Marc's eyes. Gary waited, then asked: 'Is there more?'

Marc nodded and he looked wretched.

'I told you – Sam's gay.'

'True; but is there something else?'

'I don't know,' Marc said almost inaudibly, looking once again at his feet.

'Yes,' Gary said, 'I think you do.' There was silence. All Gary could hear was the drizzle falling softly and steadily on his head and the squelch of Marc's rubber boots, as he moved his feet backwards and forwards on the muddy grass.

'Let me help,' Gary said. 'Sam's gay – you told me that.

Frank doesn't know – he mustn't know – and you also want to tell me that…' Gary trailed off, waiting for Marc to finish the sentence.

'… that…' Marc said, '… that…'

Marc looked to his right at an unexpected noise. Gary followed his frown and saw Frank bounding towards them, with a serious and determined look on his face. He said a brief 'Hi, Marc' before approaching Gary.

'I've come to make up,' he said. 'To say I'm sorry. We've known each other for more than twenty years. We've practically grown up together. Gary – I want us to remain friends. I don't want to lose you.'

Frank's lower lip quivered as he spoke. He appeared anxious, uncertain and contrite. Gary had never known Frank to apologise like this before for anything or to humble himself in such a way. He knew that Frank really meant what he said. Marc looked crestfallen by Frank's intervention. He visibly withdrew back into himself and lowered his head, so that his eyes were hidden by his hood. Both waited expectantly for Gary to speak.

'Fuck off, Frank,' were the words which emerged; words which surprised even Gary himself as he said them.

'What did you say to me?'

'You heard me alright. I'm talking to Marc, can't you see?'

'How dare you talk to me like that, you smug, self-centred little shit,' Frank jerked his chin backwards in disgust. 'You've got real issues, mate. I don't know how you're going to sort them out, but don't ever say I didn't try to help.' He spat at Gary's feet. 'I'm going home. Don't bother to phone me, because I don't want to speak to you ever again.'

He stormed off, waving his middle finger in the air.

'Go fuck yourself, Frank,' Gary shouted after him. 'See if I care.'

'Go after him, quickly,' Marc said looking alarmed but not comprehending what he'd just heard. 'It's more important to stay friends…'

'No, son,' Gary said still shaking with anger. 'It's more important that you tell me what you want to say.'

'I can't, dad, I can't.'

Gary felt sorry for Marc, who stood in front of him looking utterly despondent. This was to have been his moment and Frank had nearly hijacked it; but Gary was determined not to let Frank succeed. 'Yes, you can. I know you can – and *you* know you can.'

'I can't.'

Gary could see tears in his eyes. He stretched out and held Marc's arm. He continued calmly in a reassuring tone of voice: 'Let me help you, Marc. You told me Sam is gay, that much I understand. You want to tell me that Sam is gay and that…'

'… that… that…'

'That…' Gary repeated, sipping the cola again as he willed his son on.

'You know, don't you?'

'Know what, Marc?' Gary looked Marc in the eyes; but neither of them could see the other very well because tears were streaming down their faces.

'That I'm gay, too, dad. I'm gay.'

'Are you sure? How do you know?'

'I spent last night in Sam's tent. Don't worry, we didn't do anything dad; but it wasn't the first time.'

Gary raised his can. 'I propose a toast,' he declared. 'A toast to my son – a young man with the guts to tell his dad something very, very important. I'm proud of you Marc.' He took another sip of his drink.

'I don't understand,' Marc said, wiping his eyes. 'Is that it?'

'That's it, you've said it. I understand and it's OK. I hope you can work it all out.'

'I wanted to tell mum.'

'You've known that long?'

'I've known since I was nine or ten.'

Gary was stunned but tried to prevent it showing. 'Well, on your mum's behalf, I can tell you…' Gary paused and gulped, 'I can tell you that she would have been proud of you too. She would realise how brave you've been. You know, she really loved you, Marc.' Gary hugged him tightly for several seconds.

'You don't mind, dad? I'm not a disappointment to you?'

'How could you be? Most kids wouldn't tell their parents at forty, let alone at fourteen like you.' Gary toasted him a second time. 'It's fine, Marc. I'm cool about it. I want you to be happy.'

Marc winced at the use of the word 'cool' but he looked relieved. 'Thanks, dad. I was really scared; you can't imagine. I really appreciate it.'

'But, for God's sake, don't tell Frank,' Gary said. 'Not yet, anyway.'

Marc gave a nervous laugh. 'It doesn't look like I'll get the chance to do that any time soon.'

TWENTY-NINE

Several minutes passed before Marc broke away to try and find Sam before he left the festival. Gary looked at his watch: he was due to meet Claire in about half an hour, but he'd never make it in time. He poured away the rest of the drink into the swampy grass and crushed the can in a single violent movement. He felt better immediately, as he transferred his stress into the now deformed metal. He felt exhilarated by the strength that he had shown in that movement, by the combined power of his arm, wrist and fingers and by the loud retort of buckling aluminium.

The can had submitted irreversibly to his will and it was satisfying. Gary reflected on Frank's revelation about Natalie and, involuntarily, his fist tightened on the crushed can. He continued to apply pressure until his hand shook and a sharp pain made him look down. The metal had split and blood from his palm was spreading slowly over the distorted blue sides and curved silver base of the can.

Gary flung it into a nearby recycling bin and licked his hand. It throbbed but the cut was fine and clean. Despite the pain, Gary didn't mind. The cut was a foreseeable consequence of what he'd done and it had been his free choice, not something imposed on him by someone else, or by events.

He walked in the drizzle nursing his injured hand. How had he missed the signs that Natalie had fallen out of love with him? He tried to remember specific times they had spent together, but it was impossible now to recall any details, especially when he didn't know what he was searching for. Had she ever said anything to him? Had she ever *not* said anything he might have expected to hear? That was even more hopeless, trying to prove a negative.

Looking back, he'd never understood Natalie's reaction when he returned from the yoga course. She had berated him for being selfish, abandoning her and not caring about the children. He'd tried to say that it had been her idea for him to go, to help him with his depression, but she wouldn't listen.

Maybe he shouldn't have gone. Maybe he should have predicted how she would feel. Maybe he should have taken her along or, better still, sent her on the course in his place. After all, her suggestion was like a gift – and he knew from experience that people often gave things as presents that they really wanted for themselves.

Gary reached the intersection of two muddy tracks. His hands were now deep in his coat pockets, his shoulders were hunched and all his attention was focused on the wet toes of his boots. His worried concentration was broken by a cheerful sound of twanging strings and childish giggles. He looked up.

Beneath the dense green canopy of a tree he saw six children standing in a row. Gary guessed that they were about ten or eleven years old. They wore raincoats and boots, but they had removed their hoods because of the shelter afforded by the leaves. Each child held a brand-new, brightly-coloured ukulele and together they were strumming the notes of a familiar tune. After two false starts a girl with tumbling golden locks and rosy pink cheeks stepped forward.

'... Two, three, four,' she shouted and together the children launched into the opening riff of 'Teenage Kicks'. With whoops of delight and toothy grins, they strummed wildly and sang at the tops of their squeaky voices. Their smiles and laughter were charged with irrepressible charm and optimism. Gary smiled at the lyrics, which dealt with emotions and desires far beyond the understanding of the angelic performers. So this was the result of all that early morning practice he'd heard.

'A bit young to be busking,' said another bystander.

'At least they can say they've played Glastonbury,' Gary replied, 'which is more than most of us.'

An energetic burst of driving rain forced Gary on his way. He skipped along the track feeling warm and reinvigorated. He splashed in puddles and kicked out at the raindrops. It's a great feeling, he said to himself, when your clothes are dry and your raincoat keeps the water out.

He didn't fully understand the positive mood swing that had now taken hold of him, but he put it down to three things. Partly, it was due to his anticipation of the end of the festival, a sense that he had survived everything life had thrown at him over the preceding days. Secondly, he had a feeling that the worst was over; that as soon as the lashing rain stopped, things could only improve. Finally, he began not to worry about other people, but to look forward to Beachy Head, the closing headline act of the weekend: a band he'd idolised since his teenage years, but had never seen perform live. He relished the prospect of watching them on stage so much, that he found himself trembling with expectation.

Isolated from the world around him by the hissing rain,

Gary began to day dream. He hummed along to favourite tunes playing in his head and tapped his fingers lightly on his thigh. He gave an occasional skip and jump to coincide with a dramatic musical moment, or a particularly pleasant memory. If the rain became too heavy he would take occasional shelter under a tree or the cover of a nearby stall. When the rain relaxed, he would set out again, weaving around people walking in the opposite direction.

A couple approached him, pushing a wheelbarrow of wet camping gear through the watery mud. A young child walked alongside them wearing a bright yellow waterproof coat, with matching rubber boots and sou'wester hat. Like Gary, the child appeared to be in a dream world of her own, singing and talking to herself, as her parents pushed the barrow with grim but determined faces.

Behind the girl trailed a silver helium-filled balloon on a string. It bobbed up and down in jerky movements, in time with her steps. Gary caught the reflection of his own face in it as the girl passed by. It was a happy, smiling face; a little careworn perhaps; certainly wet and dirty in places, and covered in stubble; but radiating contentment.

Gary hardly recognised himself.

The rain stopped suddenly and the sky became brighter. Pungent odours of vegetation filled the air. Gary inhaled deeply, instinctively stretching and yawning at the same time. He threw back the hood of his raincoat and revelled in the cool air. At once, he felt hungry and thirsty.

Clutching coffee and a pastry, Gary ambled slowly towards the jazz tent. He was in no real hurry to rejoin Claire or the girls, despite their earlier arrangement. He glanced up to see dirty grey clouds racing by in the sky. He thought it was a bit strange because at ground level there was hardly a whisper of a breeze. The clouds in front of the sun glowed and, gradually, a gap appeared which allowed wan sunlight to filter through. Gary could feel no appreciable warmth on his cheeks, but he welcomed the sun's efforts. The clouds continued to thin out until the final veil obscuring the sun vanished altogether. Strong, golden light then swept over the festival, surging into every dark corner and throwing long shadows everywhere.

Gary gazed at the contrasting light and dark in the sky. The sun's rays streamed underneath the dense, dark grey crust of cloud overhead painting any stray dangling wisps a livid crimson-purple colour. The distant hills, once pale and colourless in the morning mist, were now an unnatural, saturated yellowy-green.

A colourful rainbow arched across the distant sky. Framed against the steel grey cloud it was an object of incomparable beauty. The colours shone intensely. Awe-inspiring, Gary thought, as he checked off the individual colours, from the richest red to the deepest violet.

THIRTY

Hannah was already waiting for him at the entrance to the jazz tent. She looked pale, nervous and unsteady. Gary was concerned by her appearance and asked if she was alright. When she didn't reply, Gary led her into the tent and sat her down on a chair. Having fetched her a glass of water, he pressed her to say what was wrong.

Hannah sipped the water and some colour flowed back to her face. 'Nothing's wrong,' she said quietly. 'You're late.'

'I don't see Claire and Lucy here, so no harm done. Are you sure you're OK?'

'I've just been feeling a little queasy.' Gary looked her over for signs to explain what was going on. He noticed that she was sitting slightly more erectly and that her chin was raised a little higher than usual. Her eyes burned with pride and defiance: nothing new there then, he thought. She sat with her hands behind her head but, try as he might, he couldn't work it out. 'Was it something you ate?' he asked.

Hannah snorted. 'No, it's not that,' she said.

'So you know what it is?'

'Of course,' she smiled.

'Well,' Gary said in a voice somewhere between worry and bemusement, 'I don't know, so will you let me in on the secret?'

'If you want,' she said, teasing him with her playful eyes

that were full of joy and daring. She then lowered her hands and slowly began to lift her raincoat. At first, Gary was confused, then annoyed. He shook his head, wondering why she was being so childish. He looked up and saw a broad smile break across her face. She continued to pull up her coat and, with it, the bottom of her jumper and blouse, to reveal her stomach.

Gary gasped with horror as he caught sight of a small diamond and silver ball protruding from her navel, encircled by angry red skin.

'Please, no,' Gary cried. 'Tell me it's not real!'

'It's real alright,' Hannah replied, soaking up every moment of her father's reaction. 'I got it done this afternoon. Isn't it beautiful?'

'Hannah, how could you?'

'Your reaction is fantastic,' she said with delight.

'Seriously, Hannah, who did this to you?' Gary's voice was no longer simply shocked and concerned, but it was laced with anger. 'I want to know – they're not allowed to pierce you without my consent. You're only fifteen and that's not old enough. Tell me where you went.'

Hannah tossed her head back in laughter. 'I can't remember where it was. It's not as if they advertise.'

'You had absolutely no right to do that. I'm going to call the police – it's an assault.'

Hannah stopped laughing. 'Don't be stupid,' she said coolly.

'You don't understand – you could get an infection, a reaction, who knows. I'm serious.'

Hannah rose to her feet and deliberately knocked her chair to the ground. 'It's my body, not yours,' she said, staring into Gary's eyes.

'You're my daughter…'

'It's my life.'

'Until you're eighteen, I have responsibility for you.'

Hannah ignored him, but took a step closer. 'I don't tell you how to live your life, so don't tell me how to live mine.'

'You're not listening…'

'What's the big deal?' she shrugged. 'You've got a hole in your ear; I've got a hole in my belly button. You survived; so will I.'

'That's not the point,' Gary said angrily.

'I like it. It feels good to me. It's what I want to do, now.'

'Hannah…'

'If I change my mind I'll take it out. So, get a life and learn to live with it.'

Hannah picked the chair up from the ground and sat down on it with her back to Gary.

Gary touched Hannah's shoulder.

'Leave me alone,' she said.

'Don't you understand why I feel the way I do? Why I'm so concerned for you?'

'Give it a rest,' Hannah sighed. Then she turned and looked straight into her father's eyes. 'Mum wouldn't have made such a fuss.'

Gary stepped back and let go of her shoulder. 'What's she got to do with it?' he protested.

'My mother had more sense,' she answered with real hostility in her voice, 'than to get worked up about nothing.'

'Your mother wouldn't have agreed to let you get pierced like that. I can tell you that for nothing.'

'I never said that; only that she wouldn't have made a fuss like you.'

'Why are you being like this?'

'I'm not being like anything. You've got the problem, not me.'

Gary's head started throbbing from anxiety and stress. He pulled another chair over and sat down on it. He rested his elbows on his knees and looked up at Hannah. Her face was taut with irritation. 'It'll take some getting used to,' he offered as an olive branch.

'I don't see why.'

'Please, Hannah, I've had a hard day and this is difficult for me.'

'What about *my* day? Got off to a great start, didn't it, cleaning up after you. Mum wouldn't have done that to me.'

'But there you go again...'

'How dare you?' Hannah cried. 'Why shouldn't I mention my own mother when I want to? I miss her too, you know, in case you hadn't realised.'

Gary could see tears beginning to fill her eyes. 'We all miss her terribly,' Gary said.

'Well, you should have thought about that before.'

'What do you mean by that?' he asked, confused. Hannah was now shaking with anger.

'I know what happened,' she said slowly. Gary shrugged his shoulders: he didn't understand what she was trying to say. Had she overheard his falling out with Frank? He didn't think she could have done but, even if she had, surely she'd sympathise with him? He had a sense of foreboding about the course of the conversation. He wanted it to stop, without Hannah revealing her knowledge, but he knew that wasn't possible now. Almost involuntarily he opened his mouth and asked: 'What do you mean, you know what happened?'

Hannah didn't waste words or time. 'It was your fault. *You* killed her!' she said starkly.

'What?' Gary groaned in a state of shock. 'Are you saying I murdered your mother?' He couldn't believe what he'd heard; the accusation tore his heart. He felt breathless and his head began to spin as well as throb.

'No, but you *caused* her death.' Tears were streaming down Hannah's cheeks.

'But Hannah, it was an accident.'

'You were coming to a concert at the school and you were late as always. Mum was rushing around after you. If you'd been on time, she wouldn't have fallen down the stairs.'

'I wasn't late and she wasn't rushing.' Gary was gripping his chair tightly with his injured hand and he felt the pain shoot through his forearm. 'How do you know anyway? You weren't even there.'

Hannah wiped her eyes, but didn't soften her look. 'I called mum on my mobile to find out where you were. I spoke to her before she died.' Gary fell back in his chair with surprise.

'You never mentioned that before,' he gasped.

'I did, but you didn't listen. You never do. She told me that you were running late and she couldn't get you out of your room. She was rushing around trying to get everything done and she said it was driving her mad.'

'I wasn't late.'

'You're always late for everything. You only ever think about yourself.'

'Did mum tell you that?' he asked quietly, as he started to shake. He pictured Hannah's schoolbook at the top of the stairs, with its bright blue, white and red cover.

'Yes, she did. And she didn't know if she could stand it any longer.'

'Hannah, it wasn't like that…' Gary began. The textbook was in French – a language Natalie had loved and a subject that Hannah loathed. It lay at the top of the stairs and it shouldn't have been there. He'd told Hannah a thousand times. He remembered a cry of surprise, several rolling thuds, a sharp crack and then silence.

He saw himself rushing to the top of the stairs to discover Natalie's crumpled body at the bottom, her neck and head lying at an ungainly angle. Hannah's school book, tattered and bloodied, lay beside her as if the passing angel of death had placed it there gently as a memento.

'Can you imagine,' Hannah continued, 'the last conversation I ever had with my own mother? 'I can't talk now, Hannah. I'm in a rush because your dad's late again and I can't get him out of his study. We'll get there as soon as we can, but please go!' That's how it went; something like that.'

Gary shook his head. 'It wasn't my fault.'

'Those were my mum's last words to me: 'Please go!' She didn't want me, because she had to deal with you. You might as well have pushed her off the edge of the stairs. You were killing her anyway – can't you see?'

Gary's brain was too full of shifting images and painful memories to take in Hannah's words. He wanted to answer her accusations, but he just couldn't do it. He felt confused and angry.

It was now clear to him that his relationship with Natalie was not as he had previously imagined. His so-called friends had criticised his conduct and he felt bad about that; but no one had ever accused him of actually causing Natalie's death. And how dare his own daughter level that accusation at him now? What did *she* know about the true circumstances of the accident? What had he done to deserve these words? What should stop him now from revealing the truth about Natalie's death?

'It wasn't my fault, Hannah,' he growled. 'There was more to it than that.'

He watched her thin lips quiver slightly as a look of curiosity and then anxiety passed across her face. 'What do you mean?'

'Je sais,' Gary said deliberately in French. 'I know.'

'You don't know anything,' Hannah replied. 'You're just making it up.'

'Hannah,' Gary said, 'I have to tell you the truth about why your mother died.' He spoke coldly and evenly. Hannah was still shaking and fear crept into her eyes.

'The truth?' she whispered.

'Yes,' Gary said. 'Where the *real* blame lies. Hardly anyone knows, but it's something you'll have to live with for the rest of your life.'

He paused for dramatic effect. He looked at the angry young woman in front of him and watched as her defiant frame folded in on itself, so that once again she was just a little girl; *his* vulnerable child. He hesitated. He'd gone beyond the point of no return and he wished he could rewind the last couple of minutes, to take the conversation in a different direction. He felt like an executioner with a duty to perform, but having doubts about the guilt of the condemned. Would speaking the truth have a similar terminal consequence for Hannah? Maybe, but she had thrown down the gauntlet with a wild and unjustified accusation.

It was a poisonous untruth. What would their future

relationship be worth if he allowed it to remain unchallenged, hanging like an axe over his own head? It would be an intolerable state of affairs: the future built on a perpetual lie. Hannah might always blame him for Natalie's death, but would she be better or worse for knowing the truth? Inside, he already knew that she would be worse off but if he suppressed the truth, then he would have to live the lie and bear false accusations for the rest of his life.

He opened his mouth, uncertain what he was going to say. He wanted to put the record straight so badly: a few simple words would do it. But he also felt the need to protect his daughter from the dirty, nasty real-life consequences of childish errors.

'I didn't want to tell you, Hannah, not until you were a lot older and able to understand these things better,' he began. 'I think you're right. Your mum was rushing around a bit and I think I was probably late as usual. I was sitting in my study, it's true. I'm sorry for all that. But the reason your mum died was because she slipped and stumbled at the top of the stairs.' He paused.

He pictured Hannah leaving the schoolbook on the landing, intending to collect it later. He imagined Natalie stepping on the book and her foot slipping, launching her down the stairs. It was an act of carelessness on Hannah's part, an act of wilful defiance. Whatever his culpability was for being late, Hannah's placing of the book at the top of the stairs was the direct cause for Natalie's death. He knew that knowledge would crush Hannah.

'She slipped and stumbled,' Gary repeated, 'because…'

He watched tears rolling down Hannah's cheeks, as if she already knew what was coming. Gary felt so terribly sorry for her, despite all that she had said to him. He was determined to finish his sentence but, at the very last moment, something diverted him, as if he were on a railway track and the points had changed unexpectedly.

'…because…' Gary continued, '…because she'd been drinking. You see, Hannah, your mum had a bit of a drink problem. She was suffering from an illness, if you like. The truth is: she'd had a drink or two that day and then she stumbled and fell down the stairs. That's where the blame lies; not with me, or you or anyone else.'

Hannah frowned as she took in this new information. She looked relieved, then unconvinced.

'Why didn't you tell me before?'

'It's hard to accept that someone has a problem with alcohol.'

'You said I'd have to live with it for the rest of my life.'

'Did I?' Gary said, unsure if he had or not. He began floundering for an explanation: 'Well, I meant that… well, you know… these things… alcohol problems… sometimes run in families. They say it's genetic. I didn't want you to worry that you might become an alcoholic when you grow up.'

'Will I?' she asked.

'No, no; almost certainly not. But who knows? There's always a chance. Do you understand now, why I'm so worried about your drinking?'

Hannah was silent, deep in thought. Gary knew it hadn't been much of an answer, but it was the best he could come up with. He tried to guess what she was thinking: at first, she looked confused, but then an expression of scepticism crept over her face. She opened her mouth to say something, but Gary raised his hand.

'There's more,' he said.

'What?'

'Thinking back to the day of the accident, I've remembered what mum's last words were. As she passed my study I heard her shout through the door...' Gary gulped as tears broke from his swollen eyes. '... she shouted: 'If I didn't love those children so much, I'd have left you years ago.' So you see, Hannah, I was a bit to blame but, whatever she said to you on the phone, her *last* words were that she loved you. That's what you must remember. She didn't want you to go, she wanted you and you're the reason she stayed.' He paused and added quietly through his sobbing: 'I wasn't enough.'

Hannah began to weep and she embraced her father. 'Oh, dad!' she whispered. 'I'm sorry. I didn't mean to make you cry. I don't blame you, but I thought for a moment you were going to blame me.'

'Hannah, you're *not* to blame,' Gary said. 'It was just an accident; but, if anyone's to blame at all, it's me.'

THIRTY-ONE

Claire and Lucy arrived at the jazz tent to find Gary and Hannah in each other's arms. 'What a lovely sight,' Claire said. Gary and Hannah pulled themselves apart, laughing with embarrassment, avoiding Claire's eyes and wiping their faces. 'A grand reconciliation?' Claire asked innocently. 'I didn't know you two had fallen out.'

Hannah laughed nervously and blushed. 'We were just talking about mum,' she said. 'It was pure emotion.'

'Oh, I'm sorry to interrupt.'

'Not at all,' Gary said. 'Your timing was pretty perfect.'

Lucy reached over and lifted Hannah's raincoat, which had rolled back down.

'Oh my God, you did it, Han!' she screamed. 'Mum, *please* can I have a belly bar like Hannah?'

Claire looked horrified. 'You must be joking,' she said. 'Hannah, are you mad? Is it painful? Aren't you worried about infection?'

'You adults don't get it,' Lucy said leaping to Hannah's defence. 'It's beautiful and it's really cool!'

'Gary, did you agree to this?' Claire asked sharply.

'Absolutely not,' he replied. 'She never asked me and, if she had, I'd never have given my consent.'

'But how could you have allowed it to happen?'

'What do you mean? I haven't seen her all afternoon.'

'She's only a child, Gary.'

'Claire – this is not my fault. She did it herself.'

'But what are you going to do about it?'

'I thought I'd pin her to the ground and rip it out forcibly – is that what you mean?'

'You're the adult. You're the parent. You have to do something. I would never let Lucy put herself at risk like that.'

Gary was dumbfounded. Once again, he felt out of control of the situation. He was at a loss to know why he was being blamed for Hannah's actions, and he resented Claire denouncing his parenting skills in such a public fashion. Hannah and Lucy were silent, watching the scene play out.

'She's nearly sixteen and it's her navel,' he replied slowly.

'She's fifteen. She's just a child.'

'I agree, but she acts practically like an adult and more importantly she took the decision, not me.'

'It wasn't her decision to make, Gary. Can't you see that? You're abdicating your responsibility if you don't do something.'

'Well, I can't take it out physically, can I, if she won't agree?'

'Don't be spineless! There are plenty of ways to persuade a fifteen-year-old to do something you want. Surely you don't need me to tell you how. There are carrots and sticks that every decent parent knows how to use. Her mother would never have stood for this. It's appalling!'

'Mum,' Lucy said. 'What's wrong with you? It's not that bad. It's great.'

'No one asked you,' Claire said to her daughter crossly. 'You don't understand. This is a matter of principle.'

Gary saw that Hannah was looking miserable. He could

see that her stomach looked red and sore, and he felt sorry for her. It was a terrible decision, but a very brave one. To face the pain alone must have taken a lot of courage. He wished to the bottom of his heart that she hadn't done such a stupid thing, but part of him admired her: she had asserted her individuality albeit, he thought, in a most repulsive way.

'Yes, Claire, you're right' he said with emphasis. 'It is a matter of principle. I don't agree with what she's done but, at the end of the day, it's her life. But when you think about it, don't you think it's pretty impressive? I mean that a young person like Hannah can weigh up the pros and cons of such a momentous decision, can make that decision and then carry it through despite the fear and pain it involves. I'm impressed with that. Aren't you?'

Claire was speechless and her mouth hung open. 'So, Claire, let's move on, shall we?' Gary added with finality. Hannah stared at her father with wonder and delight. She wanted to thank him but, before she could say the words, Claire regained her composure.

'Oh, I completely give up on you Gary,' she said. 'You're enough to drive anyone mad, and mostly you do.' She turned to Hannah. 'I hope you don't live to regret it young lady, but don't forget it was your choice.'

Claire pulled down the hem of Hannah's jacket to cover the piercing.

'Anyway,' she added a little more calmly, looking back at Gary, 'that's decided it. You ought to know that we're going early.'

'Why early?'

'As if you haven't noticed the rain and the wind and all this mud – it's just no fun anymore. The catering's nearly finished and half the staff are going early too. There's nothing to stay for.'

'What about Beachy Head at ten o'clock? They're the highlight of the whole weekend.'

'For God's sake, Gary, grow up! They're just a band, and an old one at that. I can watch them on the telly when I get home.'

'But you'll miss the atmosphere. Look, don't go; it'll be so much more fun with you here, and Hannah will miss Lucy if you do.'

'We're tired and cold and we want to go back.'

'What about Frank?' Gary said in desperation. 'He'll want you to stay a bit longer.'

'Frank's gone already.'

'What? Without saying goodbye?'

'Gary, it's not surprising he didn't come and find you to say goodbye.'

'I suppose not,' Gary admitted. 'Did he take Sam with him?'

'Of course.'

'Marc'll be disappointed.'

'Yeah, he seemed pretty upset when he saw them go. Funny, I didn't think he and Sam got on that well together.' Gary raised his eyebrows but said nothing. Then he asked: 'Can't I persuade you to stay? Just for me?'

Claire sighed. 'Oh Gary, I wish I could but Lucy's had enough and so have I. You'll still have Hannah and Marc to keep you company. We're definitely going. I'm desperate for a hot bath; and I just can't wait to get into clean pyjamas and slump in front of the telly with a glass of wine. Can't you understand that?'

'It does sound good,' Gary said shrugging his shoulders. 'I wish I could be there too.'

Claire's expression became stern like an annoyed school teacher. 'It's too late for that,' she said, but not as strongly as either of them had expected. She held his hand and squeezed it gently. 'Look, we've got to go.'

She kissed Gary on the cheek and hugged Hannah lightly, avoiding contact with her midriff. 'Let's meet up again back in East Dulwich,' she said to Gary, 'when everything's back to normal.' She took Lucy's hand. 'Enjoy the band, Gary. I'm sure they'll be great. I know how much you've been looking forward to them.'

When Claire and Lucy had gone, Hannah managed a sulky 'Thanks for sticking up for me, dad,' but it sounded half-hearted. Gary understood that she was miserable to be without a friend.

Marc arrived several minutes later with red eyes. Although the tears had long gone, he wiped his face without thinking as he entered the tent. When he heard about Hannah's pierced navel he turned up his nose and uttered a dismissive 'Gross!'

'Cheer up you two,' Gary said as brightly as he could. 'Let's go and eat something nice, watch a couple of bands that you like, and then it's Beachy Head at ten. They'll be fantastic you know.'

'Sam's gone,' Marc replied. 'I don't want to stay.'

'You'll see him again soon,' Gary said.

'Not if Frank's got anything to do with it.'

'Why, what did Frank say?'

'He's really angry with you, dad. He said he couldn't stand being here any longer with such a sick and twisted family. I tried to persuade them to stay, but he said he didn't want to see me around again, either. He said I was bad for Sam and he hoped that I grew up to be more of a man than my father – well, you.' Marc's eyes moistened. 'What am I going to do?' he wailed.

'Come on, it'll all blow over,' Gary said. 'It's not the end of the world.'

'I don't want to stay if Sam's not here.'

'Nor do I,' Hannah added, 'if Lucy's gone too.'

Gary looked at them, one after the other. 'We'll miss Beachy Head if we go now.'

'It's about to rain again, anyway,' Marc said.

'I thought it was clearing up nicely.'

'No. The clouds have all come back.'

'I don't want to see any more bands in the rain,' Hannah said.

'But what about Beachy Head?'

'Dad,' Hannah said, 'you don't really want to see them. They're just a bunch of old men; and completely past it.'

'But I've waited all my life to see them.'

'Dad,' Marc said, 'they're going to come on with their walking frames and before you know it they'll hobble off to draw their pensions.'

'Rubbish; they're not like that at all,' Gary objected. 'They're fantastic musicians – iconic you could say – and they'll be full of energy. I've played you some of their songs and you know how good they'll be.'

'It's old music,' Hannah said.

'Since when have you started hating old music?' Gary asked. 'I always thought you two listened to anything. This is a chance not to be missed.'

'They're boring,' Marc said. 'I can miss the chance.'

'So can I,' Hannah added.

'But this was one of the attractions of coming. I wanted to see them play live. It's something I've never done, something I really want to do. Please, kids.'

'You told us this was our treat,' Hannah said, casting glances at Marc. 'It was our holiday, because of what happened to mum…'

'… so we could, you know, get over the accident and everything,' Marc continued.

'Well,' Hannah said, 'we've done that – it's been successful, you might say – and we don't need any more…'

'… not in the rain,' Marc emphasised.

Gary had been caught in a clever pincer movement and he was desperately disappointed; but he'd try one last throw of the dice. 'You know, kids, this is really important to me. Your mum and I listened to Beachy Head when we first started going out together.'

'Yuck,' Marc growled. 'Just thinking of it makes me feel sick.'

Hannah shook her head. 'You're so selfish, dad. You're always thinking of yourself. Can't you see we've had enough and we want to go? Watch them on TV but, please, please don't make us stay against our will.'

Gary raised his arm to make another point, but then let it fall again. 'What's the use?' he asked rhetorically. He stuck his hands in his pockets. 'You're the selfish ones,' he muttered, but neither Hannah nor Marc replied. They looked on expectantly, hoping to see some concrete sign that Gary would convert words into action. 'Well,' he said at last, 'I suppose we'll have to take the tent down.' He paused for a reaction but there was none. 'Will you come and help me?'

'Dad, I'm really tired,' Marc said in a weak voice.

'So am I,' Hannah said, weaker still. 'And I still feel queasy from my belly button. It really hurts now.'

'What? So I have to take it down on my own?' Gary asked, now totally fed up.

'You put it up without us and we don't know what to do.'

Gary looked at them both for any indication that they might help him. They stood motionless, putting on 'tired' faces. 'Kids, you're all the same,' Gary sighed. 'At least come and help me pack up the sleeping bags and the rucksacks.'

Reluctantly, Hannah and Marc followed Gary to the tent. By the time they arrived, the rain had started to fall again in alarming quantities. Their campsite was a desultory sight. Several of the neighbours' tents had already gone. Light yellow rectangular patches marked out where the tents had been and where the grass had been starved of daylight. Their tent stood alone like a pink nylon cathedral of arched walls and thin black fibreglass buttresses. The field was dotted with black dustbin liners half-full of rubbish and with pieces of abandoned camping equipment.

They stuffed the sleeping bags back into their nylon bags and clothes into rucksacks. Hannah and Marc carried their kit back to the jazz tent, while Gary set to the task of dismantling the tent on his own.

As rivulets of water streamed over his face, he eased the tent pegs from the slimy earth. He tied up the bright blue guy ropes and then disengaged the fibreglass poles from the rings which held them. The tent deflated gently and sank slowly to the ground. Gary struggled to detach the poles from the soaking fabric.

When the poles and nylon outer sheet were folded and

packed, Gary loaded them into his wheelbarrow and trudged off to fetch the teenagers. On the way, he stopped for a strong coffee. He apologised to the stallholder in a tired and weary voice, when he discovered that he had no loose change and could only offer a large banknote as payment.

'Forget it,' the stallholder said waving the note away. 'Have it on me.'

'Are you sure?' Gary asked. 'Trade must've been terrible in this weather.'

'Oh, not so bad if you've been selling hot food and drinks,' he replied. 'It's those poor buggers in the marketplace selling clothes and sunglasses that I'm sorry for.'

'Yeah, must've been a washout for them.'

'Literally. But maybe it'll be better next year. It's not always like this. So, you're not staying for Beachy Head then?'

'I'd really love to, but the kids staged a rebellion.'

'What do kids know, eh? All fads and fashions. They'd miss the opportunity of a lifetime, if they thought it wasn't cool or if a little rain fell on their poor little heads.'

'To be fair there's been quite a lot of rain,' Gary said. 'But I suppose I could make them stay until after Beachy Head; I am the driver after all. If I decided not to leave, there'd be nothing they could do.'

'Well, it's a thought.'

Gary shrugged. 'Are you going to watch them?' he asked.

'You bet, come hell or high water. I saw them years ago, when they recorded their live album. They're brilliant.'

Gary picked up the wheelbarrow and thanked him for the coffee.

'Don't miss them,' the stallholder said as he moved to serve another customer. 'You'll regret it, if you do.'

Gary collected Hannah and Marc. He wanted to canvass the idea of staying until Beachy Head had finished their set, but when he saw the fatigue on their faces, he changed his mind. With rucksacks on their backs they joined the exodus of bedraggled people leaving the site. None of them looked back as they passed the turnstiles and ascended the slippery slope towards the car parking fields.

As he tried to push the wheelbarrow up the stony, rutted track Gary felt guilty for bringing the children to the festival. Had it been just a selfish act on his part? he wondered. His intentions had been good, but had the children really enjoyed themselves? He wasn't sure, because there was no obvious outward sign. He reflected on his own experience: set aside the events of that day, he could honestly say that he'd had a good time.

They stopped halfway up the slope to catch their breath. The rain was falling steadily, but less strongly than before. The remaining light in the overcast sky was waning and it seemed as if a premature dusk would soon engulf them. Hannah looked back at the festival, still seething with life and booming with noise from one side of the valley to the other. Gary was surprised to hear her mumble a wistful 'Bye, bye, Glastonbury' before turning and continuing to climb the track.

Gary's wheelbarrow became stuck and he struggled to push it any further. A man approached and asked if he could help. Gary saw his partner waiting patiently in the rain with two young children. Gary was reluctant to be a burden to anyone – apart from his own children, of course, but he couldn't help that; and he tried to refuse. The man ignored him and lifted the front of the wheelbarrow over the rock that was causing the obstacle. Together, Gary and the stranger manhandled the wheelbarrow to the top of the slope.

'I am so grateful,' Gary said. 'I wasn't getting any help from the teenagers,' he added waving ahead towards Hannah and Marc.

'It was a pleasure,' the stranger replied, turning down the slope to join his family; and, as Gary watched him disappear amongst the crowds, he was touched by yet another unselfish act of kindness.

THIRTY-TWO

It took Gary longer than expected to find the car. Although he would have preferred to stay, there was a certain indefinable relief at nearing the end of the adventure. The rain had now stopped and Gary had the impression that it would stay dry for the rest of the evening. The clouds had lifted and here and there Gary could see some golden sky, even though the sun itself remained hidden.

There was stillness in the field where the cars were parked, reminding Gary that most festival-goers were still on site having fun. Gary felt no resentment; probably, he thought, because striking camp was irreversible.

Once everything was loaded in the car Gary eased the boots off his feet and put on light trainers. His toes tingled with pleasure. The engine started first time and Gary let it run for a moment or two, before he released the handbrake and rolled gently forward on the grass. He aimed for a marshal in an orange tabard who was directing cars through a gate at the end of the field.

They were soon on the road and driving back towards London. Darkness fell and in no time Hannah and Marc were snoring gently on the back seat with their mouths open and heads touching. Gary switched on the radio and played some quiet classical music. He was glad to be behind the steering wheel, following broken white lines on the smooth black tarmac. It may only have been a car, but Gary loved being in control of something once again.

As the car traversed roundabouts and sped along dual carriageways, Gary felt a sense of elation. The long weekend had been eventful, in ways he hadn't foreseen or wished for. But, he thought, there had been a great deal of honesty and openness between people: a lot of truths had been spoken and myths dispelled.

He had been hurt by people who he had mistakenly reckoned to be his friends. Their words had brought about the end of an era in his mind. In a curious way their revelations had helped him to draw a line – several lines, in fact – under the past. They allowed him now to move on with his life.

He was elated too by his children. Not by what they had done, but by their self-confidence and their ability to make big decisions about their own lives. He was especially pleased that Marc had shared his innermost secret with him. Despite these positive thoughts, Gary also had a tremendous sense of loss. His love for Natalie had faded forever; he would probably never speak to Frank again; and he feared that Claire would always be distant.

He wondered what would become of Hannah and Marc. Could he provide the stability and guidance they both needed? Would Hannah come to accept any boundaries he might set, any authority he might try to impose? Should he even try? Would she ever respect him?

Had he done enough to support Marc? It was especially difficult for him: so much emotional turmoil, at such a young age. Did he need a father figure, or would a strong mother figure be better? What could he do about that in the short term, anyway? What could he do about Marc and Sam? Would he have to call Frank next week? He really didn't want to, but should he for Marc's sake?

Gary was absorbed by these thoughts as he cruised along the country roads and then along the empty motorway. When he reached the outskirts of London, his mind switched to thinking about dense traffic, pedestrians, road signs and traffic lights. He was keen now to reach home, before the children woke. He was very tired himself and felt a need for sleep.

A flash of light in his rear view mirror told him that a camera had caught him speeding. He glanced at the dashboard: 36 miles per hour. Just his luck, he thought. There was nothing for it but to switch the radio off and concentrate more on driving carefully.

Gary parked the car almost exactly outside the house and turned off the ignition. He listened to the engine cool and to the steady breathing from the back seat. Very gently he shook Hannah's shoulder and asked her to wake up; she groaned, lifted her head a few inches and then slumped back to sleep.

He then tried Marc, who woke more easily, and together they unpacked the car. Gary opened the front door of the house and kicked away the pile of junk mail on the floor. He switched on the lights: the hallway was exactly as he'd left it but he sensed that something was missing; that there had been a profound change while he'd been away.

They took the camping equipment into the kitchen and lay it on the vinyl floor. 'It's good to be back,' Marc said wearily, helping himself to a glass of water. Gary went back to the car and shook Hannah again. 'Come on, love, wake up. You're too heavy to carry,' he said.

He unclicked her seat belt and tried to pull her closer to

the door, but she hardly moved. Then he noticed something fall out of her pocket. He picked it up off the seat and examined it by the light of the street lamp. He stopped short: it was an unused condom. Unused and still intact! He was horrified by the implications and only partially relieved by the realisation that, at least, she must have had precautions in mind.

'Oh, Hannah,' he wailed quietly, as he put the condom away in his own pocket. He shook her more firmly and then helped her out of the car. She stumbled into the house, eyes closed and her arm around Gary's stooped neck.

The children were dishevelled and dirty: there was mud all over their damp clothes and they stank of wood smoke and sweat. Marc sat at the bottom of the stairs with his head in his hands. Hannah propped herself up against the door frame. Gary suggested they have showers before bed, but they both protested that they were too tired.

'But the sheets are all clean,' Gary said.

'Oh, please dad,' Hannah said. 'We really, really need to sleep.' Gary thought of Natalie: she would never have allowed it.

'Fine,' Gary said. 'Go to bed, but leave your clothes on the landing.'

Gary looked around the hallway: there were bits of grass and mud strewn everywhere. He looked up to the ceiling. 'Sorry,' he said aloud. 'It was necessary.' He didn't believe in an after-life, but it suited him now to address Natalie because, despite everything, he still felt her presence in the house, though somewhat diminished. Even so, for the first time ever, he resented it.

Gary climbed the stairs quietly with two steaming mugs of hot chocolate. He followed a trail of discarded clothing to Hannah's bedroom and he knocked softly on her door before entering.

Hannah was in bed lying on her back. She sat up when she smelled the chocolate. 'You remembered this time,' she smiled as she took the mug. Her face was still flecked with mud and, for the first time, Gary noticed a livid red bruise on her neck.

'I remembered before,' Gary said. 'It just went cold.'

'Cold hot chocolate's no use to anyone,' Hannah said. She brought the mug to her lips and took a sip before putting it down on the bedside table. 'I need to let it cool a bit,' she said. She lay back down and pulled the duvet over her shoulders. 'Turn out my light, will you?' she mumbled. Gary went to kiss her, but Hannah turned and covered her head. 'I love you,' he said in a gentle voice. She grunted and pulled the duvet tighter around her.

Gary took the second mug to Marc, who was sitting in bed composing a text on his phone.

'To Sam?' Gary asked and Marc nodded.

'I don't know if I'll ever see him again; and I think his dad hates me.'

'But I love you Marc; you know that, don't you?'

'Yes, dad, and I love you too.'

'I'm sorry it was all so wet and muddy.'

'It was gross, dad, really gross,' Marc grinned as he slurped his drink. 'Anyway, it won't be so bad next time.'

'What do you mean?'

'Oh, Hannah and I have already decided that we're going back next year. You can come with us, if you want; but you don't have to.'

Gary went down to the living room and was struck by how

cold and quiet it was. It seemed larger and emptier than he remembered and it was less inviting. He switched on the television, hoping to catch the end of Beachy Head. As the picture formed on the screen, he heard only cheering crowds and a presenter hailing the band's performance as one of the best she'd ever seen. Gary tutted and switched it off.

He felt exhausted. He kept telling himself to go to bed but his body wouldn't respond. He looked at the photographs of Natalie on the mantelpiece: young Natalie, happy Natalie, married Natalie, Natalie with the children, Natalie with friends. There were so many pictures and so many memories.

A feeling of anger and disgust rose within him. He stood up and removed the pictures one by one and put them into the waste paper basket. He sat back down satisfied with his work. A new beginning, he thought. Everyone can now get on with their lives, unfettered by the past. He was sure the children would understand and approve.

He poured himself a whisky. He loved the sensation of raw heat as the liquid ran down his throat. The peaty aroma reminded him of smoky campfires at the festival. He tried to think about all the things that had happened over the previous few days, but it all seemed a blur. Several hours of driving had put distance between those past events and his current situation. He felt disconnected from them and even more so from his previous life with Natalie.

He also felt badly betrayed, by both Natalie and Frank; but he couldn't feel anger about it now, because a large part of him felt responsible for what had happened. True, Natalie had let him down, but wasn't he now doing the same to the children? What kind of father was he anyway? A father who was selfish and late for everything, and who took his children camping in the rain as his idea of giving them a good time. A rubbish father: that was the truth. He felt guilty and inadequate; what had they done to deserve him?

He switched off the lights and went upstairs to wash. Before going to bed, he pushed open Hannah's bedroom door. She was still lying on her back, almost snoring through her open lips. Gary lent over and kissed her cheek. She stirred and kissed him back. 'Are you OK, dad?' she whispered.

'Yes, I'm fine. I'm very tired but glad to be back home.'

'Dad,' Hannah said grasping his hand, 'you don't need to worry any more. It's all over, you know.' Gary looked at her in the half-light and could make out the whites of her eyes. He wanted to ask what she meant, but he was afraid of the reply. In some ways, he felt that it was all just beginning.

'We had a fantastic time, you know,' Hannah continued, sensing his fear. 'It was a really great experience. Thanks for taking us.'

Gary squeezed her hand. 'And don't worry about this morning – I won't tell anyone what happened. Your secret's safe with me. I forgive you, dad.'

Gary relaxed his grip of her hand. He stroked her head and kissed her forehead. 'No,' he replied, 'you're right. I won't worry about that. Thanks.' He pulled the duvet up to her chin, kissed her again gently and added: 'Your mother would've been proud of you. You're such a strong, independent young woman. I'm proud of you, too. I love you, Hannah. Now, go to sleep and I'll see you in the morning.'

Gary closed her door shut and stood for a minute on the silent landing, staring into space. All he could hear was the beat of his heart. Memories flooded into his mind, as his eyes followed the curve of the banister down the stairs. He turned back to face Hannah's door. 'I forgive you, too,' he whispered.

He returned to the living room and sat an in armchair. He buried his head in his hands and sobbed quietly. After a couple of minutes he stopped and rubbed his warm swollen eyes. He looked at the bare mantelpiece and felt as though a part of his life was missing. More significantly, a part – practically the whole – of the children's lives had been removed from sight. 'Erased by you, you selfish bastard,' he said aloud.

He eased himself out of the armchair and reached into the waste basket. He pulled out a silver-framed photograph. It was a large black-and-white portrait of a laughing Natalie: head thrown back, an alluring array of white teeth, eyes sparkling with delight and dimples, with Gary at her side inclining his head towards her. He recognised it as a picture taken by Frank in the year before Natalie died; it was one of Frank's favourites.

Gary had often stared at it trying to work out what Natalie was thinking as she faced the camera. He'd always assumed the picture was a display of how much Natalie had loved him; but no longer. Now he understood that she was gazing into the eyes of the photographer. It was a larger print of the pared picture he'd found in Frank's wallet.

He hated Frank for betraying him and his memories of Natalie. He didn't want to believe that Natalie was capable of duplicity, but the evidence was there in her eyes for all to see. It didn't help that it was the children's favourite picture of their mother.

It was a torment for Gary to look at Natalie's face any longer, but he already knew in his heart that he couldn't and shouldn't put it back in the waste basket. He brought the frame close to his lips and kissed the glass, before placing the frame back onto the mantelpiece. He touched Natalie's lips with his finger. Then he took out the other pictures from the waste basket one by one and arranged them on the mantelpiece, almost exactly as they had been. The last picture was of Natalie and Frank. He held it for a long while before placing it gently with the others.

He felt that Natalie's eyes were mocking him, but he spoke to her directly: 'This isn't about you and me, or about you and Frank,' he said in a soft voice. 'This is about the kids. You're on the mantelpiece on sufferance, so behave yourself.' He smiled at his own little joke.

Absent-mindedly he squeezed his finger, but was surprised to find that his wedding ring wasn't there. He wondered whether he'd put it somewhere for safe-keeping. He racked his brains, but simply couldn't remember.

I hope it's not lost, he thought. It's sure to turn up soon. Then he relaxed. Maybe it didn't matter anymore; maybe it was time to move on.